AWAKENING PRANA!

AWAKENING PRANA!

9 STEPS TO REGENERATIVE SELF-TRANSFORMATION

ANNIE B. BOND
FROM THE STONEMAN DIARIES

Awakening Prana
BOOKS
RHINEBECK, NEW YORK

Awakening Prana!: 9 Steps to Regenerative Self-Transformation
© 2024 by Annie B. Bond

All rights reserved. No part of this book may be used or reproduced in any manner without the consent of the author except in critical articles or reviews. Contact the publisher for information.

This book is intended as an energy healing kriya, not as a medical manual. It is not intended as a substitute for any treatment that may have been prescribed by your doctor. If you suspect that you have a medical problem, we urge you to see medical care.

Paperback ISBN 978-1-960090-62-1
eBook ISBN 978-1-960090-63-8

Library of Congress Control Number 2024906594

Graphics by Shannon Baldwin (Running with Foxes)
Book design by Colin Rolfe

Distribution by Epigraph Books

Awakening Prana Books
Rhinebeck, New York 12572
info@awakeningprana.com

For my grandson, Archer.
May you walk in beauty and may beauty surround you.

CONTENTS

FOREWORD *by Suzanne Giesemann*	ix
PREFACE	xi
INTRODUCTION	1
We are Bioelectric	2
Bioelectric Technology	3
Science of Regenerative Medicine	4
The Transformative Technology of Awakening Prana! Regenerative Self-Transformation!	7
Our Batteries are Drained	7
Reconnecting to the Matrix of Light	8
Our Energy Flow is Blocked	9
THE ENERGY BODY	11
Let's Switch On	11
Awaken Your Energy Body	12
Car/Energy Body Analogy	17
Energetic Flow vs. Energetic Clogging	18
PART I	
Learn about the Regenerative Self-Transformation	21
Behind The Sequential Nine Steps of the Awakening Prana! Kriya/Step	21
Step I: The Elements	23
Step II: Connect/The Higher Self and Soul	40
Step III: Charge/Yin and Yang	55
Step IV: Power Up/The Vortex	75
Step V: Release	82
Step VI: Meet/Source	89
Step VII: Increase Voltage (Pranic Tube)	99
Step VIII: Conduct Energy	109
Step IX: Awaken/Connect to the Matrix of Light	114

PART II

Activating the Nine Sequential Steps of the Awakening Prana! Kriya … 123
    The Journey: Healing Technology Summary … 124
    The Power of Intention … 124
    About Meditation … 125
    The Sound Healings … 126
  Step I Activations … 128
  Step II Activations … 133
  Step III Activations … 138
  Step IV Activations … 144
  Step V Activations … 149
  Step VI Activations … 154
  Step VII Activations … 159
  Step VIII Activations … 166
  Step IX Activations … 168

CLOSING … 179
DEFINITION OF TERMS … 181
ACKNOWLEDGMENTS … 183
ABOUT THE CREATORS … 185

FOREWORD

We want our teachers to know the material they are sharing with us inside and out. In other words, to truly "walk the talk." Annie B. Bond surely does so and proves it with this gem of a book. As a result of being chemically poisoned, she has known imbalance at a level most people will thankfully never experience. In her years-long effort to heal herself, she had an awakening. This led her to teach all of us how to awaken the vital life force within us and direct it in such a way that we can achieve balance and full vitality.

I was blessed to have been guided to Annie by what I thought was sheer happenstance. I was seeking an energetic "tune-up" before teaching a weekend class at the renowned Omega Institute near her home in Rhinebeck, New York. Within minutes of reclining on her healing table, I knew I had been given a gift from Spirit. One does not need to have the keen ability to see the aura that Annie does to feel the sublime energy she radiates both during her private sessions and when simply in her presence.

During what turned out to be the first of several healing sessions over the years, Annie identified blockages that went beyond my original goals for our time together. She skillfully cleared them and left me "upgraded" in ways that revealed themselves not only immediately, but in the coming days and months. She spoke in language that was a bit foreign to me at the time, labeling different energies with feminine and masculine characteristics and describing directional flow that gave me a new perspective on how we process and are affected by all experiences.

I watched Annie use the solitude of the pandemic to establish a vital new connection with Spirit in the form of a wise teacher she calls Stoneman. It was fun and thrilling to watch her put the latest teachings she received into designing clear diagrams that you will find in these pages. She devised clever analogies to make the teaching easily comprehensible.

This book is the result of meticulous research into the nature of our true nature that occurred not in a library or online. Instead, Annie listened within, asked questions of Stoneman, and refined her understanding of prana. Ultimately, she came up with the brilliant nine-step process you will learn here that has the potential to balance and revitalize you in ways you didn't know were possible.

As one whose passion is to be the clearest possible "instrument" for communicating with higher consciousness, I know the value of working with our energy daily. Annie's processes are my go-to tools for clearing dense energy and raising my vibration. I'm sure that once you read about them and then try them for yourself, you'll agree that there are no accidents: You were meant to find these methods.

Prepare to enjoy true radiance as you transmute whatever may be holding you back from being the best possible version of your highest Self.

SUZANNE GIESEMANN, author of
The Awakened Way – Making the Shift to a Divinely Guided Life

PREFACE

"Healing from your upbringing and culture is not easy. Setting the intention to do so in a heartfelt way is half the battle." —**Annie B. Bond**

Have you ever heard of a shaman death? When life trauma is so powerful it all but takes you out? I've had one. "Shaman death is the symbolic death of the initiate to the old ways of life and personal identity." The basic idea of ancient initiations was to break down all the former notions of "self" that were held by the shaman-to-be, notes the Bat writeup in *Medicine Cards*, by Jamie Sams & David Carson. The experience for me was especially searing because I wasn't in training to be a shaman, a healer, or anything spiritual. I was an artist, recently married, and starting what I thought was a straightforward, creative life.

My shaman death has had a ripple effect for the last forty-three years. It came from when I was poisoned by a gas leak in a restaurant in 1980, when I was twenty-seven. The exposure sent me and eighty other people to the hospital. I was ultimately in the hospital for three months, with central nervous system damage from the gas, but wasn't on the road to recovery until I found one of the first environmental medicine doctors in existence, and was officially diagnosed with multiple chemical sensitivity. I was your basic bubble case—every synthetic chemical I breathed was toxic to me—and needed a chemical-free environment to recover. I was blessedly not sensitive to natural materials. Even though it meant moving ten times in four years, I developed an unerring drive for clean air and that didn't stop until I found a "clean" home. There I recovered.

Yes, there are a few silver linings. Would I go through all this again? Unlikely (!), but because of my force-fed deep insight into the number of chemicals we live with, because I had to live away from them, I knew a lot about the topic and I became a best-selling author of five books on green living and was the seminal editor of early green living publications and was named "the foremost expert on green living" by "Body & Soul" magazine in 2009. I did experience the death of the old ways of life and personal identity, and neither were symbolic. And, I did become a shaman.

One of the ways I was able to protect myself from chemicals, and to ferret them out, was by observing how my body reacted to exposures. This is how I got well. Given I was in survival mode, I was very focused and alert to these nuanced shifts and then how to mitigate the chemicals. I studied these reactions for many years, for hours on end. A sore throat and fatigue? Likely formaldehyde. Hyperactive? Hydrocarbons. Black depression from certain types of pesticides, and I would feel like a dying bug around pesticides in general. Even if I couldn't smell the chemical, I could identify what the chemical was by how I reacted to it, and then try to search it out. I knew a house was being painted with oil-based paints before I smelled it, for example, because I became hyperactive and couldn't think. Then I tracked down the cause.

In his book, *Outliers*, Malcom Gladwell introduces the "10,000 hour rule." He quotes the neurologist Daniel Levitin who wrote: "The emerging picture from studies is that ten thousand hours of practice is required to achieve the level of mastery associated with being a world-class expert—in anything…" He also quotes Lennon to show how hard the Beatles worked to achieve what they did (easily 10,000 hours before they were famous).

Little did I know that I was giving myself a profoundly deep teaching about the energy body. When it was flowing and when it wasn't! Tracking how my body and mind felt as a reaction to what I was breathing. Tracking how the energy of the chemicals felt in my body. That expertise was surely gained after 10,000 hours of experience. And how it felt without the chemicals. The vibrancy.

This is how I became a green living expert.

I was reminded about this expertise of my tuning into the energy of outside influences on my body when I had what I hope is my first and only case of Covid. While finishing this book, forty-three years after the poisoning I tracked Covid's energy flow through my body, an energy I knew from giving healings with those who had it (yes, I became a healer, see below). I had seen that the virus has a distinctive lower vibration density, one that has evolved through the variants, and I could "see" it in their energy field, and now in mine—and I could do something about it.

It was the switch to tracking vibrational energy vs. synthetic chemical energy in myself that drew me to energy healing almost two decades after I was poisoned. People as sick as I became often push the envelope. Western medicine wasn't helpful for my central nervous system. I really wanted to feel well! I became a Reiki Master! I signed up for a comprehensive energy school!

Historically, first I focused on inner energy for finding clean air (which I found in a home after five years), and then, over the following decades, I moved into tracking my energy itself, tracking the energy of what I now know is my energy body. Tracking low vibration energy inside of me because of trauma to remove it—and higher energy, to support it—so that I could reach vibrant health!

As I pushed into energy work, I had a lot of improvement, particularly in working with Kundalini energy (Torus) for my central nervous system. I started connecting to my energy body as a spiritual system, and began to unfurl emotional trauma, as well. The work became a call to myself. I had gone off-center. I needed to find my way back. The wounded healer concept was new to me. However, I fit the definition perfectly.

Energy body healing works with the vibrations of light, energy, sound, and consciousness. The healer feels, sees, and hears the vibrations with their intuitive skills and works with spirit to cleanse and clear old energy patterns and even illness that clients hold and carry in their physicality.

It turns out I could "see" trauma and emotional issues as a blueprint in the energy body. The flow was clogged. All my 10,000 hours of tracking energy inside of myself—even though synthetic chemicals—paid off, and I found myself to be very clairvoyant in this way. I also have had many mystical experiences, including being awakened in the night having what I identified at the time as a healing from the Divine Mother. I'll never forget the tenderness, the luminosity, and the compassion. I came to realize a few months later that it had been a visitation from my soul, bringing me such reassurance and reconciliation with the truth of who I am. The experience changed the course of my life as because of it I created the Divine Mother modality.

I've never looked back. I'm forever pushing the envelope to feel well, to be in flow, in harmony, to find serenity. Instead of an unerring drive for clean air I now have an unerring drive for a "clean" energy body. I find myself completely focused on the profoundly spiritual technology of our energy body, the fluid flow of Source, and all that blocks its flow. Most energy healing modalities teach how to clear and restore the linear chakra system. *Awakening Prana!* goes deeper—to the underpinnings of our vibration system, to jumpstart our well-being, to return us to an awakened connection to the All That Is.

DIARY OF A HEALER

During a period of a few decades, I have worked with energy techniques on myself almost every day, and given literally thousands of healings. I've slowly but surely developed an energetic practice (as mentioned, above) that has brought me enormous healing. In body, mind, and spirit. This book and practice is the culmination of these teachings.

The teachings have been facilitated by the very wise sage Stoneman who has nudged me along at every step.

Twenty years ago I came across a stone in my driveway that looked like the Old Man on the Mountain.

I was intrigued by the eyes, and, having a creative streak, I would prop the stone next to my computer, look into the eye that is shaped like a heart, and start typing what I felt he was saying to me!

One thing led to another and the years went by until I began to realize that I turned to this stone and automatic writing with it when I was searching for wisdom about healing.

I started calling the stone "Stoneman," and my "The Stoneman Diaries" now span many computers and many years worth of writing. A number of years ago, I realized that the wisdom I was receiving when I wrote with Stoneman was extraordinary.

Bit by bit I began to shoulder that I was channeling. I soon began to realize there was a Being I was connecting to in Stoneman, a Hathor in fact. (I have been a huge fan of *The Hathor Material*, by Tom Kenyon).

I fully stepped into channeling "The Stoneman Diaries," and his wisdom is behind much of my understanding of the energy systems and energy body that I teach in the Awakening Prana Healer Schools. I am honored and humbled to bring my work with Stoneman to the world.

Here are some of the benefits I have received:

1. Quickly navigating stressful situations. They clear almost immediately and I move on.
2. Finding a footing to circumvent challenges before they cling. The wind seems to blow them away.
3. Receiving insights without needing to search. I use my intuition to navigate and then integrate insights.
4. Becoming whole and balanced from integration.
5. Living in synchronicity with my Higher Self, accessing it regularly.
6. Ruminating and negative thoughts about myself cease quickly.
7. I am physically healthy. My field is clear, continually filling with light, breaking up old lower vibration density causing physical challenges. I have healed from Lyme Disease (a serious tick-borne disease) and central nervous system damage from industrial gas, and then pesticide poisoning that hospitalized me for three months.
8. Learning to ground well, and strengthening my connection to the polarity of Mother Earth and Father Sun transformed me. Opening this channel enabled my energy body to come into balance and allow healing to flow into my blueprint, the All That Is About Me.

Now I have learned the practice from Stoneman, and developed a technique so that the current of the Source energies can finally flow unimpeded to my body, mind and spirit. I feel so transformed it is almost hard to recognize myself as being the same person I was before this work. I have authenticated and adjusted the practice during over a thousand healings.

This book is for:
1. Anyone suffering from a physical ailment.
2. Those suffering from environmental, parental, social, cultural, spiritual or workplace trauma.
3. People who feel fragmented or disconnected from the world around them, as if they do not "fit in."
4. Spiritual seekers who are stuck and need a deeper level of connection.
5. Anyone who wants to experience the natural Elements with spiritual depth, and embody the wisdom of the natural world.
6. Those who feel split from their masculine and/or feminine sides and seek to transform and integrate these aspects.
7. Readers who long to connect with their heart, to give and receive love more profoundly.

INTRODUCTION

"We are slowed-down sound and light waves, a walking bundle of frequencies tuned in to the cosmos. We are souls dressed up in sacred biochemical garments and our bodies are the instruments through which our souls play their music." —**Attributed to Albert Einstein**

The quest for a simple solution to regenerate health and well-being has been the driving force of my research into energy healing practices over the last few decades. A long-time energy healer friend and I have had countless discussions over the years venting our frustration that healing is slow and takes such a long time. Years, in fact, for many issues. There must be a faster way! Healing needs to be simple *and* successful.

As new techniques have come to me while working with myself and clients, and with efficacy top of mind, I've gained empirical insight about what helps flow and regeneration. These footholds have led from one insight to the next.

Over years, the pieces of a new modality have emerged. One that works quickly to bring healing to the body, mind, and spirit. One that centers on the simplest of understandings: that we are bioelectric. Negative (-) and positive (+) currents are needed in equal balance, to charge our batteries so our energy bodies can fully flow as a dynamic system. A system that can continually bring healing and rejuvenation to body, mind, and spirit. My understanding is mirrored in the emerging regenerative medicine field.

The way negative (-) energy currents manifest and are represented in our biology is as a *feminine* energy/current, and the way positive (+) energy currents manifest is as a *masculine* energy/current. They are charges—they charge our battery.

The negative (-) and positive (+) energies are the Source currents—of everything—they are our battery charges. Just think of the way babies are created. "Created" is the optimal word.

When looking at these (-) and (+) battery currents in myself and my clients, I found that most of our batteries are drained and won't charge because there isn't enough current. We need the replenishment of one of these currents, if not both! We may be depleted in the healed feminine energy, or the healed masculine. We also need them in equal balance.

Once fully replenished, and with the batteries recharged, healing is quick, comprehensive, and regenerative. We become less separate from life force energy, more connected to the All That Is.

WE ARE BIOELECTRIC

In medicine, electricity is being used to treat ailments of the body and mind. "Volt jolt," known as transcranial direct-current stimulation (TDCS), is one way, others include deep brain stimulation for Parkinson's and "electroceuticals" to reverse diabetes. Findings show that "[a] little bit of electricity enhanced memory, mathematical skills, attention, focus, and creativity—it had even shown promise for post-traumatic stress disorder and depression," writes Sally Adee in the introduction to her book *We Are Electric*.

Bioelectricity is the study of electrical phenomena in living organisms. How does a salamander grow back its tail? How do bones regenerate? Because of a bioelectric *system*, a technology that makes our presence in biological form work, says Robert Becker, M.D., the author of *The Body Electric*. The system requires both (-) and (+) charges and the activation results in healing and wholeness.

I'd take this further, to note that the negative (-) current is feminine, or Yin, created by the Divine Mother energy of Source, and the positive (+) current is masculine, or Yang, created by the Divine Father of Source. This bioelectric system is our sacred nature.

As humans became increasingly disconnected from nature—from Mother Earth, the carrier of the feminine principle—and from Father Sun, the masculine principle—we collectively disengaged from *the system* that activates the currents of life force energy within us.

Many have increasingly depleted themselves of the negative charge, the Yin energy of the sacred element Earth, also called Shakti, and it needs to be replenished, filled up, and to come into balance with Yang. Stop and think of the implications—feminine energy creates matter!

In modern times, many others have depleted themselves of the Yang energy of the sun, of the sacred element Fire and Source, and it, too, needs to be replenished, filled up, and to come into balance with Yin. Again pause, and reflect—Yang energy is consciousness!

We aren't firing on all cylinders. Source is always there, but in our depleted state we have limited our access. In balancing the feminine and masculine principles in ourselves we will be returning to a dynamic system that will regenerate, renew, and restore our well-being. We will not experience frequent depletion in the form of:

- Illness
- Autoimmune disorders
- Cancer

- Depression
- Anxiety
- Fatigue, exhaustion
- Lack of joi de vivre, fatigue
- Lack of motivation
- Lack of direction
- Broken relationships
- Trauma and retraumatization

(-) Feminine, Yin, is matter. (+) Masculine, Yang, is consciousness.
Yin and Yang are foundational concepts present in Chinese philosophy. The terms have been defined and redefined throughout Chinese philosophical history. It is easier to see how Yin and Yang operate in the world than to define the terms theoretically. However, three essential premises underlie Yin/Yang: 1. Yin/Yang is the integrated tapestry of existence—nature and mind. 2. Yin/Yang signifies waxing and waning throughout the cosmic and human or material realms. 3. Yin/Yang ensures the continuous and dynamic balance of everything.

> "As the Zhuangzi (Chuang-tzu) claims, "Yin in its highest form is freezing while yang in its highest form is boiling. The chilliness comes from heaven, while the warmness comes from the earth. The interaction of these two establishes [harmony], so it gives birth to things. Perhaps this is the law of everything, yet no form is seen." —**Zhuangzi, Chapter 21**

One cannot extract Yin from Yang or Yang from Yin; no functional hierarchy exists. Neither is superior or separate. On the contrary, they signify the cosmos' unified equality, dynamism, and harmony, providing a lens to view the world. (*Internet Encyclopedia of Philosophy*, a peer-reviewed academic resource)

In our diminished capacity, true human potential remains untapped. It's as if we've been disconnected from the fuel line of our car. We need to reconnect the fuel line and fill up the car with gas. (-) Yin and (+) Yang energy creates the spark for it so we can re-embody with regenerative energy healing.

We all know life force energy; it is sometimes called "prana," the vital life force that permeates all things. This is what we have access to when our dynamic energy body is in flow! We are connected to Source. When it is gone, there's death to our physicality. Most of us are limping along, increasingly separated from our power source. We could be far more vibrantly alive if we only understood how to replenish. Connecting will make us radiate!

BIOELECTRIC TECHNOLOGY

Electrical impulses are as familiar to us as flipping a light switch. Consider the following terms to understand how electricity is commonly used in the field of electrical engineering and related disciplines. Whenever we do something as simple as turn on a light, the following principles become functions: charge, current, voltage, conductivity, circuit, power.

Medical science has shown that at a gross level, our bioelectric bodies respond well to various electromagnetic wave frequencies. They penetrate our circulatory systems, introducing the higher frequency that damaged and dense areas require for repair. Examples of two modalities are Electromagnetic Field Therapy (EFT) and Electrical Muscle Stimulation (EMS).

Electromagnetic frequencies or pulses (EMF) have been used for over a hundred years to stimulate metabolic healing, support detoxification, improve lymphatic flow, stimulate cellular regeneration, heal broken bones and balance the nervous system. They gained international recognition during Soviet Space Explorations when cosmonauts used pulsed electromagnetic field therapy (PEMF) to decrease bone lower vibration density loss. Interestingly, removing people from the Earth's gravitational and magnetic fields increases bone lower vibration density loss. (Thom & Drobot, 2018)

Electrical muscle stimulation (EMS) uses electrical impulses to stimulate muscle contraction. It is widely used in sports medicine, strength training and for reviving immobilized patients. Impulses delivered through pads that adhere to the skin mimic pulses from the central nervous system. They cause muscle contractions, creating movement. The movement heals the muscles. So we know, scientifically, that the bioelectric body exists and that electrical impulses can heal, producing a form of regenerative medicine.

SCIENCE OF REGENERATIVE MEDICINE

Awakening Prana! Regenerative Self-Healing will withstand the test of time because it dovetails with research in regenerative medicine. Regenerative medicine is the "wave of the future." The following sections explore well known scientists Kevin Tracy, and Michael Levin's research. We will see how *Awakening Prana! Regenerative Self-Healing's* steps follow Sally Adee's predictions in *We Are Electric.*

Kevin Tracey is a pioneer in the field of bioelectronic medicine. His research has focused on the molecular basis of inflammation and the nervous system's role in controlling the immune system. He has contributed significantly to understanding how the body responds to infection and injury and how this response can be modulated to treat disease. Tracey is a highly respected scientist and leader in the field of bioelectronic medicine. He is the President and CEO of the Feinstein Institutes for Medical Research, a leading biomedical research institute in New York. He is also a Molecular Medicine and Neurosurgery Professor at the Zucker School of Medicine at Hofstra/Northwell.

One of Tracey's most important discoveries was the identification of the inflammatory reflex. (Famm et al., 2013) Using nerve-stimulating electronic devices to treat inflammation and reverse disability is laying the foundation for a new discipline called bioelectronic medicine. It is being tested in clinical studies of patients with rheumatoid arthritis and other diseases.

Tracey reports, "It is based on a deceptively simple concept of harnessing the body's natural reflexes to develop an array of effective, safe, and economical alternatives to many pills and injectable drugs. By precisely targeting the biological processes underlying disease, this nerve-stimulating technology should help avoid the troublesome side effects of many drugs." (Tracey, Scientific American, 2015)

Electroceuticals are still under development, but they have the potential to revolutionize the way we treat many different conditions. Some examples of electroceuticals that are already in use include pacemakers, cochlear implants, and deep brain stimulators used to treat various neurological disorders.

Electroceuticals are also being investigated for treating many other conditions, including chronic pain, Inflammatory bowel disease, Alzheimer's disease, heart failure, diabetes, and cancer. They offer several advantages over traditional treatments, such as drugs and surgery. They are often less invasive and have fewer side effects. They can also be more effective in treating some conditions.

Michael Levin is a biology professor at Tufts University, director of the Tufts Center for Regenerative and Developmental Biology, and associate faculty member at the Wyss Institute for Biologically Inspired Engineering at Harvard University. Levin's fascination with bioelectricity evolved into a quest to answer one of life's longstanding mysteries: How do animals know what shape to take when they grow a head or repair their bodies? He points out that although the genome is thought to be life's instruction manual, those assembly instructions aren't in our DNA. His logic follows the laws of chemistry until the laws begin to break down. He explains that "If you take a human or many other kinds of embryos and you cut them in half, you don't get two half bodies the way that you would get if you cut a car or a computer or something else in half, you get two perfectly normal monozygotic twins, and the way that happens is because that collection of cells can tell that half of it is missing and it can tell that it needs to rebuild what's missing? That process right there is literally a kind of intelligence, and once you've understood that the body, much like the brain, is a collective intelligence and the morphogenesis is the behavior of that collective intelligence, you can start to ask all sorts of interesting questions. How can you train it? How do you know what it's thinking? How do you communicate with it? (UC Chicago News Podcast, 2023)

I ask questions similar to Levin's about morphogenesis and the role of collective intelligence. After all, I healed my nervous system in ways that defied modern allopathic treatment. My premise is that regenerative medicine does not have to depend on machines. We can access our bioelectric technology through working with the energy body and its connection to Source, nature and the Elements.

Levin's discoveries have enhanced healing capacity in allopathic medical environments. For instance, researchers at the University of California, San Francisco, use Levin's work to develop new treatments for spinal cord injuries. At the University of Washington, researchers are using Levin's work to develop new treatments for heart failure. The Wyss Institute utilizes Levin's work to develop new ways to regenerate cartilage and bone.

Min Zhao, a dermatologist at the University of California, Davis, studies how electrical gradients at wound sites are superior healing guides. Utilized to guide electric signals that can regulate how human stem cells migrate to repair wounds. A wound-induced electric current—triggered when cells are damaged and ions pour out—starts to flow the instant skin is cut. "It happens faster than any chemical changes," Zhao reveals "When I first started working on this, I thought the electric field would be just another of hundreds of physical and chemical factors. But when we put all these chemical signals together and compared them, we found that the electric field's physiological strength overrides the rest." (Madhusoodanan, Jyoti, PBS, Nova Next, 2018)

Sally Adee, an award-winning science and technology journalist and author of *We Are Electric*, sees a future validating my premise, taking regenerative medicine beyond the electroceutical industry.

> "But that's now. There are things in the pipeline that look nothing like these tools. They won't be made of metal. They will interface with us on a deeper level. And they will likely be made of the stuff we find in the natural world, which runs on the same electrical programming as we do." —**Adee, Sally, "We Are Electric," 2023, p. 240**

Now let us take the bioelectric discussion one step further . . .

Every life form has a feminine and masculine aspect.
The first time I was drawn to work with the bioelectric technology of the energy body as a healer was when I was guided to ask male/Divine Father energy to flow down the centerline of a male client. I lay my hand over the top of his head in a vertical way, with my palm in the back and fingers over the center of his brow. He needed shoring up of his male energy, and through such an important channel. He said he was thoroughly stabilized by the healing.

Little did I know at the time that I was starting a profound bioelectric practice to bring masculine and feminine energy into balance and replenishment for significant rejuvenation and healing.

Yin and Yang
The concept of Yin and Yang suggests that these two opposing forces are interconnected and interdependent. They are not absolute or separate entities but rather aspects of a whole. Yin and Yang are believed to exist in everything and are constantly in a state of dynamic balance. They complement and transform into each other, and their interaction is seen as the driving force behind natural cycles and changes.

It's important to note that Yin and Yang are not meant to be seen as good or bad, but rather as *complementary and necessary aspects of existence. They are magnetic.* The balance between Yin and Yang is key, and imbalances or excessive dominance of one over the other can lead to disharmony and imbalance. The philosophy of Yin and Yang has had a significant influence on various aspects of Chinese culture, including traditional medicine, martial arts, feng shui, and even daily life.

It is important to note that this book is not about gender. *Awakening Prana! Regenerative Self-Healing* focuses on transcendent, dynamic energy that anyone can access to heal and feel complete.

THE TRANSFORMATIVE TECHNOLOGY OF AWAKENING PRANA!

Ancient wisdom meets modern technology in this set of steps, techniques, and exercises that are designed in sequence to raise your vibration. Your energy body will revitalize while you embody your physicality, grounding in daily life. The method creates regenerative self-transformation, radiating through your body, mind, and spirit.

The steps are a shamanic journey through kriya and kripa—dynamic energy sequences and grace through prayer.

- Kriya - step within a yoga system
- Kripa - divine grace in eastern philosophy.

The result? At long last we find a system that can quickly bring transformation, regeneration, and radiance to lives burdened by trauma, dis-ease, and suffering.

I present a unique kriya, the Awakening Prana! kriya of sequential steps (I - IX). Each will be discussed in detail throughout Part I and Part II. I explain each step in Part I, and coordinate the sequence to ignite embodiment through sound, meditation, and invocation, in Part II. They coalesce into the complete Awakening Prana! kriya by Step IX, when we are ready to receive data transmissions- light codes from Source for our transformation.

OUR BATTERIES ARE DRAINED

Yang Imbalances of Yin (-) and (+) Yang
There are many ways in our lives that our batteries are low and even drained because the currents of Yin (-) and Yang (+) aren't flowing at full capacity. Here are four primary depletion areas we can identify and balance. Reading this book offers a system to detect depletion, and restore equilibrium and balance.

We detect Yin and Yang depletion by looking at the following four categories:

Category A: Body. Our physicality, nature, and relationship with the Elements.
Solution: We are made of the Elements. Connecting to them (Step I).

> "The simplest thing you can do to change the health and fundamental structure of your body is to treat the five Elements with devotion and respect."
> –Sadhguru, *Inner Engineering*

Category B: Mind. Our distracted minds, wounded egos.
Restless, unfocused, and scattered state; hamster wheel thinking of the wounded ego, all block our deeper connection to our truest nature.
Solution: Healing the mother (Yin) and father (Yang) wounds (Step II).

The ego is the part of us that is constantly striving for something, whether it is happiness, success, or recognition.

> "The ego is the Source of our restlessness and discontent." –**Tara Brach**

The collective also bombards us with its imbalances. Objectification of women, pressure on men to be macho, political division, hatred and prejudice.

Category C: Spirit. Our disconnect from our souls/higher selves.
When we are disconnected on this level we deprive ourselves of guidance, wisdom, and unconditional love.
Solution: Asking our soul mother and father in to help and restore balance (Step III).

We restore equilibrium and balance when we connect to our pilot:

> "The soul is the pilot of the body, and the Higher Self is the soul's pilot." –**Plato**

Category D: From Source. Our trauma's lower vibration density blocks the flow of Life Force.

Ultimately we have to experience and embody the Source, All That Is, The Great Spirit, the Presence of Love, the Atman, or Brahman, according to our definition of spirituality.
Solution: Steps I-IX, breaking down the lower vibration density blocking our connection to Source, to OM, to Source's Life Force.

> "God is not a person, but a presence. We can feel God's presence in our hearts, minds, and souls." –**Deepak Chopra**

RECONNECTING TO THE MATRIX OF LIGHT!

The definition of axiatonal involves <u>aligning</u> of <u>energies</u> in the <u>body</u> with a <u>cosmic grid</u> of energy. To Source.

Note that for this book I've chosen to call the highly vibrant essence, of which the Cherokee say there is no name because it is so beyond our imagination, Source. I feel that this terminology is inclusive of a wide spectrum of belief. Insert whatever word/concept is resonant for you: Source, Creator, Infinite Reality, Creation, the All That Is, Mother/Father God, God, Brahman, Buddha, Waheguru, Allah, or Yahweh... .

I've studied everything I could get my hands on about the "axiatonal grids" over the last few years, including the seminal writing about it in *The Book of Knowledge: The Keys of*

Enoch, pondering every single line in section 3-1-7. I have pages of diagrams trying to track how the energy flowed from what I learned.

The Axiatonal Teachings
The axiatonal system teachings define a cosmic energy "lattice" of axiatonal light lines and grids. Humans have become disconnected from the energy lattice.

In a nutshell, and in my own words, the axiatonal lines and grids focus on what I call:

- Source currents, the currents of prana that carry life force energy, our quantum DNA, the radiance of Source, to the axiatonal grids, what I call
- the receptor points for this regenerative light to come into our physicality, at the meeting point of our energy body and our bodies.

The Source currents bring the quantum self to the receptor points. The Torus, explained in more detail further on, carries the flow of the Source currents to the places in need of healing and transformation.

The Matrix of Light
The axiatonal system teachings explain that there is a cosmic grid that the axiatonal lines and subgrids tap into. A system that has become disconnected from the light because of the premise of this book, that we have lost the bioelectric capacity to connect to such a matrix of light. Especially from the sacred feminine.

Awakening Prana! finds its path through untangling how and where we lost our bioelectric capacity, and how we can reclaim it. We have lost the *bioelectric capacity* to connect to such a matrix of light because we are out of Yin and Yang balance. It focuses on the connection to the Source of the grid and gives the tools for how we can reclaim this capacity.

This practice recognizes we are part of a huge matrix of light that includes the ley lines on the planet and the lines of the Torus running through us. Building human capacity for connecting to this matrix of light by repairing Yin and Yang imbalances as shown in the 9 Steps is the key to regenerative energy medicine.

OUR ENERGY FLOW IS BLOCKED

The flow of our energy body, and our connection to Source energy, is blocked from lower vibration density that has built up because of trauma, programmed behaviors, and other ways we cut off from flow. Lower vibration density in the energy body is a concept that is used in a variety of different healing modalities. It refers to the amount of blockages or stagnant energy that is present in the body's energy field. It occurs because the bioelectrical engine system isn't running well and lower vibration density builds up and blocks flow. These blockages can be caused by a variety of factors, including stress, trauma, and negative emotions.

What Creates lower vibration density?

The hamster wheel thought process that I experienced and have witnessed in my clients came from layers of trauma. The layers became embedded in my physicality, chakras and nervous system, but the original trauma is held in perpetuity in the auric fields. From there it manifests at the cellular level unless brought into coherence through therapy, energy work, or, believe it or not, positive thinking ("we create our own reality").

Any type of trauma impacts our cells; it disrupts our electrical current system. Osteopath John Upledger, the pioneer of craniosacral therapy has demonstrated how our cells retain memory during over four decades of study. His motto for students became, "Let the cells speak." (Upledger, 1997) However, cells can only speak when we provide the proper environment for them.

Who ya gonna call? The battery current of the feminine and masculine aspects of Source.

THE ENERGY BODY

LETS SWITCH ON!

An analogy helps people understand the energy body and how it functions, while providing a useful framework for working with and balancing energy. Take a moment - think of a car and its components.

CAR ANALOGY

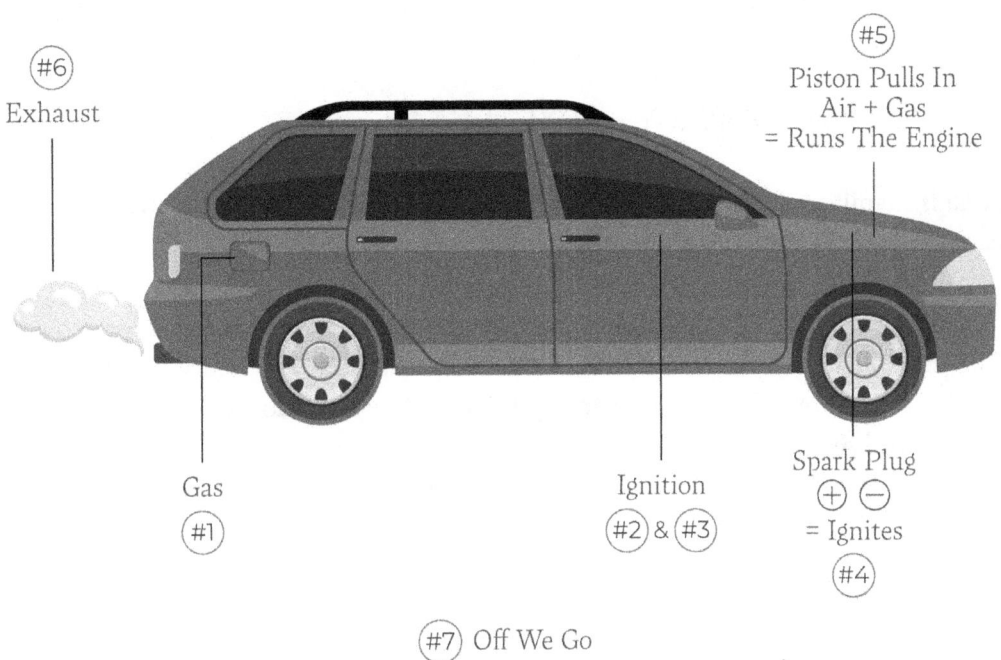

The car parts correspond to our energy body components. It's fascinating! Here's how it works:

#1. **Gas** - represents life force, the energy animating the body and keeping it alive.

#2. **Car Key** - represents the connection between the driver (the energy body) and the car (the natural world).

#3. **Ignition** - represents the electrical current that ignites the engine, or life force for the energy body.

#4. **Battery** - starts the engine by providing electricity to a small electrical motor known as the starter motor. The energy body has (-) and (+), too.

#4. **Spark Plug** - represents the spark that ignites the fuel in the car engine, while Source activates the energy body.

#5. **Piston** - represents the component pulling air and gas into the engine, causing it to run. The energy body has something similar.

#6. **Exhaust** - represents the release of exhaust fumes from the car engine - the energy body is the letting go of negative energy.

#7. **"Off We Go"** - represents the car starting and moving forward.

Now take the analogy a step further. Let's create a framework for reclaiming our vitality in phases, step, by step. Look at the corresponding phases of energy currents in living beings propelling us towards healing.

AWAKEN YOUR ENERGY BODY!

A car is a familiar object. We have understood it from our childhood. Now, let us use the car analogy as a foundation for understanding the energy body.

What about the energy body? How can we grasp it?

Just like we have a dense system of bones and blood, we have an energy body network. The energy body consists of a number of subtle interconnecting systems and structures:

Here is an overview, with more in depth about each part following.

The **Central Axis** is the key. It is All That Is About You. It carries the energy of your truest nature, your link to Source, and your sacred nature. It is your keepsake throughout lifetimes.

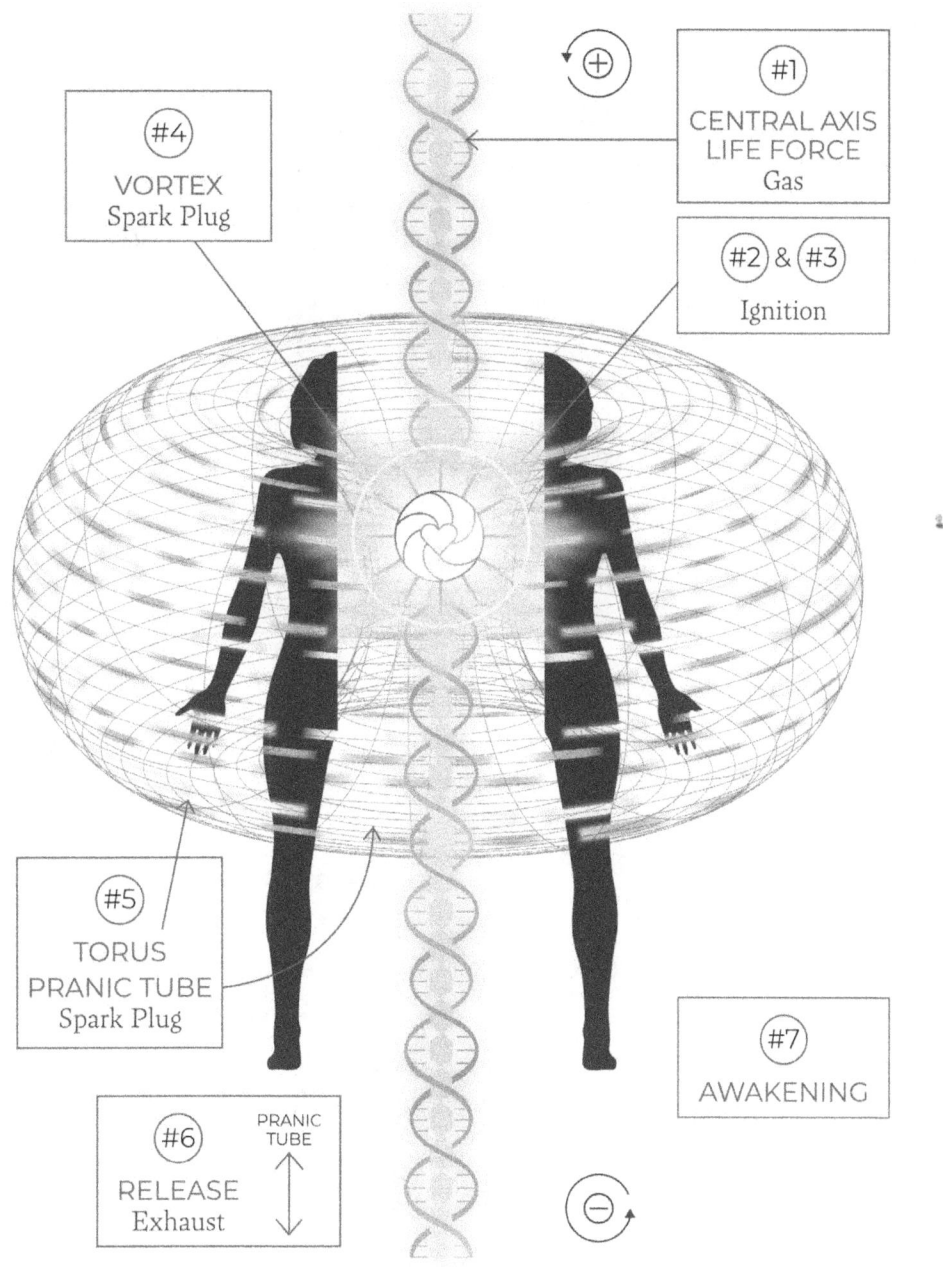

The **Torus** surrounds the human body and resembles a donut or a ring. It has a hole in the middle. The Torus is formed by a vortex around the Central Axis.

The inside surface of the Torus is called the "inner tube," the "sleeve" of the Torus, and the inner sleeve is the **Pranic Tube**, also known as the central channel. The Pranic Tube is an energy channel that pulls in Yin energy from the root base of the body and Yang energy from above to the crown of our head, and rotates around the **Central Axis**, creating the Torus.

THE TORUS

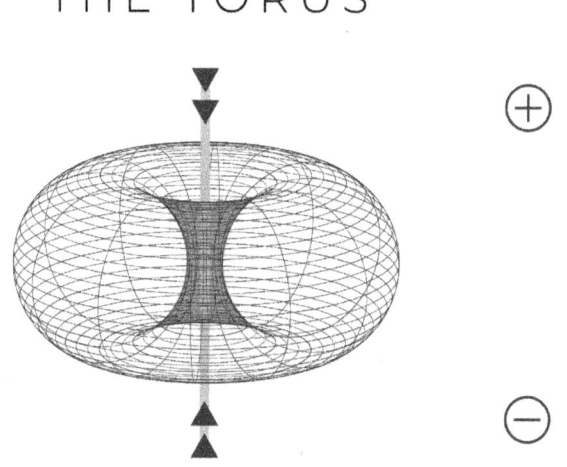

Torus Is Created From The Yin And Yang Vortex

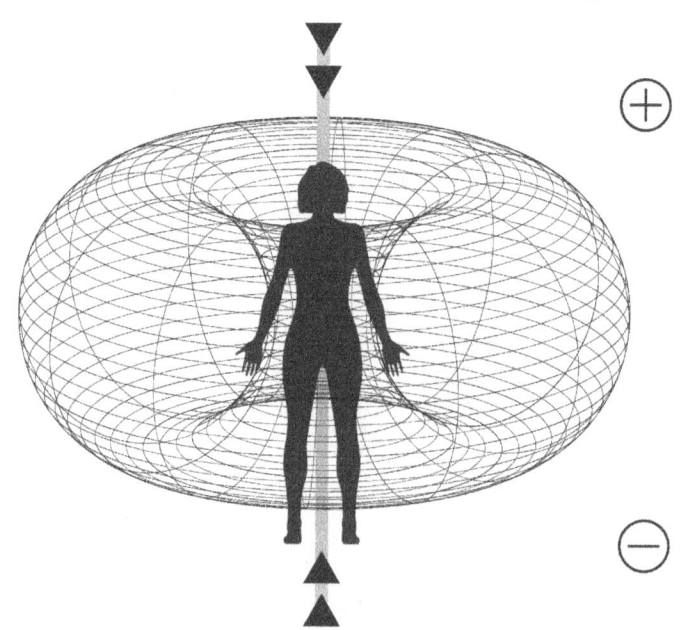

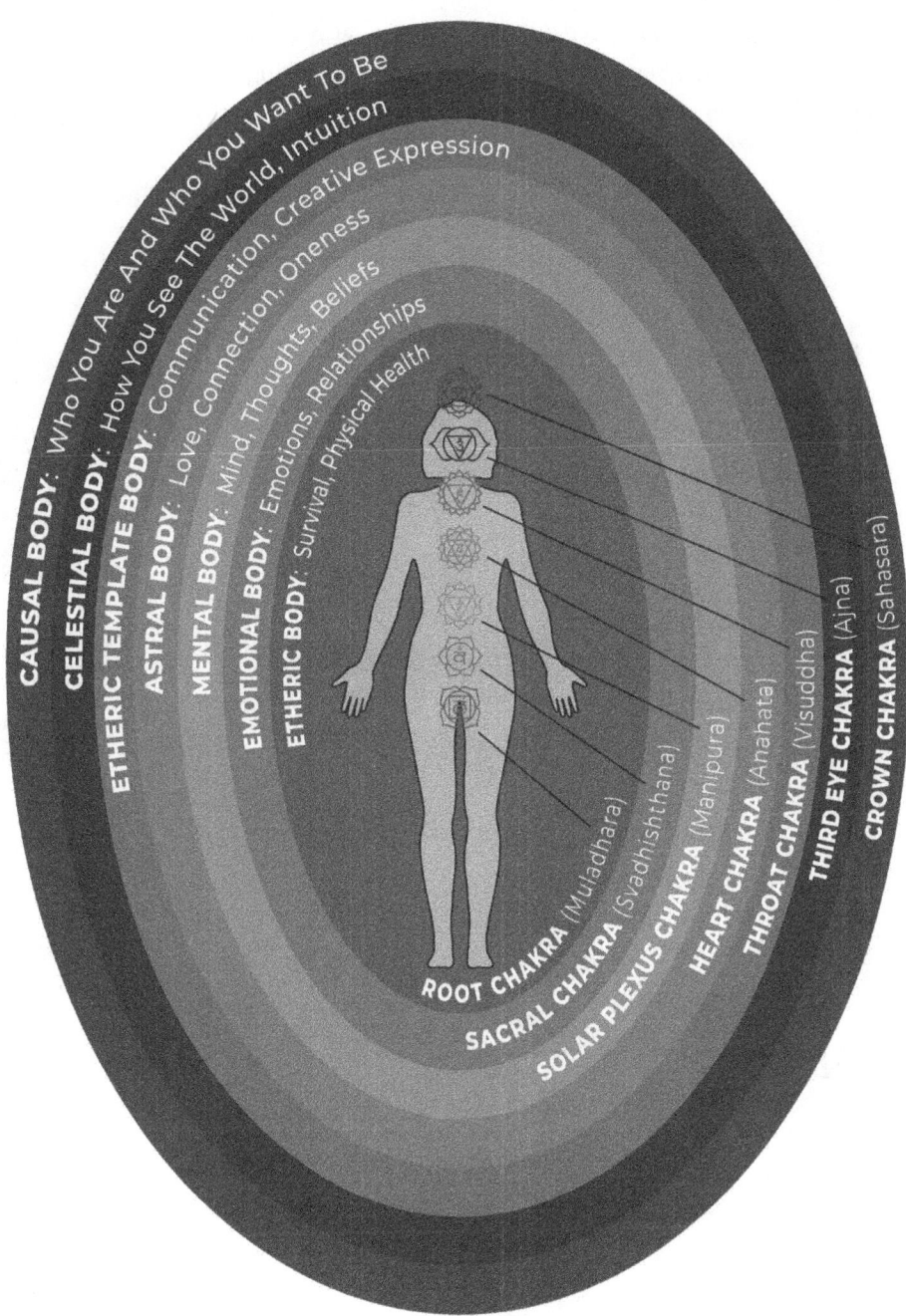

Auric fields are the layers of energy that surround the physical body, including the emotional, mental, and spiritual aspects of a person. There are several layers of **auric fields**, each with a different color and vibration, and they correlate to the chakras.

The **Elements** Earth, Fire, Water, Air, and Ether make up our physicality and energy body structure.

Our **Higher Self** is our liaison with our soul and The All That Is.

Within the Energy Body:

Chakras are energy centers located along the spine that relate to different developmental fields of consciousness. There are seven main chakras, starting from the root base of the body and extending to the crown of the head.

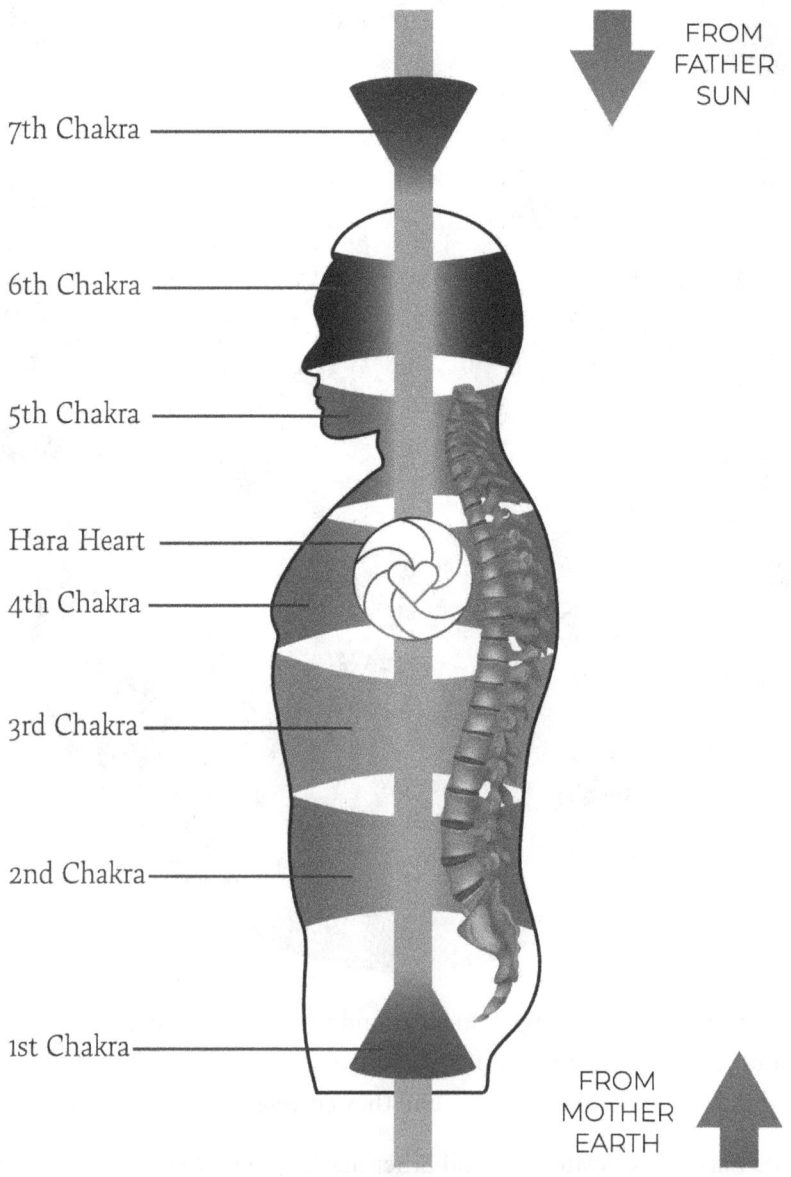

CAR/ENERGY BODY ANALOGY

Note how the steps of the *Awakening Prana!* healing as noted, below, relates to the car's engine.

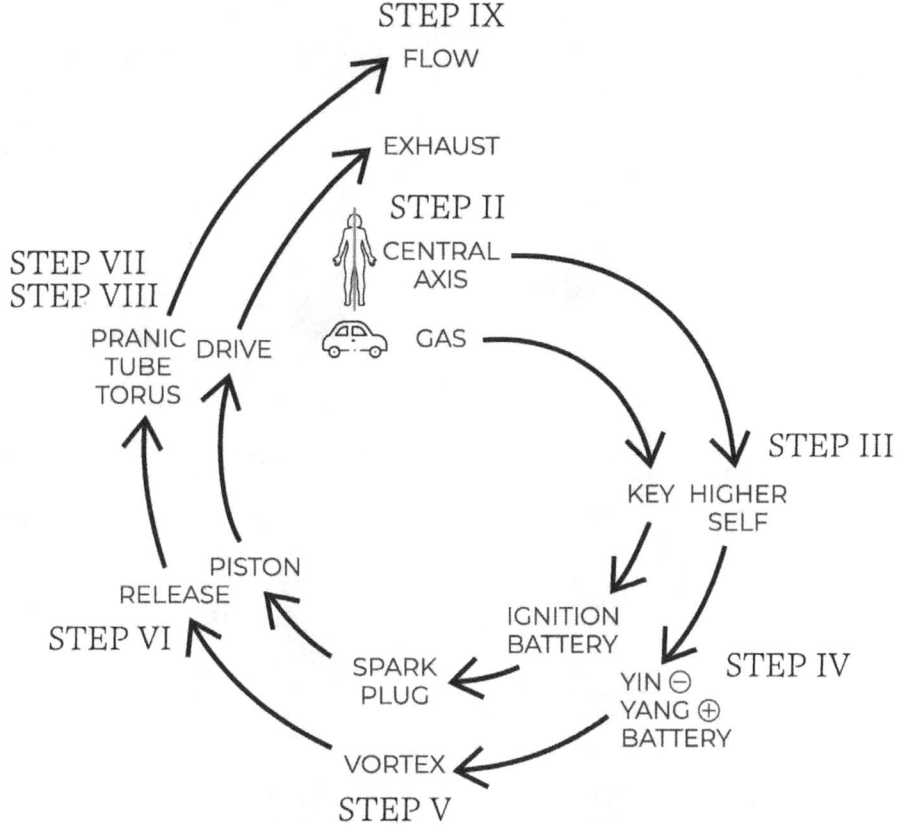

ENERGETIC FLOW VS. ENERGETIC CLOGGING

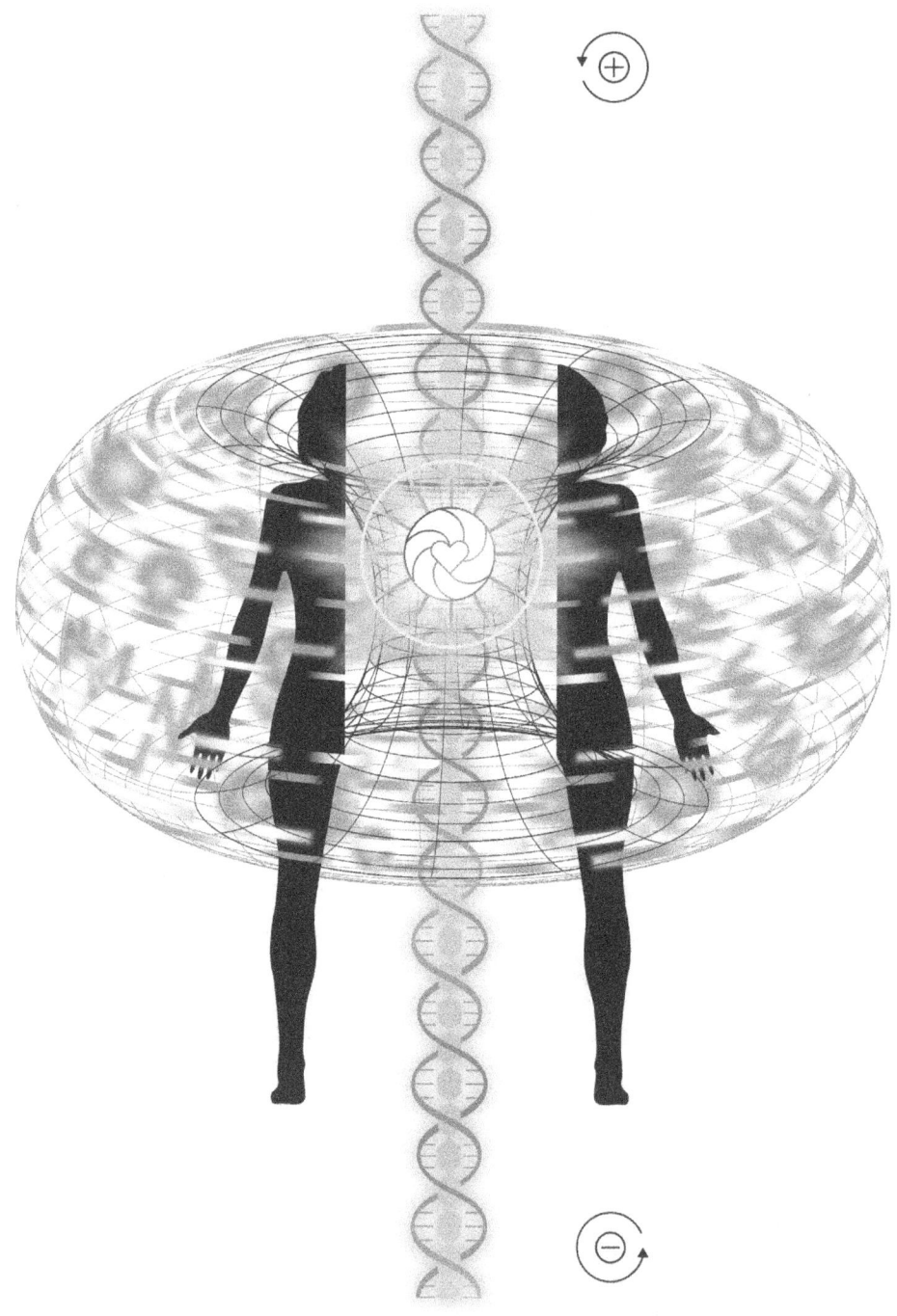

BEFORE Clearing and Releasing

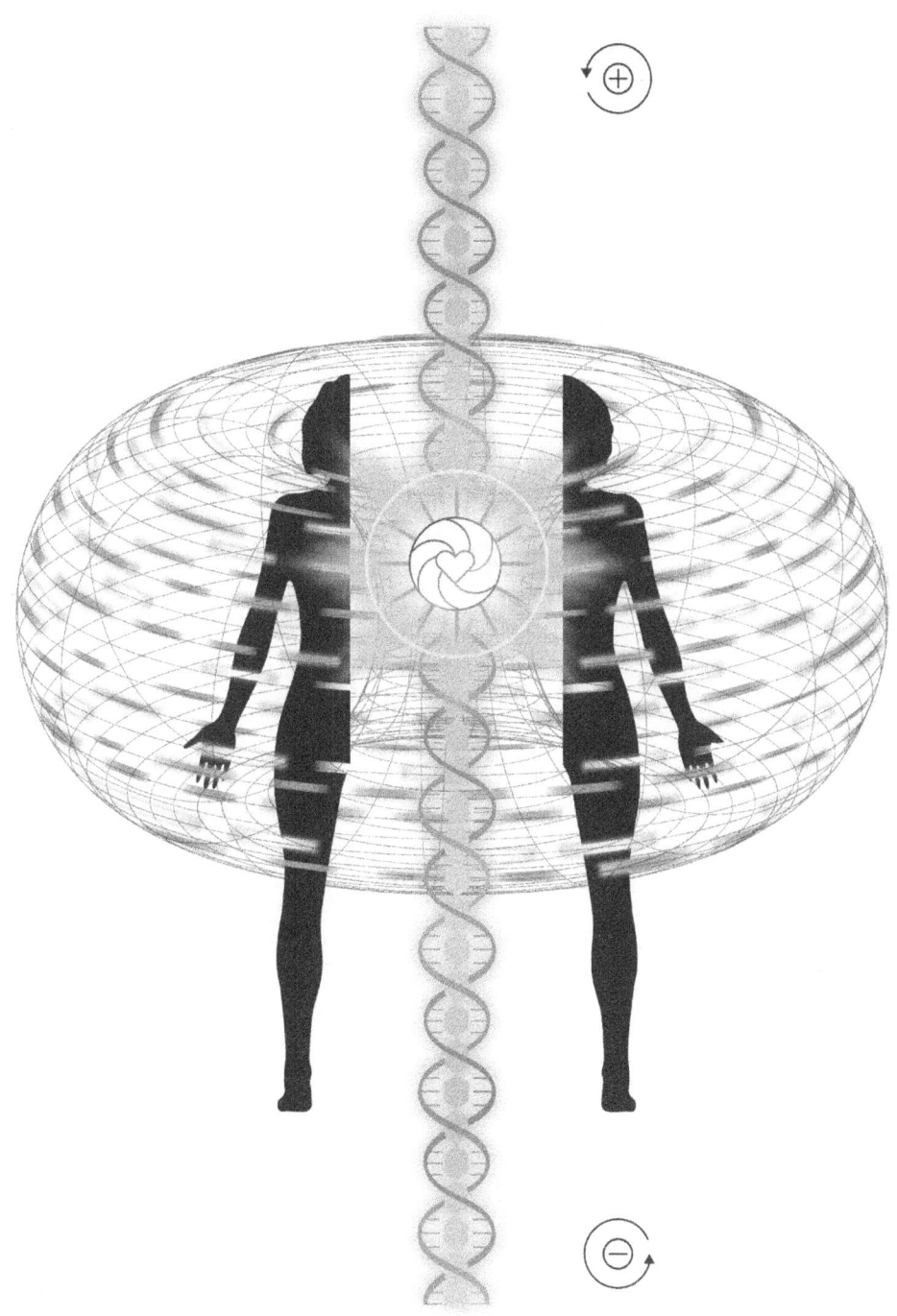

AFTER Clearing and Releasing

PART I

· · · · · · · · · ·

LEARN ABOUT THE REGENERATIVE SELF-TRANSFORMATION

Here is a sequential overview of the 9 Steps, techniques, and exercises that are designed to raise your vibration.

BEHIND THE SEQUENTIAL NINE STEPS OF THE
AWAKENING PRANA! KRIYA/STEP

Step I - Embody (the Sacred Elements)
Being here now, being grounded, connecting to Earth, Fire, Water, Air, and Ether in a spiritual and physical way.

Step II - Connect (Higher Self/Soul)
Developing a relationship with your Higher Self helps you gain self-agency, wisdom, and discernment.

Step III - Charge - Replenish Batteries (Yin and Yang Equal Balance)
Establishing a balanced electrical charge, You need equal amounts of the (-) feminine, Yin current with the (+) masculine, Yang current to fill your batteries.

Step IV - Power Up - The Motor (Ignite/Activate the Energy Body Vortex)
We experience an alchemy of change and replenishment as the (-) and (+) charges ignite a Vortex of powerful prana energy. Without the Vortex, the energy body would not move. The Vortex creates movement and flow of prana throughout, creating a Torus (see Step VII).

Step V - Release (Remove lower vibration density)
Here the lower vibration density of our suffering is pushed out of our energy body, allowing the flow of radiant, life force.

Step VI - Meet (Source)
Experiencing the Source of our perfect blueprint, our Life Force energy, and The All That Is.

Step VII - Increase Voltage (Pranic Tube Draws Prana)
The Vortex of Step V creates a powerful push/pull of energy from above (Sun) and below (Earth), through our central channel, as well as from the Source energy from our Central Axis, increasing our voltage.

Step VIII - Conduct Energy (All Systems Go; Toroidal Flow)
The building of the energy body from Steps I-VII brings us to the Torus around us, a donut-shaped Vortex of energy that is responsible for the flow of energy throughout our body, as well as our connection to the universe. The Torus is a conductor of healing energy.

Step IX - Awaken (Come into Complete Flow with Source)
At last we are fully connected to Source energy. It freely flows to us bringing with it the regenerative energy of our quantum DNA and the sound, color, and healing powers of Source.

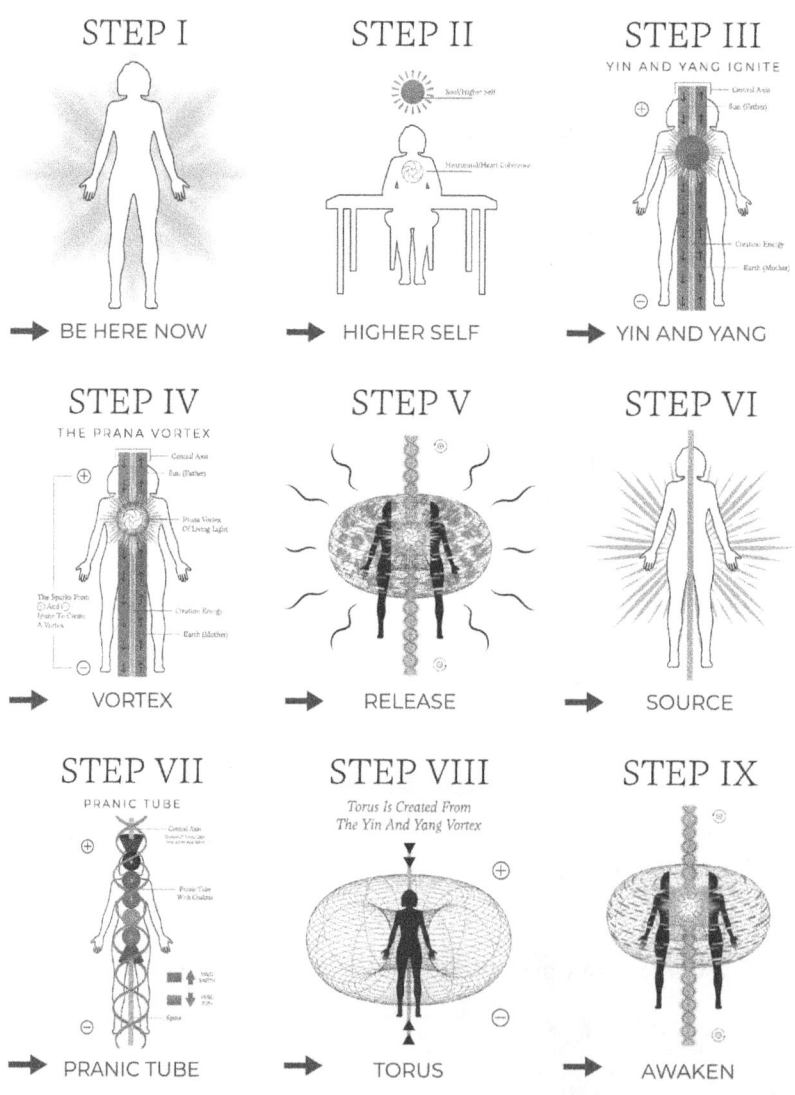

STEP I: THE ELEMENTS
BACKGROUND ABOUT THIS STEP OF THE SEQUENCE

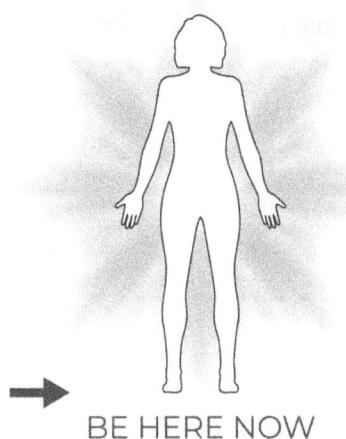

BE HERE NOW

"Love every leaf... Love the animals, love the plants, love everything. If you love everything, you will perceive the sacred mystery in things."
—Fyodor Dostoyevsky

The Sacred Elements establish the dynamism of our energy body! They establish the current of life force inside of us, they build the structure of the system. Lack of flow results in part from our disconnection from nature.

The sacred geometry form of the Sacred Elements deeply interconnects everything in the Universe. There are timelines and there is master jigsaw work involved in their sacred geometry and how they connect with each other. Without the Elements we couldn't embody the life force Source currents into our physicality. Earth, Water, Fire, Air and Ether bring flow and movement to our energy body and physical body.

Being grounded on the planet, embedded in our earth star chakra, being in our bodies, "being here now, being embodied," is the key to integrating this step. When we are grounded, we feel more connected to ourselves, others, and to the world around us. The term "embodied" means to be fully present in your body and in the world around you. It means to be aware of your physical sensations, your emotions, and your thoughts. It also means to be connected to your surroundings and to the people in your life.

The teaching of "Be Here Now" can be traced back to many different spiritual traditions, including Hinduism, Buddhism, and Taoism. However, it was popularized in the West by the American spiritual teacher Ram Dass in his 1971 book of the same name. It is a message that encourages us to live in the present moment and to appreciate the here and now. It is a reminder that the past is gone and the future is not yet here; the only thing we have is the present moment.

> "Living in right relationship with the elements is a journey, not a destination. It takes time, effort, and commitment. But it is a journey that is well worth taking." —**Rebecca Tsosie**

DIARY OF A HEALER

Working with the Elements is a fundamental part of every single healing I give. If you think of it, the elements move energy. Water washes it, Fire burns it, Air blows it, Earth magnetizes it. I call them in—and yes, I personify them—to aid in shifting lower vibration density. A person may be holding lower vibration density in their chakras and their physical body. I've found that if a person is extremely sick, they are almost always depleted of Ether. Asking Ether to bathe them in healing radically boosts their health. Water is a wonderful element for clearing the emotional arena and Earth for the physical.

I've found working with the Elements especially powerful for clearing Covid. Early variants of the virus looked impenetrable—like the glued together way broken car windshields look—locking people in and making them suffocate. Water helped penetrate that glue, Fire burned through it, Air blew through it, Earth pulled it apart, and Ether brought eternal love.

What and Why of the Elements

> "We shall have to find ourselves within nature before God is able to find us."
> —**William Barrett**

Humans are:

72% Water
12% Earth
6% Air
6% Ether
4% Fire

The five Elements of nature, Earth, Fire, Water, Air, and Ether are in constant flow and interaction with each other. Each element has its own unique qualities and characteristics, and each element can transform into another element.

- Earth is the element of stability and grounding. It is associated with the physical world, the body, and the material realm. Earth provides us with a foundation to stand on and a place to grow. It makes our bones.
- Fire is the element of transformation and passion. It is associated with the sun, the heart, and the will. Fire can be used to create or destroy, and it is a powerful force of change. Fire keeps us warm.
- Water is the element of emotion and intuition. It is associated with the moon, the womb, and the unconscious mind. Water is fluid and ever-changing, and it can represent both our deepest fears and our greatest potential. It makes our blood.
- Air is the element of intellect and communication. It is associated with the wind, the mind, and the breath. Air is the element of communication and creativity, and it allows us to connect with others and with our higher selves. Air enables us to breathe.
- Ether is the element of spirit and consciousness. It is associated with the stars, the soul, and the sacred. Ether is the Source of all Source, and it is the element that connects us all. Ether is our spirit.

The flow and interaction of the five Elements is a complex and ever-changing process. Each element plays an important role in the balance of our bodies. Each element also plays an important role in the balance of nature.

- Earth provides us with a foundation, fire helps us to transform, water nourishes us, air allows us to communicate, and ether connects us to the sacred. Earth is the foundation of the system, and it provides the raw materials for the other Elements to transform.
- Fire is the heat that drives the transformation process, and it helps to create new forms from the old.
- Air is the medium through which the transformation takes place, and it allows the different Elements to interact with each other.

- Water is the lubricant that keeps the system flowing smoothly, and it helps to distribute the energy of transformation throughout the system.
- Ether is the spirit of the system, and it binds all of the Elements together into a unified whole.

The flow and interaction of the five Elements is a dynamic process that is constantly changing. However, the basic principles of transformation, communication, and connection remain the same. These principles can be applied to our own lives, and they can help us to create more balance and harmony in our world.

The healing you receive from the Elements is deep and true. Try to connect. Start with the meditation in Part II; sometimes you'll feel the energy shift inside of you. You are receiving healing. The shift could be energy body based but it could also be physical.

When you connect to:

- Earth you could sense your bones and muscles,
- Water you could feel fluidity,
- Fire you could feel a shift in your digestion or body temperature,
- Air you might tune into your breath and nervous system,
- Ether you might feel a lightening of tensions as there is an increased flow of the internal energy channels.

Tom Kenyon seared a new way of looking at the Elements Earth, Air, Water, Fire, and Ether into my brain about twenty years ago, when I read his book, *The Hathor Material*. He describes channeling in the Hathors from an "ascended intergalactic civilization." Stoneman tells me: "We are highly ascended beings who are rooting for the Earth as she comes into her ascension. We've been working with your planet since well before Egyptian times, back to the Lemurians. We have seeded the sound healings of many ancestral lineages, especially Native American, Tibetan Buddhist, and Taoist. Today we are working with a louder sound, bringing it to those of you who can hear it and translate it to seed the new path of the WAY."

The Hathors revealed to Kenyon that the Elements are huge, powerful sacred beings who have agreed/offered to "hold" their energies here on this planet so that we could exist. One could look at them each as a form of sacred consciousness. They bring form to our understanding of the connection between matter and consciousness. Kenyon channeled, "...[Y]our body is a sacred temple, for it is the space in which the four Sacred Elements of Earth, Fire, Water, and Air/Space offer themselves to you in service."

DIARY OF A HEALER

I've taken shamanic journeys to meet each of the Elements as if they were individual Beings—each journey gave me extraordinary experiences. A shamanic journey is an altered state of consciousness in which a person enters the spirit world to seek guidance, healing, or information. There are many different ways to induce a shamanic journey; I initiate mine through drumming to induce a deep trance state and ask a spirit animal to accompany me, ensuring guidance and protection.

Imagine the Elements as huge benevolent beings of consciousnesses that have agreed to give us form on the planet. Earth, Water, Fire, Air, and Ether.

When I met Earth the first time I encountered a wise and kind grandmother-aged Native American woman with long braids. She was busy but turned to tell me that she could magnetize down and transmute all poisons such as heavy metals—toxic poisons sent to her. How heartening!

When I met Water she appeared as a goddess-like woman in a pool of water in a glade in the woods. In full glory, she twirled her arms dancing, casting sounds over the gently rippling waves.

Fire presented himself as a man with a beard of flames. He exuded kindness, I felt enveloped in compassionate understanding.

Air and Ether had the most diffuse personifications; after all, Air has just a bit of matter and Ether, none.

While encountering Air I felt connected to the kind of air at the top of a mountain: crisp, containing expansive universal bell tones, like a singing bowl. Air creates a visionary outlook, it seems to help me have a bird's eye view putting my mind into perspective mostly!

The first time I went to meet Ether I saw a pulsing system like the Milky Way, and it was pulsing with love in a similar way that people claim to have felt in NDEs. The second time changed me—and the way I give healings—forever. In my mind's eye I saw great spiders unwinding webs from around giant trees. Ether told me that they were unwinding the webs of illusion. Imagine yourself a tree and there is a web of illusion around you—and the mistaken belief systems you may have—and Ether is here to unwind them from their stranglehold.

The Elements will assist you. So, ground yourself well, drink lots of clean water, be warm, breathe fresh air, and remain in your heart!

The Elements Directly Lead to Yin/Matter/Divine Mother

According to many indigenous belief systems and eastern spiritual traditions, the feminine is associated with the Elements Earth, Water, and Air. These Elements are often seen as representing different aspects of the natural world. Therefore the foundation of embodying the Elements, translates into embodying the Divine Mother.

Working with the Elements for Metaphysical Healing

On a metaphysical level, working with Elements in energy healing results in an extraordinary collaboration. The Elements are top level healers we can call upon to help release stuck, dense energy.

- Earth magnetizes it down to its bedrock.
- Water washes it away.
- Fire burns it away.
- Air blows it away.
- Ether removes it.

On the giving side the Sacred Elements restore the energy body.

- Earth builds the foundation.
- Water cleanses and purifies.
- Fire kindles and transforms.
- Air opens pathways.
- Ether bathes the energy body in eternal love.

> *The Elements wash, they magnetize down, they burn, they blow, they remove, they build, they cleanse and purify, they kindle, they transform, they open pathways.*

Elemental associations are part of ancient philosophical frameworks and we can co-create healing with them in various holistic healing steps and alternative medicine systems such as acupuncture and Ayurveda.

DIARY OF A HEALER

The Need for Ether for Those With an Advanced Illness

I've had a few clients over the years who have been very, very sick. With every single one of them they have been significantly depleted of the sacred element Ether. Hovering around as high as 60% depleted for those near death. Asking for the sacred element Ether to bathe them in its energy has been transformative and in some cases helped the client pivot to a road of recovery.

THE ENERGY PROPELLING ALL SENTIENT BEINGS

Life Force comes to us through channels of energy that flow through the human body and connect it with the universe. Let us look at elemental healing through another lens: the platonic solids.

The Platonic Solids

Sacred geometry is the study of the geometry of nature and the universe, and how it can be used to understand and connect with the divine. It is the belief that certain geometric shapes and proportions have special spiritual and metaphysical significance. The platonic solids hold sacred geometry and the face of the elements. Earth's face, for example, is a cube. Air is an octahedron. The platonic solids are organized in the way they are regarding their sides because of lower vibration density, not because of agency. For instance, the dodecahedron with twelve sides is Ether even though it has no lower vibration density and it has fewer sides than the icosahedron, which has twenty sides and is Water, an element that carries a lot of lower vibration density.

The complexity is hard to understand but the miraculous thing is to see how within these shapes the Elements create all things. They are on the face of all Elements! All matter is like a gigantic jigsaw puzzle of sacred geometry. The puzzle pieces of the Elements fit together, one force supports and sustains another. The winds that blow around the earth occur because the sun creates pressure differences in the air and the earth's rotation propels the air through the Southern and Northern Hemispheres. The earth under your feet is there because of the fire element in molten lava, melting and creating new land forms.

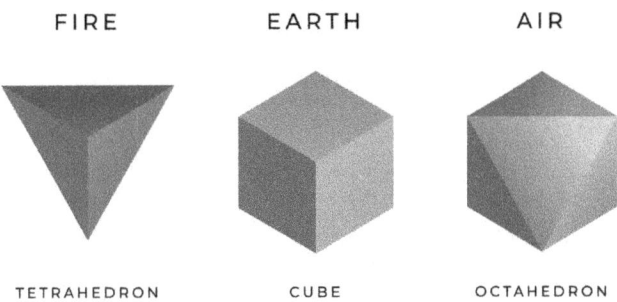

FIRE — TETRAHEDRON
EARTH — CUBE
AIR — OCTAHEDRON

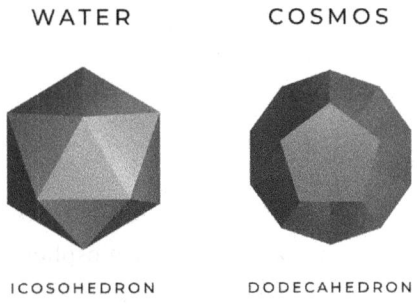

WATER — ICOSOHEDRON
COSMOS — DODECAHEDRON

The Elements and Platonic Solids Correspond to the Chakras
- Hexahedron/Cube (6 sides) - Earth Element - First Chakra
- Icosahedron (20 sides) - Water Element - Second Chakra
- Tetrahedron (3 sides) - Fire Element - Third Chakra
- Octahedron (8 sides) - Air Element Heart - Fourth Chakra
- Dodecahedron (12 sides) - Ether - Fifth Chakra

THE ELEMENTS: BOTH MATTER AND CONSCIOUSNESS

Earth is mother, earth is matter. Matter is that which defines us. A baby, a fern, a loaf of bread. Who births a baby? It is who births all forms. The mother. *Yin energy is the energy of the Mother, of matter.* It is form and nurturance. A key to understanding the imbalance of the Yin on the planet is to realize that all of the five Sacred Elements except for Ether are mostly Yin; they contain matter, and matter is the realm of the sacred feminine. It is an important point.

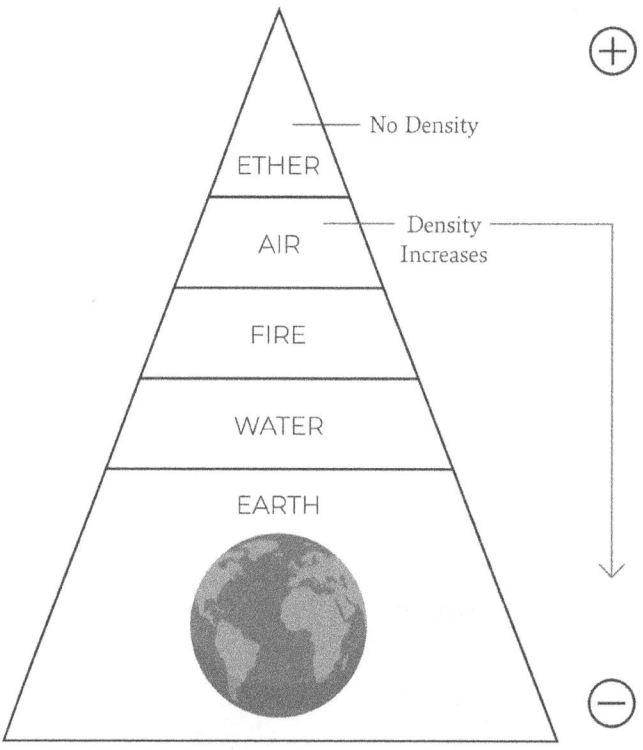

Air has the least amount of matter. Many confuse Air with Ether, yet they are quite different. Air is contained within Ether in planet Earth's atmosphere. Ether is space and extends throughout the universe, beyond the edge of our galaxy.

WARNING ALERT

• • • • • • • • • • • • •

Are you grounded? Grounding is our first connection to the Elements, before taking healing deeper.

EXPERIENTIAL EXERCISE

Grounding is Essential

How do you feel grounded? One simple way is to simply imagine yourself a tree, with roots drinking deep into the Earth. The roots not only go down but they also drink up the nutrients. The branches reach up to the sun and drink down the light.

Being Grounded Connects Us to the Earth

It often isn't easy to be on the planet. Physical and emotional issues prevail and when in trauma it is easy to dissociate from the body.

The lower chakras are involved in safety and security, relationships, ego, and personal power in the world, and when trauma happens in these areas we "shoot" out of our lower chakras into our higher ones, becoming ungrounded in the process.

Symptoms of being ungrounded include being spacey, symptoms of ADHD, or being "in one's head," full of self-doubt, unable to make decisions, generally in a fog. Hamster-wheeling to me means all of the variations on the above.

For healers, when we are ungrounded we go into self-doubt, which is always a heads up to step back, and take time to become grounded. Grounding is absolutely essential because when we are fully embodied we are more connected to Source. When we are more connected to Source we carry a deeper wisdom about everything. With deeper wisdom comes clear intuition. Clear intuition leads us back to the Source of All That Is.

DIARY OF A HEALER

The Portrait of Someone Ungrounded

Too much trauma makes many want to be out of their bodies. This might be especially the case if a person is experiencing physical pain, but you'd be surprised about how many leave their bodies because of unbearable emotional pain. In either case, it is easier to *not feel*.

Ungrounded people are definitely "in their heads," but they are often very spacey, disconnected. Dissociated. They tend to reside in their higher chakras and try to abandon the issues of the lower four relating to security, safety, relationships, personal power, and love.

For more about how to ground, see Step I in Part II. My website, awakeningprana.com, has many invocation-based meditations, sound healings, and guided meditations to help ground.

BALANCING THE ELEMENTS WITHIN US

Let us think of it this way. If human bodies are approximately 72% water but we are not paying attention to the water element, or even abusing it, what does that tell us about our bodies? However, the relationship completely changes if you think of water as being this amazing spiritual being that is coming to put life on the planet. It adds a totally different dimension. Realizing the difference has brought tremendous joy to me, and my Level II teaching where we go on a shamanic journey into the Elements. We travel into the journey and experience each element as a vibrational Being—an extraordinary and transformative experience!

THE ELEMENTS IN OUR LIVES

The Elements in our lives give us:
1. Embodiment, physical manifestation.
2. They are the building blocks of the All That Is About Us.
3. They move! The Elements move our energy body and provide the dynamism for both of our energy body and much of our physical body, as well.

Being Grounded Connects Us to the Earth

It starts with the little things. You bite into an ear of corn grown by an heirloom seed, and a symphony of sweetness and flavor bursts forth in your mouth. While visiting a friend, you sleep in an all-wool, nothing-synthetic bed and wake up more fully rested and refreshed than you've felt in months. The experiences add up bit by bit, and you realize that you thrive when surrounded by nature—natural materials, nature's sounds, and naturally produced food. We are a society craving the real Elements.

Opening a relationship with the Elements is a journey bringing untold benefits. Feel your heart open when you see a beautiful waterfall, and open your heart to the water running through you, roughly 70% of your body. Feel your heart open as you appreciate a hummingbird feeding on nectar from a flower, and open your heart to the Earth inside of you, your bones, and your physical structure.

The Law of Reciprocity and the Elements

John Beal is a disabled Vietnam veteran who was given four months to live after a diagnosis of inoperable cancer. He survived three heart attacks and post-traumatic stress disorder from his experiences in war and experienced pain and deep spiritual suffering. John says, in a quote from Yes! Magazine, "I went down to the stream behind my house and just cried, wondering how I'd care for my wife and four kids. . . Then the idea came to me: If you're going to check out, so to speak, try to leave this place better than it was when you found it. I looked at this wreck of a stream (a backwater tributary of a Seattle shipping channel laced with toxic waste), filled with refrigerators, computers, old tires, torn garbage bags, broken swing sets, and stinking carpets, and all I wanted to do was clean it up."

Beal cleaned and restored the polluted stream behind his house and even the entire watershed of which it is a part. A few decades later, he was still alive and well and had recruited hundreds of people to help him. He discovered that environmental restoration is restorative in itself, and it kept him alive. He also noticed a redemptive feeling in others who worked alongside him on the river restoration. "I've seen remarkable things happen to people who connect with Mother Earth. They see a light go on. . . When you are so overwhelmed by your depression, anxiety, or sense of illness, connecting with nature—to something larger than yourself—takes away the worry; it calms the fear." John healed and restored the earth, body, heart, and home.

There are deep, overarching markers that can clarify the whole picture of pollution in our environments if we only focus on the eternal nature of the Elements. Any imbalance of an element alerts us to pay attention, as industrial chemicals are deadly substitutes for the real things. As an industrial society, we have tried transforming the Elements into synthetic materials. However, the result has been disastrous. Think of climate change. There are endless contrasts between nature in its full radiance and nature in a polluted state. Working with the Elements, rather than against them, can recharge cellular life, providing balance rather than depletion.

The Law of Reciprocity and the Elements

> "[That] plant does the same thing for the birds, other small creatures, and the people you love and keep close to. The true goal of the global bioplan is for every person to create and protect the healthiest environment they can for themselves, their family, the birds, and sex and Wildlife. That personal bio plan then gets stitched to their neighbor's, expanding outward exponentially. If we each start with something as small as an acorn and nurture it into an oak, a master tree that we have grown and protected if we have that kind of thinking on a mass scale, then the planet is no longer in jeopardy from our greed. We've become the guardians of it. It's a dream of trying to get a better world for every living thing." **—To Speak for the Trees, by Diana Beresford-Kroeger**

DIARY OF A HEALER

My first, and I hope only, bout with COVID just happened to hit during my birthday week celebration with my family at Cape Cod. Sick, I spent at least four hours daily at Nauset Beach, one of the world's most beautiful white sand beaches. I credit my seamless recovery to the sand, sun, ions (see about negative ions below), and proximity to the pulse of the sea. (The Elements Earth, Fire, Water, and Air.) I add that I also had a song in my heart the whole time to be so close to those I loved (Ether).

John Grabs All

A wise and thoughtful Cherokee medicine priest, David Winston, told me that the deeply broken and disharmonious relationships within ourselves, families, communities, and the Great Life result in the "John Grabs All" mentality towards the Earth. Our greatest challenge, David believes, is to heal so that we may find our way back onto the path to fulfill our sacred spiritual contract and become responsible human caretakers, using our problem-solving abilities to leave the earth in a better place than we found it. Jane Goodall, and her protection of chimpanzees against the poachers exploiting them, vividly exemplifies John Grabs All versus being a caretaker of the planet.

What does this have to do with "being here now?" When we embody and honor our body and the planet we live on, we are grounded and can experience heaven on earth. Many have experienced more awakening the more grounded they are.

Air

Air composes the Earth's atmosphere and feeds our hearts with every breath we take. Without air entering our lungs, we would die in seven minutes. Air oxygenates our blood. Breathing in the air of our natural environment fully integrates us as beings on this planet. Air is invisible, yet essential. It is the air that makes the earth habitable for us.

Air Conservation

Plant a tree! During just one year, a tree can absorb 26 pounds of carbon dioxide and exchange this with 260 pounds of oxygen. This amount of oxygen can support a small child for one year. An adult requires 675 pounds of oxygen per year. Two trees can produce this quantity yearly. (Feuerstein, 2007) We take approximately 20,000 breaths per day.

Air, Prana, Spiritual

We take the air we breathe for granted and do not often recognize what it contains. It is life force energy itself. The prana, chi, or ki spoken of in the ancient medical traditions of India, China, and Japan generates the energy needed for all life. It contains life's essence. So, actions that connect us with the Elements become essential. Breathing fresh air is a simple way to connect with Source, All That Is.

In spiritual symbolism, air represents consciousness—the power of the mind. Air and thought are both invisible, yet they are very powerful. The air element also represents freedom, like the free flight of a bird. Feathers are often used in ceremonies to represent the air element and as a spiritual element symbolizing freedom.

Nearly every culture on earth has burned dried plant material to invoke spiritual connection. Smoke rises in the air, and indigenous cultures use smoke to symbolize the higher realms. The act of burning sacred smoke as a plea for help, as an intercession to a deity, or as an offering to the sacred is an ancient one. Indigenous people worldwide have used pipe ceremonies (where they smoke sacred plant medicine) to unite heaven, earth, and man.

As long as there have been people to pray, they have sent their prayer smoke up to the place of the Most High. Our lungs breathe in air, and the oxygenated blood goes to our hearts. From there, air goes deep inside to our deepest essence. The great Buddhist breathing meditation Vipassana goes to this deepest essence.

Vipassana was rediscovered by Gautama Buddha more than 2,500 years ago. In a Vipassana meditation, a person focuses on the breath, paying attention to it as it goes in and out of the body. While the mind presents thoughts and distractions, you keep returning to focus on the breath. Gautama Buddha felt that this meditation would cure all ills. Multiple meditations focus on the breath from cultures all over the world. One of my favorite ones is Native American, described in *Prayers and Meditations of the Quero Apache* by Maria Yraceburu. Breathing meditations help you move your personality—with all its shoulds and oughts and directives—out of the way so that, for once, you can just be.

Air and Your Body

Air represents movement, communication, and breath. It is linked to the respiratory system, which involves the exchange of oxygen and carbon dioxide in the lungs. Air is also associated with the nervous system, as it signifies the movement of nerve impulses.

Breathing fresh air, as well as increasing our breathing capacity, is essential for life. It is that simple. (Feuerstein, 2015) Next to nitrogen, oxygen is the most common component of the Earth's atmosphere. By mass, it makes up 86% of the world's oceans and 49% of the earth's crust. Through the process of photosynthesis involving phytoplankton, almost 70% of the oxygen on the planet is produced. Mainly trees produce the remaining 30%. It is estimated that there are three trillion trees presently on the planet. This is half as many as when human civilization arose. (Pennesi, 2015)

> "What I hadn't expected and wouldn't fully recognize until much later was that I also felt ready to care for things beyond myself. After learning that I was just as I was and without having to do anything to earn it. Seeing the same thing in other people was a small next step. One small more step, and it was clear that everything in the natural world possessed innate value and was owed the same duty of care I granted myself and that other people held dear. This belief that a person should love others and nature as much as they love themselves was at the very heart of Celtic philosophy. It had been drilled into me with every lesson. I can say now, after years of looking through the eyes tinted with gores, heather, and sea breeze, that I can imagine no more fulfilling and joyful way of seeing the world." —**Kroeger**

We hear so much good and bad about ozone that we should set the record straight. Stratospheric ozone is good because it shields the Earth from the sun's rays. Most of the media reports focus on holes developing in the ozone layer; when a hole opens up (due to the release of man-made chemicals), harmful UVA rays can pass down to the earth and cause damage to life, such as increasing the rate of skin cancer in humans.

When it is inhaled into the lungs, it reacts with the fragile airway lining, causing inflammation and other damage that weakens multiple body systems. Altogether, air pollution weakens cardiovascular, immune, and respiratory functions. It weakens crops and contaminates lakes, rivers, and oceans. Ozone depletion shortens our life span and affects our quality of life. For the last twenty-four years, the American Lung Association has reported the effects of air pollution in their yearly report, State of the Air. <u>State of the Air | American Lung Association</u>

Earth

The Gaia hypothesis by James Lovelock and others developed when NASA invited Lovelock to conduct research in the early 1960s. Lovelock realized that the earth is a self-regulating system involving both living and nonliving systems, organisms and glasses, and biological and chemical processes.

The essence of Lovelock's studies show that the earth is in constant interdependent flux. It is a collection of self-regulating ecosystems, and unless human beings can fit into the larger picture rather than dominate it, we are going to destroy the very system we depend on for life.

Earth is inseparable from our being. In recent years, the step of grounding or earthing has become more prominent in the daily media. This term means contacting the earth with bare skin, like walking barefoot on the grass. Grounding increases our white blood cell count, cytokines, and additional molecules that control inflammation. Researchers studied cases of muscle injury, using delayed onset muscle injury to measure the effect of grounding on pain. This study showed that participants who made skin contact with the earth regularly experienced pain reduction. Also, their levels of neutrophils, lymphocytes, and other chemicals related to decreasing inflammation and increasing immune system response improved. (Oschman, JL, et al. 2015)

The people of Winnipeg, Manitoba, have come together to protect their elm tree—Ulmus Americana—replacing yellow insect bands that trap the elm bark beetle in its sexual stage, the bark beetle spreads deadly fungus and aggressive pathogenic strain of fungus we are trying to curtail. These efforts have inspired others to do even more; they are sparks that set off the fire of Reawakening. If you have a large tree on your street, ensure your local Council knows you value it. Every opportunity to vote is an opportunity to put someone who cares about us in a position of greater power and authority. We are just shy of eight billion people on Earth now. (Kroeger, 2021)

While most of this step is about the depletion of our connection to the Earth, I wanted to give mention of the *incredible* energy body system of the Earth, and how its Yin and Yang balancing is so key to its abundance. Below is an excerpt from one of my all-time favorite books, *To Speak for the Trees*, by Diana Beresford-Kroeger. She has observed and recorded the science of "mother trees" in the forest. She details her discovery in the following journal entry:

> "I first observed this organizational structure in northern forests, but soon discovered that all forests are based this way. The Brazil nut occupies the same position in the Amazon, providing the core around which all other species are healthy. A species of hickory is the mother of The Forest of China; Mother trees are always nut-legume or acorn producing species because those primary protein sources attract all animal life. Mother trees are a common trait shared by every forest on Earth.
>
> Of course, mother trees were the support structure for the ancient

forests of Ireland too. The Druids knew all about them. . . . So much of the knowledge I've gained in my scientific career was already there.

I observed a huge fruiting of mycelium into mushrooms. Through the growing season, animal and insect activity would be a general bustle. A huge volume of butterflies were entering and exiting the environment around the tree. Holes in the ground indicated the presence of mice and other mammals. The evening air held the clicking of bats flying into the darkness.

As I sat and watched these trees for extended periods of time, sometimes returning day after day for a matter of weeks, it was obvious that they were focal points of activity and vitality. They were the epicenter of life in the forest, so I started referring to them as "epicenter trees." Later when I learned more about the role they play in their environment, I changed my terminology. I now call them "mother trees." Mother trees are dominant trees within any forest system; they are the trees that, when mature, serve up the 22 essential amino acids, the three essential fatty acids, and the vegetable...

I expanded my field of view beyond botany and compared the function of hormones, plants, and human beings. In humans, the tryptophan tryptamine pathways generate all neurons in the mind. The action of some of these biochemicals has been shown in humans, but their existence in trees was not known. Over the three and a half years it took to complete my thesis work, I proved that such pathways existed in plants—in some more than others and trees most of all.

[ ] plants contain the sucrose version of Serotonin as a working molecule. It is a water-soluble compound in a tree. serotonin is a neuro generator. By proving that the tryptophan- trytomine to pathways existed in trees, I proved that trees possess all the same chemicals we have in our brains. Trees have the neural ability to listen and think; they have all the components necessary to have a mind or consciousness." —**Kroeger**

Water

We are water beings who live on a water planet. Many experts now call water blue gold; they have verified the precious substance. The consensus is that our decisions about water will determine the future of life on Earth.

The earth is the only known planet with a hydrosphere of water covering its surface and in its atmosphere. Seventy percent of the earth is covered with water. Almost all of this is salt water found in oceans and connected worldwide. Yet, only about 1% of the earth's water is fresh.

Oceans become salty from the mineral salts leached from soils and carried to them from streams. The water leaves the ocean during evaporation, but the salt remains there. Over eons, seawater became more saline. Yet as salty as the oceans are, they contain 96.5% pure water, and the remaining 3.5% is made up of dissolved inorganic ingredients, such as salts that have washed there from tributaries worldwide.

Earth continually recycles water. The water at the surface recirculates by leaving the earth's surface, entering the atmosphere by evaporation from the sun or plant transpiration, and returning to the earth by precipitation. Precipitation then seeps into the ground and becomes groundwater. Earth is an ecosystem, and we have the same amount of water now that there was at the time of the planet's source. Water consumed today will eventually be recycled for use by future generations. The water we're drinking now has been on Earth for millions of years! If you imagine that your great-grandchildren will drink the same glass of water you drink, you will be inspired to take better care of it.

Water entrains that which is in its environment. (Entrainment means melding.) Consider this: If calm, healing music is played to someone who is very agitated, slowly but surely, the agitated person calms down as his body's rhythms meld with the restful music. The person becomes in sync with the rhythm and pulls it into himself, melding with it. Can the same be said of water? If we become in sync with water and heal our local environments and ourselves, can we change the world bit by bit?

Water as a Spiritual Essence

The Maori, an indigenous people of New Zealand, view water as a living thing and believe that all things have a Maori or vital essence. The Maori traditionally look at water in three states.

1. Waiora, or "waters of life," includes rainwater, tears, springs, holy water, and special healing water that often rejuvenates damaged things.
2. Waimate, or "dead water," has no life essence and cannot support human life or food.
3. Waikino, or "bad water," either represents a dangerous place in a river, such as a rapid or snag, or water that is polluted physically or spiritually. The Maori believe that bad water can be changed.

Ether

Love Is the Ultimate Decontaminator!

Ether and Akasha are the same. Ether is the only element which has no form. Ether, or space, expands beyond the known world. It is the formless domain of the limitless, eternal, Higher Self. If we cannot lovingly restore our planet and our physical body, we fragment our Source connection, the essence of love. Healing Technology will help you reconnect.

I like to think of Ether as eternal love. The pulsing love of the universe.

Ether and Your Body

Ether is considered the subtlest element, representing spaciousness, expansion, and connectivity. It is associated with the spaces within the body, such as the hollow organs, empty cavities, and channels through which energy flows.

For the Activation of Step I see Section II

STEP II: THE HIGHER SELF AND SOUL
BACKGROUND ABOUT THIS STEP OF THE SEQUENCE

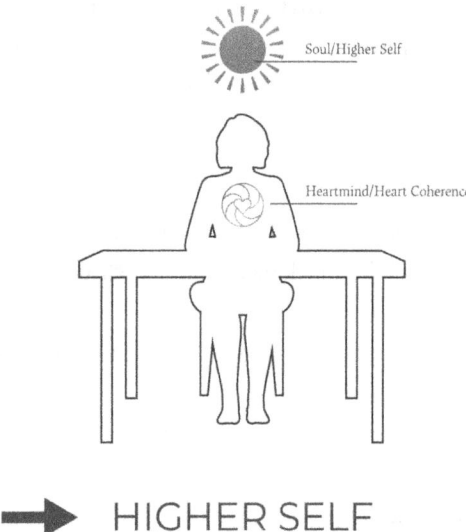

What is your Higher Self? Your sacred nature and emissary for and of your Soul in this lifetime. Your Higher Self bathes you in unconditional love and teaches you about the illusions of your life in duality and the ego.

From an energy body perspective, *meeting and building a relationship with* your Higher Self connects you to the driver of your well-being, and confirms your connection to Source, the All That Is.

It is thought to be housed in our soul star chakra, about 8" over our head.

What and Why your Higher Self
Your Higher Self helps you to learn to love yourself in the world of duality. Duality being the inherent nature of reality as consisting of pairs of opposites, such as good and evil, light and dark, male and female. Our Higher Self helps us navigate between consciousness and matter, becoming accepting and nonjudgmental about all the flaws and wounds of your ego.

Importantly, your Higher Self carries your soul's feminine and soul's father energies, not the energy of your birth parents of this lifetime.

Working with your Higher Self can help you override the unhealed male/female imbalances and wounds you may have established from your family of upbringing, and the collective. (For more about this, see Step IV.) Equally importantly, your Higher Self can teach forgiveness.

> **EXPERIENTIAL EXERCISE**
>
> A simple meditative request that I have made for decades, is to say, *"I ask my Higher Self to clear our connection, as much as is in the highest good for now."* Many times a day, if I think of it. By now I've established a strong channel to my Higher Self by doing this, resulting in improved clarity and speed of insight, healing, and information when I ask for it.

Achieving Oneness Requires Attention

Higher Self is the essence of who we are in this lifetime, coming home to ourselves, and a bridge to the wise loving consciousness that is the essence of who we truly are, our Atman or soul self. I put this circle diagram together to help explain the *relationship* between our everyday personality and our Higher Self and Soul. If you look at the circle center, that's where we almost always are. We live via our programmed upbringing in a life full of distractions. A place where we can be trapped by ego. This is our regular 3D world. There is nothing wrong with it, we all need it. However the 3D world is just ego-based. It is the "me" that goes grocery shopping and needs to get this and that. We need this part of ourselves but we can coexist with it by changing the channel to a different frequency.

BUILDING A RELATIONSHIP WITH YOUR HIGHER SELF

It was during meditation that I started to *feel* that there is a relationship I can have to a much more powerful Source. Tears rolled down my face. I don't know where I had been but I had come home. Native Americans call it the Great Spirit; an energy that carries my true self that possesses wisdom and knowledge.

By building a relationship with your Higher Self you merge closer with your essence, your soul.

Intuition is a way to connect to our Higher Selves. In fact, it is the information highway to it. If I have a clear sentient gut feeling about something, it's my Higher Self talking to me. If I have an insight it is my Higher Self talking to me. So as you can see if you look at the arrows above, when I started to build a relationship between me and my 3D world and my Higher Self, it can become a wonderful game changer in your life.

As you develop more of a relationship with your Higher Self your higher vibration starts to dominate the regular mundane self, the distractions. Bit by bit your vibration starts rising and you rise above a lot of the trauma the hamster wheel represents, and things that dragged you down or created lower vibration density.

One of the things I've learned is that the best way to constantly contact our higher selves is to ask. We ask - We ask - We ask! We have the privilege of asking because our free will can direct us to do so. When asking we become humble and surrender to a higher form of knowledge, a higher knowledge than our mundane, 3D self contains.

EXPERIENTIAL EXERCISE

Buddha said, "As we think, so shall we become." Try to embody your Higher Self more and more by asking, asking, asking. Raise your vibration so you think more positive thoughts.

ASK, ASK, ASK

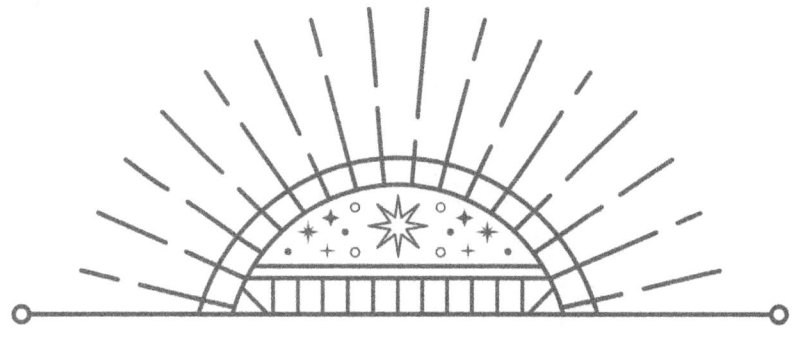

DIARY OF A HEALER

As I mentioned above, I have asked my Higher Self to be with me for years, in whichever way achieved the highest good in the current circumstance. I did this off and on all day; I did it for years. I asked my Higher Self to be with me to clear our connection. I asked my Higher Self to clear our connection as much as is needed. I always asked for as much as the highest good as needed because I was afraid that if I got too much I might lose my grip on my ego-based 3D world. I still sometimes ask to ensure it is only in the highest interest. I welcome the direct and clear engagement. It happens by asking for the clearest connection possible or required at that moment. You can explore your daily connection with similar invocations. Once it is habitual, your days become anchored in the delight of reciprocity with Source, the All That Is.

The Ego and the Higher Self/Soul

> ". . . [H]uman beings come into existence with a certain operating system already installed in us. . . . The system . . . is a binary operating system. It runs on the power of 'either/or.' People frequently call it the ego, but I prefer to stick to my metaphor and call it the "egoic operating system." —**Cynthia Bourgeault**

The ego and the soul are two different aspects of our being. The ego is our sense of self, our identity, and our personality. It is what makes us unique and separate from others. The soul, on the other hand, is our spiritual essence, also unique. It is the part of us that is connected to something greater than ourselves. Our Higher Selves mediate between the two, carrying the drive of the soul's teachings.

EXPERIENTIAL EXERCISE

My go-to great prayer to clear the static and gain insight to get off the hamster wheel, is this: "*I ask my Higher Self to bring healing to _____ (issue) and I pray for insight.*" Sometimes the answer comes immediately, but at others, especially if I am really "in my head," I have to repeat the prayer a lot, even over days, until I get the knowing of the true answer.

Intention
"I ask my Higher Self to bring healing to _____ and I pray for insight."

> "It is this query that has changed my life more than any other spiritual practice. The invocation is key as once you are given the insight you really know you have it, which in its own right is a great training in discernment. Sometimes I learn the insight immediately, and other times it can take a few days of continually repeating the request until I have the knowledge."
> —Annie

DIARY OF A HEALER

Old Programs Running Your Life

When we grow up, we are raised to fit into "norms"—of a household, of a grade in school, of a church, of a culture. Some of us have had more control inflicted on us than others, through rules, rigid beliefs, criticism, and even abuse.

I see this "programming" show up in the energy body, including in the following ways:

1. We build elaborate energetic armaments to sustain our personalities. All this personality development is the reality for our ego, one we develop to fit in and survive. This heavy and rigid energy permeates many chakras and has a strong inflexibility. It can take time to dissolve this rigidity, but it is important on the path to one's authentic nature.
2. Another way is that we internalize negative comments from our upbringing and build them into inner tyrants! The brutal and incessant voices push one to work too hard, berate oneself mercilessly for flaws, beat oneself up for not "being good enough." I see this energy—that originally belonged to others—hardened in circles inside the head by the ears, and it usually shows up when I am working on a person's fifth chakra, the home of the song of who they are, their truth. The hard energy blocks the flow of this song, their authentic nature.
3. Sometimes the "programming" for how to behave is so extreme that a person builds what looks like an energetic "motherboard"—a circuit board carrying the elements of a computer—and their personality runs off of that. I am not kidding. A month ago I pulled one out of an older client who had been accused of being "on the spectrum" as a child, and had worked as hard as he could to fit in the way he was told. It meant he ran his life like computer software, far from his authentic self.

Stepping back and looking at these three instances, one sees that the clients have become slaves to internalized and inaccurate inner narratives. The narratives are based on programming that their wounded egos developed usually from challenging family relationships. Not the true wisdom and guidance about themselves on a soul level.

I urge people who are slaves to negative thinking—and again, this could be most people, at least at times—to learn Byron Katie's Four Questions (Is it true? Can you absolutely know that it is true? How do you react, what happens when you have that thought? Who would you be without that thought?)

It takes time to learn to witness the negative thoughts and change them. Take the case of Sarah, she had a very critical mother, and the internalized negative thinking ran her life mercilessly. I spent a large amount of time asking for clearing of the dense, intractable

> energy inside her head near her ears, where she had stored all the negative she had "heard" from her mother. I even called her mother into the healing etherically, so that Sarah could release her mother's energy back to her. I counseled Sarah to work with Byron Katie's questions, and to become a witness to the machinations of her own wounded ego. I have discovered clients' intuition develops when they use the four questions to clear their mind.
>
> Next for Sarah will be to develop self-love, that healing alchemy that is all about blossoming into her authentic nature.

YOUR INTUITION IS YOUR HIGHER SELF'S INFORMATION HIGHWAY.

Intuition is a way to connect to our Higher Selves. In fact, it is the information highway to it. Your intuition is your Higher Self's information highway. Honing your intuition—your clairsentience, clairaudience, clairvoyance, and claircognizance, is a key piece of your connection to your soul, Higher Self and your Central Axis.

Clairsentience

What: FEELING. That "gut" feeling. The ability to receive information through the senses or emotions. Also, feeling things with touch (psychometry), such as with stones.

Where: The solar plexus—the third chakra—is the master antennae for clairsentience, from just below the navel to the top of the diaphragm. Also, the second chakra is the feeling chakra.

Blocks: Being in the head...

> **EXPERIENTIAL EXERCISE**
>
> Come up with a choice between two options. Now tune into how you would feel with choice #1 and then how you would feel with choice #2. This is a gut check. Which choice made you feel the most relaxed and open? Constricted and tense?

Clairaudience

What: HEARING. The ability to attain auditory information

Where: Above the ears, the temporal lobe, the fifth chakra.

Blocks: Judgment and self-censorship can quickly overpower the quiet voice of clairaudience.

EXPERIENTIAL EXERCISE

Think of a few things that you want information about. For example, your dog has a rash, what is the best solution?

Take a few deep breaths and sit in a meditative position with your spine straight. Pose the question to your Higher Self, saying you would like the answer in words, and wait for an answer in words.

Clairvoyance

What: SEEING. The ability to receive mental images, symbols, or actual events.

Where: The brow, the sixth chakra, the third eye.

Blocks: Fear of pain, of seeing, of psychic gifts. "If I don't 'see' something painful, I will be in less trauma."

EXPERIENTIAL EXERCISE

Here is a great exercise that gets ahead of your busy mind.

Take a look at the diagram of this gauge, below. Close your eyes with this in your mind's eye and ask where the arrow goes if the answer is a YES. Left or right?

YES?/NO?   NO?/YES?

> Once you know that information, make a list of straightforward yes or no questions.
>
> Sit in a meditative position with your spine straight and ask your questions, one at a time, with the gauge in your mind's eye and waiting after each to see where the gauge arrow goes—yes or no?
>
> I have students of mine that ask questions like this all day long!

Claircognizance

What: KNOWING. The ability to have ideas/thoughts directly from Spirit as in telepathy and by simple knowing.

Where: Crown of the head, the seventh chakra and also within heart intelligence.

Blocks: Anodea Judith, author of my favorite book on the chakras, *Eastern Body, Western Mind* says that attachment is the "demon" of the crown chakra. How are your attachments interfering with your claircognizance?

> EXPERIENTIAL EXERCISE
>
> My all-time favorite claircognizance exercise is to ask my Higher Self to bring me a healing around something I am upset about and pray for insight. Sometimes I need to repeat the question for a few hours, even a few days, but when I receive the insight it is an understanding of the issue from all its angles.

> ## WARNING ALERT
>
> *Are you "in your head" too much? "Dropping" into your heart and coming into heart coherence is a great way to stop the monkey mind.*

HEART COHERENCE

Heart coherence is a state of alignment between the heart, mind, and spirit. This alignment facilitates a deeper connection with your inner self and the sacred, leading to a greater sense of peace, purpose, and fulfillment. A great way to connect to your Higher Self on a regular basis is to be in heart coherence. The HeartMath Institute is a non-profit research and education organization dedicated to exploring the science of heart coherence and its applications for personal and global transformation.

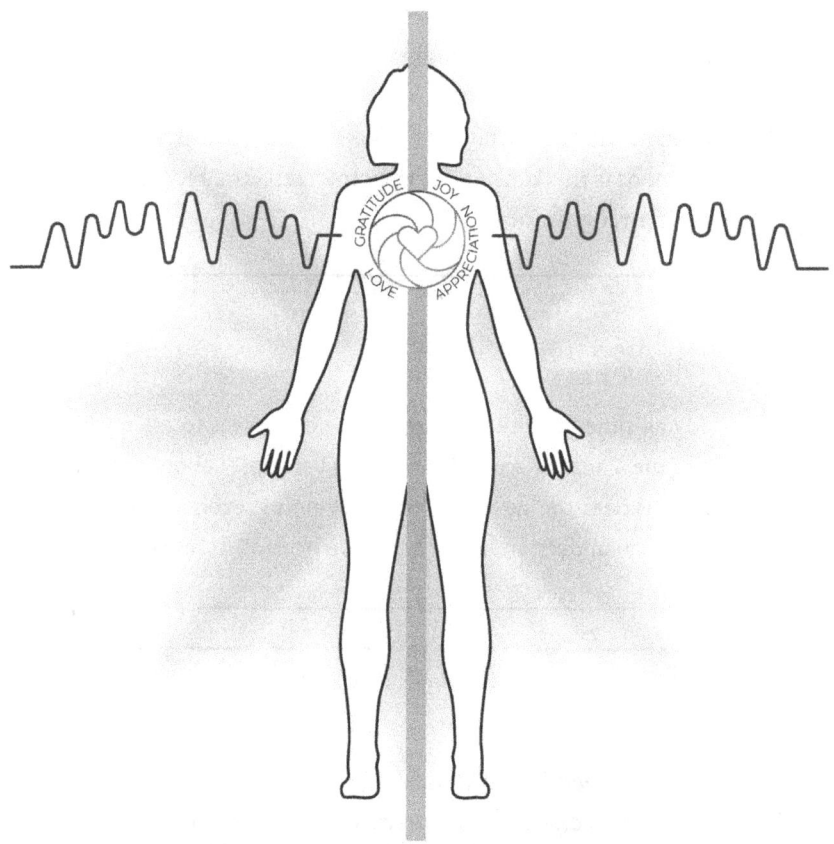

EXPERIENTIAL EXERCISE

Let us set up for heart coherence. This is an adaptation of Gregg Braden's three-step process.
- Take a few deep breaths, sit up straight, close your eyes.
- Place your awareness in your heart chakra, just drop your inner focus of energy down into your heart chakra.

> - Now tune into something that makes you have a sense of joy in your heart or a sense of gratitude or something that brings a smile to your heart chakra. (I find it's hard to have a family member because those relationships are complicated but I can think of my dog's paws. For example, I could put a smile in my heart or I could look at the trees outside and it gives me an immense feeling of joy.)
> - Let us go beyond feeling.
> - Resonate with gratitude.

> **BENEFITS**
>
> When you have that complete focus you will discover resonance in the heart. It is like a sound from a singing bowl or from the sound vibration OM. You tune into that resonance of how it feels and that's really important too. And for me personally I can stay in heart coherence longer if I tune into its resonance. I can keep practicing and going back to how it feels. I feel its effects during a slow build.

What is Your Higher Self Versus Your Soul?

While a bit of a crude analogy, I have found it represents my experience with the difference between the Higher Self and our Soul. If you think of a big horse barn, and the barn is big or huge, depending on how many past lives we've had, each horse stall is a different past life. However, our soul is the whole barn. So, for example, stall number 110 might have been me in a past life when I lived in Africa and I was a farmer. Whereas stall 111 shows me as a little boy in England, wearing those little shorts and a cap. I come to another birth scenario from one stall to the next. There are completely different circumstances of the lifetime, but the soul lesson would have been the same. I did not learn it in 110, so I will have to relearn that lesson in 111. I may have to go to stall 112 or 113 or even beyond. I have to keep going until I learn all of my lessons. Every stall is a different lifetime until I evolve completely.

Connect to the Higher Self *this lifetime*. We will ask questions like: "Why did I choose the parents I chose?" In short, we chose the parents so our soul could create a Higher Self to come into this lifetime, carrying the wisdom and teachings we needed to learn. Hopefully, we can learn the lesson that perhaps we didn't learn in the previous four lifetimes. Now, we have another chance to learn it. It is a simple way to frame what drives our healing process.

How does the whole spiritual system line up?

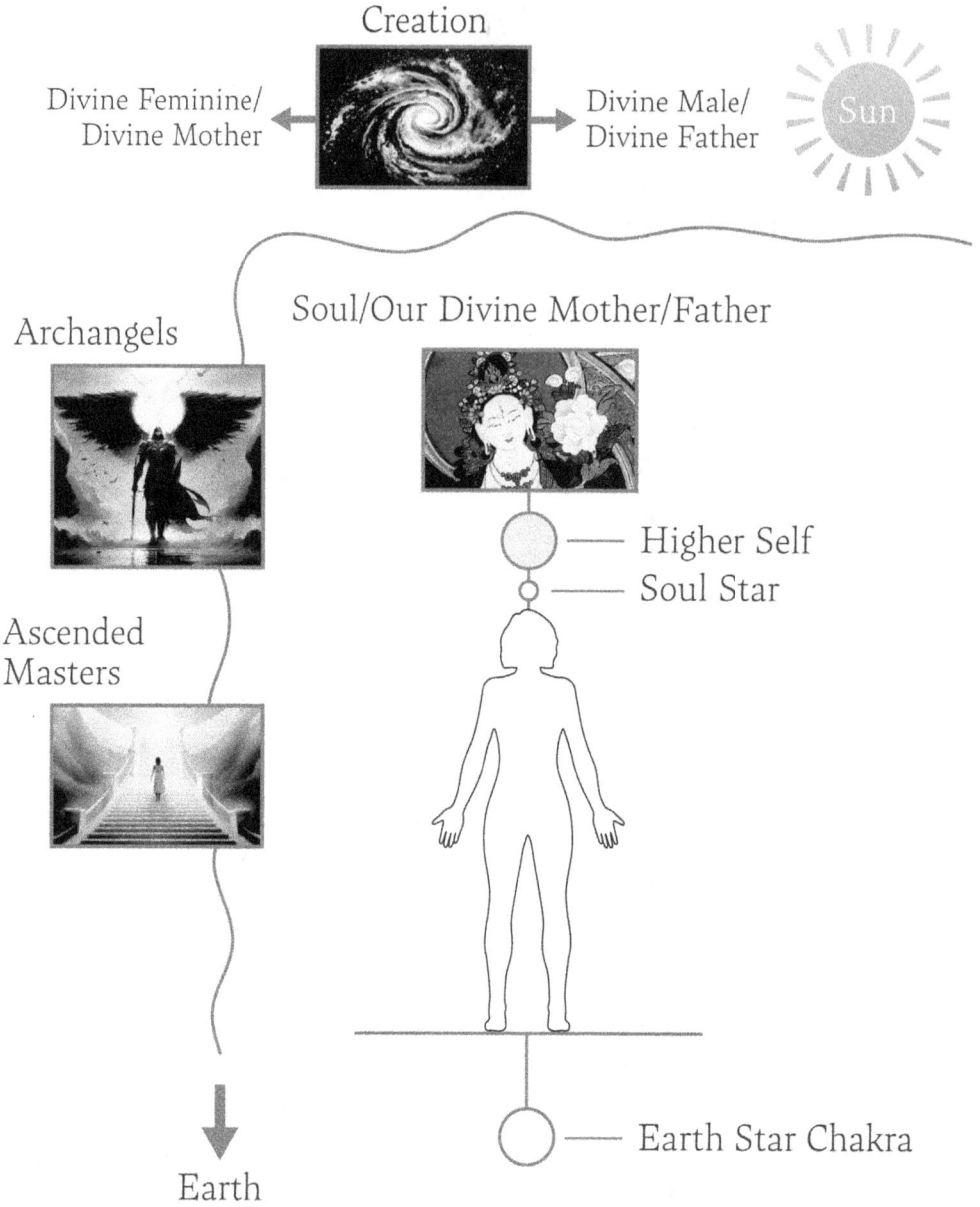

Entrainment: Your Soul and Higher Self Connection Via Your Heart Chakra

Opening to a relationship with your Higher Self and Soul means opening to your eternal essence. We are much more than our physical body and our collection of thoughts. According to the *Awakening Prana! Regenerative Self-Healing* system the unifying goal underlying spiritual growth and energy healing is coming into relationship with this wise, loving consciousness. It is our true, unchanging identity which was, is and, will always be. Degrees of misperception separate us from knowledge of our eternal being.

> **EXPERIENTIAL EXERCISE**
>
> Get in a meditative state, take a few deep breaths, settle, and ask your Higher Self to come in front of you until it is ten feet away. Get a feel for all its aspects. Now ask it to come and merge with you, and as it does, entrain to its energy to maximize the divinity within and minimize the low vibration density we carry.

Entrainment

Entrainment is the process of one system's motion or signal frequency locking into step with the frequency of another system. This can occur in physical systems, such as pendulum clocks, or biological systems, such as the human brain.

In physics, entrainment is often used to describe the synchronization of two or more oscillators. Oscillators are systems that regularly repeat a pattern of motion, such as a pendulum swinging back and forth. When two oscillators are entrained, they begin to move in sync with each other, even if they have different frequencies to begin with.

Entrainment can also occur in biological systems. For example, the human brain has a natural rhythm called the alpha rhythm, which has a frequency of about 10 Hz. When we listen to music, the rhythmic beats of the music can entrain our alpha rhythms, causing them to synchronize with the music. This can have a number of beneficial effects, such as reducing stress and improving cognitive function.

Here are some examples of entrainment:

- Pendulum clocks: Two pendulum clocks placed next to each other will eventually start to swing in sync because the swinging of one clock's pendulum creates a rhythmic force that entrains the other clock's pendulum.
- Fireflies: Fireflies in a swarm often flash their lights in sync with each other. This is thought to be a way for them to attract mates or to deter predators.
- Human brain: The human brain has a natural rhythm called the alpha rhythm, which has a frequency of about 10 Hz. When we listen to music, the rhythmic beats of the music can entrain our alpha rhythms, causing them to synchronize with the music. This can have a number of beneficial effects, such as reducing stress and improving cognitive function.
- Heart rate: Our heart rate can be entrained by external stimuli, such as the sound of a metronome or the sight of another person's heartbeat. This is thought to be one way that our bodies synchronize with each other in social situations.

Overall, heart coherence is both a physiological and spiritual phenomenon. It has the potential to benefit both the physical and spiritual levels.

Heart coherence is a state of synchronized rhythmic activity between the heart and other organs in the body. It is measured by the heart rate variability (HRV), which is the variation in the time intervals between heartbeats. When the HRV is high, it indicates that the heart is in a coherent state.

There is a growing body of scientific research suggesting heart coherence is associated with a number of benefits, including:

- Improved cognitive function: Studies have shown that heart coherence can improve cognitive function, such as attention, memory, and decision-making.
- Reduced stress: Heart coherence can help to reduce stress by increasing the production of calming hormones, such as oxytocin and dopamine.
- Enhanced emotional well-being: Heart coherence can help to improve emotional well-being by reducing anxiety, depression, and anger.
- Increased resilience: Heart coherence can help to increase resilience, which is the ability to bounce back from stress and challenges.

What Does Prayer Mean?

Prayer is a conscious choice to seek Source/Mother/Father/God in whatever form sacred presence speaks to each of us. Prayer can be addressed to archangels, ascended masters, invocations to guides, and more. Prayer is a dialogue with the sacred from moment to moment. Whatever challenges we experience with inner prayer strengthen our eternal life. Prayer brings us back to the center to transform internal and external distractions. Prayer strengthens the role of our Higher Self. The difficulties we experience in inward prayer are preparation for our outward lives.

The heart contains its own nervous system, known as the "heart-brain." The heart brain communicates with our cognitive brain and influences the cognitive and emotional states I referenced above when discussing "HeartMind." Its electrical field initiates a magnetic field.

EXPERIENTIAL EXERCISE

Centering Prayer

We can take the sound of OM, or any other sacred name we like, into a practice Father Thomas Keating developed called Centering Prayer.

1. As you breathe in, say your sacred word silently to yourself.
2. As you breathe out, relax and let go of any thoughts or feelings that come into your mind.
3. Continue for 20-30 minutes.
4. When you finish, open your eyes and slowly return to the room.

Keating emphasized the importance of simplicity and surrender in Centering Prayer. He said we should not try to force anything but simply allow ourselves to be drawn into the sacred presence. He also said that it is important to be patient with ourselves without becoming discouraged if our minds begin to wander. Centering Prayer is a simple and profound way to connect. It can be used by anyone, regardless of their religious background or level of experience.

EXPERIENTIAL EXERCISE

The Gayatri Mantra is a powerful mantra that can help us to connect with our inner divinity. It shows us how to pray to increase our spiritual understanding. We can repeat the prayer daily. Go to YouTube and look up Deva Premal's Gayatri Mantra meditation, as one example. The meaning of the Gayatri Mantra can be interpreted in many ways. Here is one interpretation:

Gayatri Mantra
- Om bhur bhuvah svah - We meditate on the supreme light that pervades the three worlds: the physical world, the mental world, and the spiritual world.
- tat savitur varenyam - We meditate on that most adorable light, the sun, which is a symbol of the sacred.
- Bhargo devasya dhimahi - May that light illumine our intellect.
- Dhiyo yo nah prachodayat - May that light inspire us to do good and to live a life of wisdom.

Throughout the day, when current events disturb our thoughts, it is helpful to entrain ourselves with a higher vibration, a healing bandwidth. Forgiveness work is very powerful, and this prayer below, adapted from John Newton's work, is one that is very helpful.

EXPERIENTIAL EXERCISE

Cleansing Prayer For All Humanity
God, Please Help All Humanity
Throughout All Time, Past, Present And Future
All Forgive Each Other
Forgive Ourselves
Be At Peace With Each Other

Be At Peace With Ourselves
Love Each Other And Love Ourselves
Now And Forever
Please - Thank You God,
Amen

Adapted from The Forgiveness Prayer by John Newton

I repeat the following prayer every time I am in my stone circle/medicine wheel:

EXPERIENTIAL EXERCISE

Prayer of St Francis

Lord, make me an instrument of your peace;
where there is hatred, let me sow love;
where there is injury, pardon;
where there is doubt, faith;
where there is despair, hope;
where there is darkness, light;
and where there is sadness, joy.

O sacred Master,
grant that I may not so much seek to be consoled as to console;
to be understood, as to understand;
to be loved, as to love;
for it is in giving that we receive,
it is in pardoning that we are pardoned,
and it is in dying that we are born to Eternal Life.

Amen.

For the Activation of Step II see Part II

STEP III: YIN/FEMININE AND YANG/MASCULINE
CURRENTS OF YOUR BATTERY MAGNETISM
BACKGROUND ABOUT THIS STEP OF THE SEQUENCE

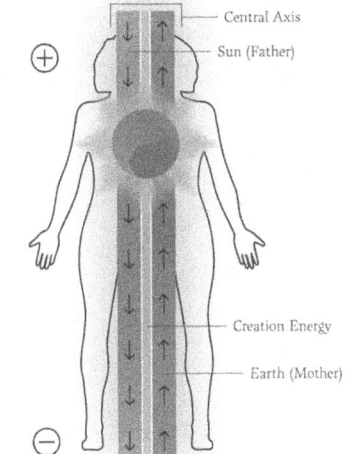

YIN AND YANG IGNITE

➡ YIN AND YANG

Electrical currents are created as the result of a positive (+) and negative (-) charge. In the bioelectric mirror of physicality we need enough Yin (-) and enough Yang (+) energy to connect and ignite to make the currents of prana, or Life Force.

Every life form has a feminine and masculine aspect. Because of magnetism they are naturally drawn to each other, attract each other.

What and Why of the Yin and Yang

Yin/Feminine Is Matter - Yang/Masculine Is Space

Yin/Mother/Shakti means Earth, Water, and partially Air. Ether has no form. Air has just a bit of form. Feminine as matter refers to the belief that the feminine aspect of the universe is associated with material existence, physicality, and the body. Mothers give birth! Accordingly, the feminine connects to nature and the earth, while the masculine domain is space and the heavens. Throughout history, the masculine/feminine energetic paradigm fundamentally resonated and integrated indigenous populations, cultural and religious traditions.

We Need (-) and (+) Charges in Balance in Four Main Arenas

As you see in the chart, below, we have a number of vector points where we can have different Yin/Yang balances and imbalances.

THE  BIOELECTRIC CHARGES

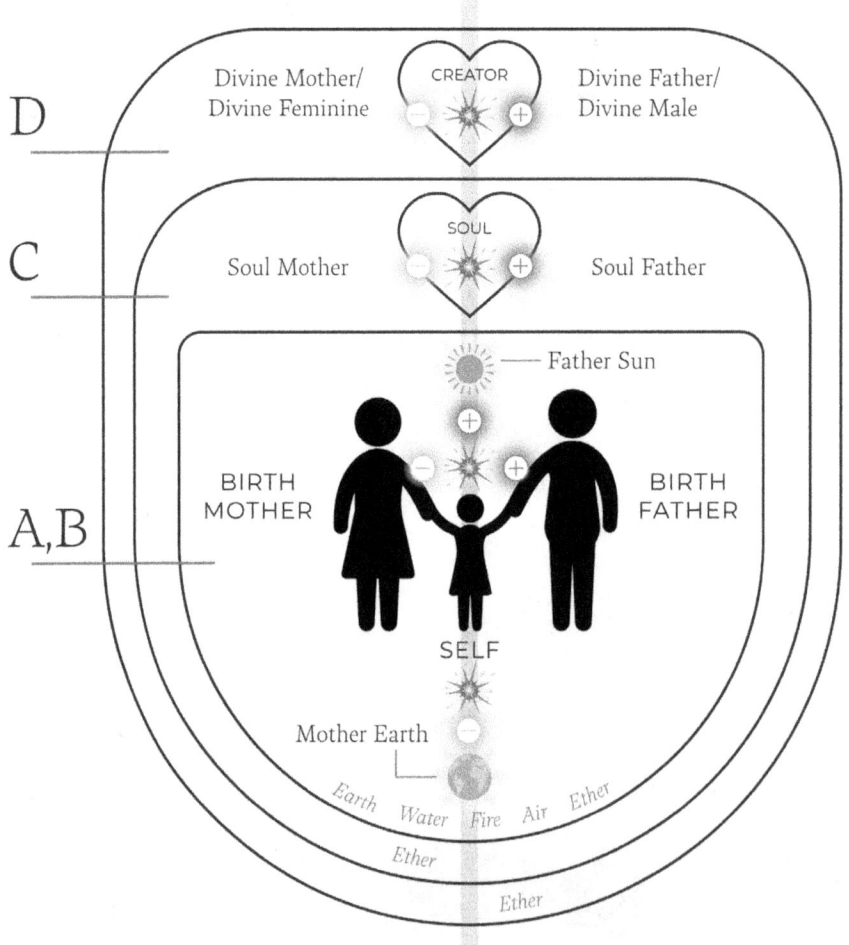

Where do we find yin and yang in our body/mind/spirit?

A. In our Bodies, On the Planet: We may experience depletion male/shiva energy due lack of connection with ourselves on the planet in relation to the Sun. Humans are also generally very depleted in the Yin energy as we dissociate from the Earth, the planet.

B.-In Our Minds: We are all born to unhealed mothers and unhealed fathers and become unhealed children. We often carry those wounds into our adulthood because due to depleted Yin and/or Yang energy we could not experience vitality. Just like we need water and sun to thrive, we need to replenish healed mother and father energy levels.

> **From the Collective:** *There is free-flowing Yin and Yang energy that comes from humanity, and with its imbalances we are often bombarded with it, putting pressure on existing imbalances. The imbalance in collective energy usually comes to us in our broken hearts. We may experience depletion of male/shiva energy due to trauma and cultural programming, thus constricting certain bioelectric functions. And Yin energy due to widespread misogyny.*

C. From our Souls: Our soul can bring replenishment with the sacred male and female aspects of itself. It's eternal balance. It lacks nothing, it is whole and complete.

D. From Source Currents, Inside of Us and Out: Source energy is perfection, total non-duality. We may be depleted of this connection but the healing it will bring carries our quantum DNA and healing of our perfect blueprint.

We become imbalanced from the traumas endemic to our culture, society, our ancestry and even our religious heritage.

THE "HOLY" TRINITY

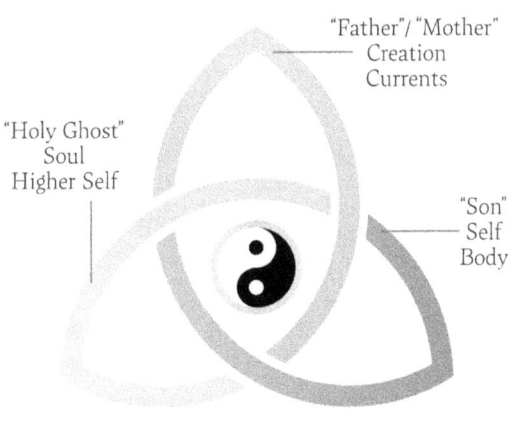

"Father"/"Mother" Creation Currents

"Holy Ghost" Soul Higher Self

"Son" Self Body

Notice that the Yin/Yang balance is central.

The so-called "Holy Trinity" reflects these areas of separate charges, all of which need Yin and Yang balance. The Trinity is a central Christian doctrine that states that there is one God who eternally exists as three distinct persons: the Father, the Son, and the Holy Spirit. This doctrine is based on the teachings of the New Testament, but it was not fully developed until the fourth century AD. The concept of the Trinity is not unique to Christianity. It is also found in other religious and spiritual traditions, such as Hinduism, Kabbalah, and Gnosticism.

Son: Our bodies, our lives on the planet
Holy Ghost: From our souls/Higher Selves
Father: Father/Mother Source Currents

WHERE AND WHY IS OUR ENERGY BODY DEPLETED OF YIN AND YANG?

DEPLETION AND MALFUNCTION ALERT

Without enough (-) Yin or (+) Yang, the Vortex weakens. There isn't a strong enough rotation so only a weak Vortex is formed. Call in the tow trucks to charge us!

- Indicators of being deficient in Yang energy are being stuck, unable to put one's right foot forward with purpose and agency.
- Indicators of being deficient in Yin energy are restriction of creative, receptive, nurturing energy, and low self-esteem.

Category A. In our Bodies and On the Planet

We need to regenerate the original flow of polarity by reconnecting to Mother Earth and Father Sun. When we become aware of ourselves as bio-electric beings, the amount of (-) Yin and (+) Yang we embody is of central importance. What is occurring? The (-) Yin Mother Earth energy comes up from below and the (+) Yang Father Sun energy comes down from above.

Mother Earth

Mother Earth energy rises up through us. Mother Earth energy is feminine. It is Yin energy containing the **Sacred Elements Earth, Water, and Air.** They are our companions on earth. They form our physicality and seal our bond to Mother Earth.

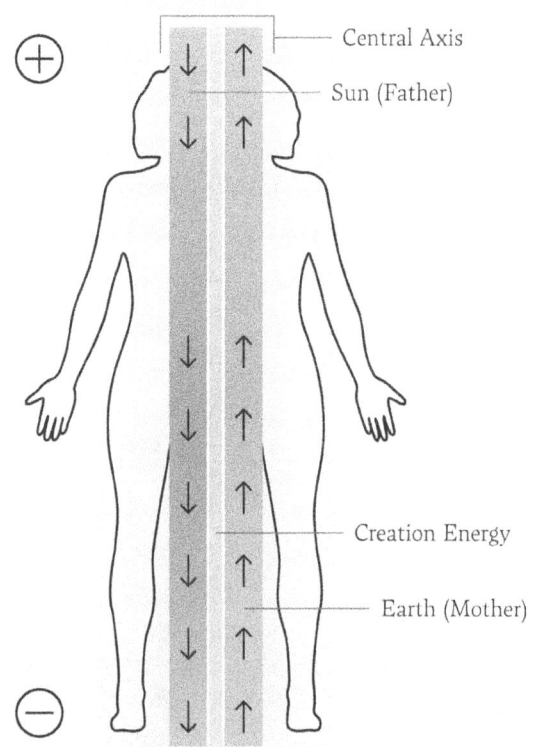

YIN COMES UP AND YANG GOES DOWN

- Central Axis
- Sun (Father)
- Creation Energy
- Earth (Mother)

Mother Earth
Father Sun energy comes down through us. Father Sun energy is male, Yang energy. The **Sacred Element Ether** helps to support our connection to Father Sun, as does the Sacred Element Fire. Sun has a name in the ancient world of Celts. It is called the song of the universe Ceolta na Cruinne. It is the song heard by the Celts before their alphabet was created.

Becoming aware, grounded, and connected to Father Son/Mother Earth means being here now. Being here now automatically activates our transformation phases.

Body
Neuroscience has confirmed what spiritual traditions have acknowledged for thousands of years:

> "Intricately linked to the ability of the prefrontal cortex to come fully online are the mitochondria, the powerhouse of your cells and the feminine life force referred to by the shamans. Mitochondria are the conductors of the genetic orchestra that regulate how every cell ages, divides, and dies. They wave the baton that helps dictate which cells are switched on and which are switched off in every one of our cells. And all the mitochondrial DNA in your body is solely inherited from your mother's lineage. That means the Source of energy that sustains your life—derived exclusively from the women in your family tree—your matrilineage." —**Power Up Your Brain, The Neuroscience of Enlightenment, by David Perlmutter, MD, and Alberto Villoldo, Ph.D.; Chapter 4, p. 33**

The feminine life force is electrically conducted through our DNA. It dictates the Source of energy that sustains all life. Yet, is that the whole story?

Category B. Mind and Collective; Parents of Origin
We are all born of unhealed mothers and fathers and we become unhealed children. We then internalize these unhealed mainstays as truth, and our energy body becomes depleted where these foundations are incomplete. Many of us spend a few decades trying to stabilize as a result.

Just as a seed needs enough of Mother Earth and Father Sun to sprout and leaf out, so, too, we need enough of the healed inner mother and father to become a healed child and, ultimately, our authentic, true self.

We must heal both the feminine and the masculine. Healing the masculine side means integrating the masculine energy into your personality. Qualities such as strength, courage, assertiveness, and leadership are essential for our survival. However one must heal first before executing them properly. Both men and women need to heal their wounds before they can integrate and embrace the whole. By the time you finish reading this book—participating with the Steps—you will have a very clear roadmap for how to balance Yin = female energy and Yang = male energy.

Yin and Yang are two complementary aspects that make up a whole. They are often represented by a circle with two teardrop shapes, one black (Yin) and one white (Yang). The Yin-Yang symbol is a reminder that everything in the universe is made up of both Yin and Yang. There is no such thing as pure Yin or pure Yang. The two are always in a state of flux, constantly changing and transforming into each other.

> ### DIARY OF A HEALER
>
> **Healing the Inner Parents**
>
> Just as a seed needs enough of Mother Earth and Father Sun to sprout and leaf out, so, too, we need enough of the healed inner mother and father to become a healed child and, ultimately, our authentic, true self.
>
> Isabelle, a young woman, came to me feeling like she was really stuck in her life, her job, relationships, and personal trajectory. She exuded a kind of radiance, yet threw up her hands saying, "I want abundance in every direction and I don't know what is stopping me!" She had suffered from depression.
>
> As she was talking about her life, she shared, without any rancor, that she didn't have a father in her life, and, in fact, very few men. She was raised by a single mother, had a sister, aunts and grandmother. No father, uncles, brothers, grandfathers.
>
> Hearing this, I expected from experience to find that she was very low in Yang energy, but you never really know until you are seeing the deeper layers of a person's energy body in a healing process. Sure enough, every chakra was very depleted of male, Yang energy, that of the father. Her energy body in general was depleted in this as well.
>
> How would this depletion manifest in her life? For one, missing Yang energy would mean missing the force to push through feeling stuck. Yang energy is very active and moves out into the world with passion. Given she had so little male energy she was also having trouble attracting it to her in a relationship, despite being a lovely, vibrant woman. She couldn't magnetize it—like-attracting-like.
>
> In a darker way, not enough Yang energy would allow her depressed thoughts to have a stronghold, as she would need the Yang energy to take charge of the thoughts and put them into perspective.
>
> In some ways, Isabelle is lucky. She didn't have a father "wound," per se. The father energy that she did receive wasn't cruel or abusive, which would have added a deep layer of trauma that needed healing. While she experienced abandonment, in her case this wound seems to have been cauterized by the powerful women in her family.
>
> If you think of us all as having two operating systems, one of them is our ego-driven system that is woven through our personalities and is the result of our upbringing and

programming, what we have from parents and society's collective shadow as well as light. It was here where Isabelle had her Yang deficiency, the lack of male energy.

The other operating system is the one of our consciousness, Spirit, our true self essence. What I also call our energy body. It is from this system that I worked to restore healed male energy into Isabelle's system, knowing it would weave into the first operating system and bring healing.

Everything has a male and female component, including our soul. When there is a need for more healed male or female energy, I ask the client's soul's healed sacred male/father and healed sacred feminine/mother energy to fill the places of depletion and imbalance. I do this through a technique I call The Trinity Activations, the cornerstone of my Divine Mother modality.

Once Isabelle has enough healed male energy to bring her male/female energy system into balance, there will be an alchemical spark of light that will bring in her sacred child and her authentic self. I've seen this light clairvoyantly. To follow up with the metaphor at the beginning of this diary, the seed can at last sprout and leaf out.

The Collective

While the above Diaries of a Healer are family-centric, one can easily substitute issues from the collective, such as someone still suffering from a shaming second grade teacher, or from the way that our culture puts pressure on men to be macho.

Category C. From Our Soul - Soul Mother and Father

Our soul can bring replenishment with the divine male and female aspects of itself. Is eternal balance. It lacks nothing, it is whole and complete. Your soul carries your akasha—the All That Is About You.

BENEFITS

As soon as Annie brought in the current of the Divine Mother energy I felt an ignition in my heart, as if my whole body woke up. It felt amazing. I am a man with a toxic mother and this felt very restorative. - CE

AWAKENING PRANA TRINITY

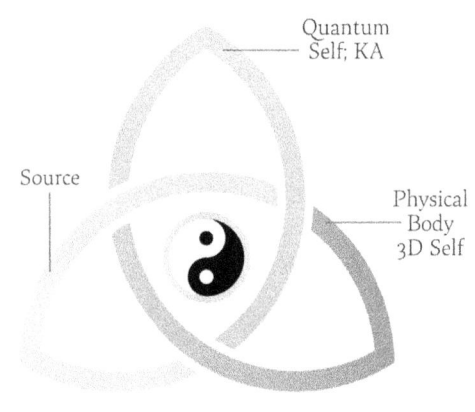

Our souls carry the perfect balance of the healed mother and father.

In the Christian doctrine of the Trinity, the energy of the soul we are talking about, is the Holy Ghost.

When I give the Trinity Activations in healings, I often meet the client's mother aspect of their soul and father aspect of their soul. These energies are not the same as their birth parents. I like to come up with human comparisons when I "meet" these energies, to make the attributes accessible for my client.

From Our Soul - Soul Mother and Father

Our souls carry the perfect balance of the healed mother and father. While traits of these consciousnesses may seem like ascended masters, note that they are attributes that are very personalized to *you*. You at your highest representation. Just like every snowflake has its own pattern, so, too, do we on a soul level. This is our unique vibration and akasha.

The Soul Mother

Common traits for client's soul mothers are those that are similar to Mother Mary, or a Mother Superior. Or maybe a healer adept, such as Mary Magdalene. Or carrying an energy like Glinda, the good witch, in the Wizard of Oz. Even a trait like the energy of Tinkerbell. Trite, maybe, but all of these are common attributes. Sometimes the energy is perceptive and wise.

Ask your soul mother to bring you healing, note the feeling and the experience, and shift. This is a great exercise to do every day.

> "I ask my soul mother to bring me a healing, whatever is in my highest good."

The Soul Father

Sometimes a person's soul father is a heart-centered energy similar to the Dalai Lama. Or Desmond Tutu. Sometimes Sometimes the energy is like Merlin, even, or someone with a soul that is very perceptive, or one that feels Buddhist.

EXPERIENTIAL EXERCISE

Ask your soul father (or soul mother) to bring you healing, note the feeling and the experience, and shift. This is a great exercise to do every day.

"I ask my soul father (or soul mother) to bring me a healing, whatever is in my highest good."

Category D. Source

From Source Comes the Source Currents

Source energy is perfection, total non-duality. When we are depleted, healing will restore the connection, bringing our quantum DNA and our perfect blueprint.

The Divine Mother

The Divine Mother is a powerful symbol of the sacred feminine and the connection between humanity and nature. She is a reminder that we are all part of something larger than ourselves and that we are all connected to the earth and all living things. The Mother has always been a primordial deity throughout the world.

The Divine Feminine

The divine feminine is a spiritual concept that refers to the positive qualities of Yin, such as compassion, empathy, intuition, and creativity. It is also associated with receptivity, nurturing, and healing.

The divine feminine is not limited to women, however. It is an energy that is present in both men and women. It is the part of us that is soft, caring, and compassionate. It is also the part of us that is creative, intuitive, and receptive.

The Divine Father

The symbolism of the Divine Father is a complex and multifaceted one, with roots in many different religious and cultural traditions. In general, the Divine Father is seen as a symbol of power, authority, wisdom, and protection. He is often associated with the sky, the sun, and the stars. In the Christian doctrine of the Trinity, the Divine Father is the Heavenly Father.

The Divine Masculine

The divine masculine is a spiritual concept that refers to the positive qualities of Yang, such as strength, courage, leadership, and responsibility. It is also associated with action, logic, and rational thought.

Just as the divine feminine isn't limited to women, so the divine masculine is not limited to men. It is an energy that is present in both men and women. It is the part of us that is assertive, decisive, and proactive. It is also the part of us that is providing, and supportive; protective, as in providing a container.

> **BENEFITS**
>
> I could feel the Yin and Yang energies moving and merging within my body during the meditation. The result was a sense of calm, as if the newly balanced masculine and feminine energies dissolved the stress that I was holding in my physical body. A deep sense of relaxation continued for several hours. - MB

You learn a lot about resistance and depletion when working with Yin and Yang in your energy body. Someone with a mother wound can have resistance to the sacred feminine energy, or certainly Mother Earth's energy. The need is to dissolve the low vibration density, the resistance, so the healed Yin/mother energy can flow. Their energy body recognizes the energy as Yin, but it takes a few minutes for it to realize it isn't the energy of the toxic female person who caused the trauma. Someone with a father wound may be so depleted of Yang energy that the need is to fill them up, like an empty well.

Male Energy Carries Female Energy - Female Energy Carries Male Energy
Masculine and feminine Elements are fundamental to how the universe operates; we could not exist without them.

Anima, according to its Latin definition, is a current of air, wind, breath, or the vital principle. It is the soul of life. It is the unconscious feminine dimension of a male, hidden, forgotten, or repressed in daily life. To regain internal balance, men need to reconnect with this dimension, the other side of their character. Once accomplished, tenderness, patience, consideration, and compassion become more accessible. However, repression, arrogance, aggression, and selfishness arise if unacknowledged.

Psychologist Carl Jung studied the **animus**, translated from Latin, which means the rational soul, life, and mental faculty. The animus represents the unconscious male domain of the female psyche; if left unintegrated, women might become inhibited, restrained, or suppressed. Lack of integration manifests in argumentative tendencies, destruction, and desensitization. However, when integrated, women can become stronger, more assertive, and more rational. (Jung, 2021)

Jung's premise had ancient roots. In fact, one of his followers, Joseph Campbell, has written extensively since the early 1940s, about how both male and female aspects resonate in the human psyche. He looked to indigenous traditions, showing how we evolved from relative degrees of harmony into fragmentation. (Campbell, 2008). More recently, Robin Wall Kimmerer, a member of the Citizen Potawatomi Nation and a professor of environmental science at the State University of New York College of Environmental Science and Forestry, artfully describes the play of masculine and feminine forces in indigenous life, pointing to our need to reconnect with nature, in order for planetary restoration. (Wall Kimmerer, 2013)

All major spiritual traditions have male and female deities who operate in a synchronicity. Indigenous traditions worldwide had male and female gods and goddesses of Source. Hinduism features the male god Shiva who exemplifies consciousness, compassion, and detachment along with Parvati who stands for beauty, love, wisdom, and Source. Buddha incarnated to teach strength of character and integrity in action. He has very similar characteristics to Shiva, while Kwan Yin exemplifies his female side, overseeing the healing domain of the physical plane.

Sikhism is a monotheistic religion, yet its teaching contains representations of male/female aspects. The feminine principle is often associated with the sacred qualities of compassion, love, and wisdom. The masculine principle is often associated with the sacred qualities of strength, power, and justice. These two principles are seen as complementary, and both are necessary for the Source and maintenance of the universe.

DIARY OF A HEALER

Transforming the Father Wound

Sam was in his mid-fifties when he came to see me, concerned that he couldn't seem to move forward with his life and work. That he felt stuck. As we talked, I learned how as a child he had been physically hit by his father, even beaten at times. It was clear he carried a painful father wound.

As with all new clients, I focused on "The Trinity Activations," a technique I developed as part of the Divine Mother modality. The healing basically works under the premise that we are all born to unhealed mothers and fathers and become unhealed children with wounded egos. We are depleted of important mother/feminine and/or father/masculine energy, a dynamic we all need to balance and thrive in abundance.

On a soul level, we have a healed mother and father, as I have discussed above, and they are not the same as our birth parents. If you will, the soul's mother and father—our sacred parents—carry the healed male and female energies and principles of balanced Yin and Yang. The Trinity Activations fill in the missing energies by bringing these to the client from the soul, be the need be for mother or Yin feminine energy, or father or Yang masculine energy.

Someone—man or woman—who is depleted in Yang energy, the masculine energy, tends to be stuck, unable to bring projects to fruition or to market, unable to bring initiatives outward to the world or to be proactive in their life.

Sam seemed to fit the profile of someone who was Yang deficient, and I expected he might be depleted in healed father/male/Yang energy. Administering the Trinity Activations revealed that he had, in fact, a significant depletion (70%!)—a genuine father wound.

The Trinity Activations brought Sam's healed father energy in to replace the unhealthy male energy he was carrying from his upbringing and fill his need for healthy male energy. His energy body was starved for the healed masculine.

As I brought in Sam's soul's father energy, I could sense its presence, its consciousness. It felt like the presence of someone like the Dalai Lama! It was extraordinary energy, compassionate, kind, and generous. The polar opposite of his birth father.

While concluding the healing with Sam, I suggested that part of his soul's purpose in this lifetime is understanding himself as a man, understanding his energy as a man, and becoming healed. He had a toxic father, and yet on a soul level, his male energy carried a very, very high vibration and grace. His journey resided in understanding the two.

The Trinity Activation resulted in Sam's rejuvenation He sprang to life and re-engaged fully with his personal development. A female client had a debilitating depression. One healing filling the depletion of healed father energy lifted the depression completely.

Note: So let's say we show up as 70% deficient in the Divine Father in my Trinity Activations healing system. We may have 70% toxic male energy where that deficiency lies. So we need to replenish 70% of that male energy that is missing with the healed sacred male energy, as we are 70% deficient.

If you expect you have a father wound or mother, you can bring a Trinity Activation to yourself by placing your hand on your heart and saying, "I ask to activate my Divine Father (or Divine Mother), my soul father, to bring me healing, whatever is in the highest good."

DIARY OF A HEALER

Healing the Mother Wound

A student of mine was working very hard to train her "clair" senses, those intuitive message systems known as clairsentience, clairaudience, clairvoyance, and claircognizance, to name the most familiar. I call these the information highways from our Higher Selves, as we can glean so much wisdom from the feelings (clairsentience), symbols (clairvoyance), knowing (claircognizance), and words (clairaudience).

That gut feeling you get when you walk into a room? Or when the hair goes up on the back of your neck? Clairsentience. Images that come to you when you are meditating? Clairvoyance. Knowing that it is time to leave your job? Claircognizance. The words you hear in your head when you are told to slow down or to remember something? Clairaudience.

Except for clairaudience, all of Sally's clairs were open at an 8/10 on a scale I use with my students, ten being the most open. Very strong. Her clairaudience, however, was a 2/10! With a number like that, the block is clearly from trauma, and if we clear the trauma, the clair can open.

In Sally's case, she would go into a paroxysm of self-doubt when she tried to work with her clairaudience. It was like she had a ten-headed hydra in her mind, each "head" telling her something else to discredit what she "heard!"

Sally had a very critical mother, and she had internalized the constant disparaging negativity to the point where she literally couldn't hear herself think. In an energy healing to look to the highest priority that needed healing to clear this trauma, I came across the symbolic hydra and removed it. Given her mother is now dead, Sally wouldn't hear the

> criticism in the real world, and she could now disentangle herself from the memories, becoming a witness to them.
>
> She also was 70% depleted of her soul's healed mother/feminine energy in her clairaudience center, which is just over the ear in the temporal lobe, and by replenishing this with the Trinity Activations I was able to help further strengthen that clair.
>
> A few weeks after this healing, her clairaudience was functioning at a 7/10! All that was needed to get this clair functioning again was removing the trauma and replenishing it with her soul's feminine energy, which was loving and supportive.

Yin (-): Yin is matter, it is what brings form.
Babies are born from mothers.

Feminine energy: Yin is often associated with qualities such as darkness, passivity, intuition, nurturing, and receptivity. Feminine energy attracts the people and things we love and value, it is the spark of the creative process, renewal, beauty of form and harmony; it harmonizes.

- Moon: Yin is often associated with the moon, as it is considered a symbol of the feminine and the night.
- Cold: Yin is associated with cold temperatures and the winter season.
- Earth: Yin is also associated with the Earth, representing its receptive and nurturing qualities.

Yang (+): Yang is consciousness, Yang brings the idea.

- Masculine energy: Yang is often associated with qualities such as light, activity, logic, assertiveness, and vigor. It is an energy of protection, action and assertion, and the ability to project into the world.
- Sun: Yang is often associated with the sun, as it is considered a symbol of the masculine and the day.
- Hot: Yang is associated with hot temperatures and the summer season.
- Heaven: Yang is also associated with the heavens, representing its active and expansive qualities.

THE DIVINE MOTHER

Older polytheistic religions worshiped Goddesses. They are frequently represented in Roman, Greek, African, and Egyptian contexts. In Hinduism, Goddesses are still worshiped in Tantric Buddhism and Tantric Hinduism. Both have a specific focus on female deities.

Indigenous populations and pagan civilizations have referred to the Mother as presiding over time itself; she creates, preserves, and destroys, engaging the eternal cycle. She

Venus of Willendorf was most likely sculpted between 28,000 and 25,000 years before Christ. Archeologists discovered her Palaeolithic excavation site close to Willendorf, Austria.

birthed humanity and oversees all aspects of Source, even the minute details of daily survival.

The ancient Greeks worshiped Demeter, known for overseeing agriculture and fertility, rendering human life and founding steps of civilized life.

Egyptian mythology features the Mother Goddess Mut. Mut means "mother." She is associated with the water element from which everything is born.

Many Christians regard Mary as the Mother Goddess. She has various titles such as "Our Lady of Sorrows" or "Conception, Miracles, and Hope. The Black Madonna is still worshiped at multiple sites throughout the Mediterranean. Throughout the ages, we can see images of a child depicted on a Divine Mother's lap.

Tantric Buddhism and Tantric Hinduism still focus on the Divine Mother. Hindus worship Durga, who creates and protects as the universal Mother, manifesting in various forms such as Saraswati, goddess of knowledge, and Kali, the goddess responsible for ego destruction. In Buddhism, we find the female counterpart of Buddha, Kwan Yin, the goddess of compassion.

THE DIVINE FATHER

In the Judeo-Christian tradition, the Divine Father is the Source of the universe and the father of Jesus Christ. He is often called "Almighty God" or "Lord God." In the Bible, the Divine Father is portrayed as a loving and just God who cares for his children. He is also seen as a stern and demanding God who expects obedience from his followers.

In other religious traditions, the Divine Father is often seen as a more benevolent and nurturing figure. In Hinduism, for example, the Divine Father is often depicted as Vishnu, the preserver of the universe. Vishnu is seen as a kind, compassionate god who is always ready to help his devotees.

The symbolism of the Divine Father can also be interpreted in psychological terms. Some psychologists see the Divine Father as a symbol of the inner masculine or the "wise old man" archetype. This archetype represents the wisdom, strength, and guidance we all need to find our way.

The symbolism of the Divine Father is rich and complex and has been interpreted in many different ways. It is a symbol that can offer us comfort, guidance, and inspiration.

> **DIARY OF A HEALER**
>
> Being at the Sedona Courthouse Yang energy Vortex with Annie showing the way gifted me with a life-altering experience of sacred masculine energy that settled around and through me, planting me in clear awareness of Yang energy. I didn't know what Yang felt like until then, nor was its presence missing in my awareness. The clear experience of Yin energy at the Kachina Woman Yin Vortex and this Yang energy at the Courthouse, gave me the gift of clearly experiencing both the Yin and Yang energies and how they feel when they are balanced. Inviting and experiencing both these energies has become a clear part of my daily energy meditation practice. I am so very grateful to Annie and the guidance that brought me to this place.
> - LK
>
> I could feel the energies moving and merging within my body during the meditation. The result was a sense of calm as if the newly balanced masculine and feminine energies dissolved the stress I held in my physical body. A deep sense of relaxation continued for several hours. - MB

OUR EGO-BASED OPERATING SYSTEM AND LOW VIBRATION DENSITY

Low Vibration Density

Horrendous things happen to people. Trauma and confusion causes the most low vibration or density. Philosophically, most wonder why are we here? What is our purpose? What do we need to do to maintain our equilibrium? We worry, we fret, we "hamster-wheel" about issues over and over, and as a result we build low vibration or density barriers from repetitive negativity, creating energetic weight. Our wounded egos show themselves as a result of our unhealed mother and father experiences. Eventually, barriers transmit to physicality in some way. They become an illness, or a sideline pattern of behavior that does not serve our highest good. Since ruminating on our stress and anxiety composes the low vibration density, we must clear out negative thought processes to ensure continuous flow and optimal health.

Rumination is characterized by brooding on one's problems and their consequences. On the other hand, pondering seeks awareness of the problem's source and how to resolve it. Brooding means asking why you seem to have problems no one else has. One might wonder why they could not handle things more effectively or what they did to deserve the problem initially. Rumination can dominate not only a thought process but create a worldview. Reframing our destructive thoughts is part of the foundation of my technology for healing. (Huang, 2022)

Forgiveness Practice to Heal our Wounds

Howard Wills is a spiritual teacher and author who has written extensively on the importance of forgiveness and releasing beliefs through which we are essentially poisoning ourselves when we hold on to anger, resentment, and other negative emotions. He teaches that forgiveness is not about condoning the actions of the person who hurt us, but rather about letting go of the negative energy that we have been holding onto.

EXPERIENTIAL EXERCISE

Here is a powerful forgiveness prayer offered by John Newton. (health-beyondbelief.com)

Comprehensive Forgiveness Prayer for Ourselves
by John Newton

You may speak this prayer aloud or silently as many times daily as you feel. Positive effects have been reported in many areas of life from this simple step. Ten or more times will bring optimal results but even one or two times each day will not only anchor the results you received in the session but also address future karma. As the prayers are encoded with a direct connection to consciousness itself and the intelligence structured within it, reading/speaking them connects you with the true source of all health and well-being, the Creator.

Infinite Creator, All That You Are: for me, all my family members, all our relationships, all our ancestors and all their relationships through all time, through all our lives.

For all hurts and wrongs: physical, mental, emotional, spiritual, sexual, and financial through thought, word, or deed. Please help us all forgive each other, forgive ourselves, forgive all people and all people forgive us, completely and totally.

For all incest, murder, suicide, rape, abortion, and infidelity through thought, word, or deed. Please help us all forgive each other, forgive ourselves, forgive all people and all people forgive us, completely and totally. Please and thank you.

For all times we abandoned or were abandoned; withheld love or had love withheld; weren't nurtured, loved and supported and times we didn't nurture love and support others. Infinite Creator, please help us all forgive, be forgiven and all forgive ourselves, completely and totally. Please and thank you.

Please Infinite Creator, for the highest good: lift out all weight, pain, burden, sin, death, debt, negativity, and limitation of all kinds; transform it into your love, and let your love flow back into us, filling and giving us all complete peace, now and forever. Please and thank you. Please and thank you. Please and thank you.

Please help us love and bless each other; love and bless ourselves. Be at peace with each other and at peace with ourselves, now and forever. Please and thank you.

Thanks to visionary Howard Wills for his pioneering forgiveness work. - John Newton

DIARY OF A HEALER

With my clairvoyant eye I see low vibration density in various ways energetically including:

- A strict religious or rule-based upbringing leaving rigid behaviors that look energetically as imprisoning a person within a jungle gym-like energy armature.
- Illness itself showing up as a heavy, dense energy.
- Dark fog representing suffering and worry.
- Sludge-like energy that can represent years of murky emotional family issues.
- Rock-like energy that can show rigid blocks to energy flow due to trauma.
- A heavy stone of grievance that can often clog the heart chakra.

Psychologists evaluate trauma based on the frequency and duration of the experience.

- Acute trauma results from a single, sudden, and overwhelming event, such as an earthquake, fire, death of a loved one, car accident, or assault. Acute trauma symptoms can include:

  ▸ Reliving the event: This can happen through flashbacks, nightmares, or intrusive thoughts.
  ▸ Avoidance: Can involve avoiding places, people, or activities that remind you of the event.

- Changes in mood and behavior: Can include feeling numb, depressed, anxious, or angry.
- Physical symptoms: Can include headaches, stomachaches, and trouble sleeping.

• Chronic trauma is repeated exposure to stressful or threatening events over a long period of time, such as in the case of domestic violence, child abuse, bullying on social media, microaggressions in the workplace, or abuse in spiritual communities, ongoing community safety issues, or military combat. Symptoms of chronic trauma can include:

- Difficulty trusting others: This can make it hard to form close relationships.
- Feelings of helplessness and hopelessness can lead to depression and anxiety.
- Changes in thinking and memory: This can make it hard to focus and concentrate.
- Changes in physical health: This can include chronic pain, headaches, and stomach problems.

• Complex trauma occurs in childhood and involves repeated exposure to multiple traumatic events, often of an interpersonal nature, such as abuse, neglect, or abandonment. Severe types of abuse in spiritual communities can fall into the complex trauma category. Symptoms of complex trauma can include:

- Dissociation: This is a mental state in which you feel disconnected from yourself or your surroundings.
- Negative self-image: This can lead to low self-esteem and feelings of worthlessness.
- Trouble regulating emotions: This can lead to outbursts of anger, sadness, or fear.
- Trouble forming relationships: This can make it hard to trust others and maintain close relationships.

Research on epigenetics shows how intergenerational trauma is encoded in our genetic structure, and this is why it is so vital to connect to our original blueprint. Volumes of epigentics research from institutions such as Johns Hopkins University, Harvard University, the National Cancer Institute, University of Cambridge, University of California, San Francisco and Los Angeles, the University of Pennsylvania and the University of Edinburgh demonstrate that it is possible to reverse our genetic heritage. It is well worth doing one's own research in this promising field.

All of us have trauma embedded from the pandemic! The list goes on, and in future teachings, I will address all of these layers and how to dissolve them distinctly.

Once healed, we embody emotional intelligence. We can be vulnerable, socially aware, have empathy, and express compassion for ourselves and others. We will become more authentic as we embrace individual and unique characteristics. Thought expression comes easily without the requirement of conforming to societal expectations. People engage in more respectful communication. Importantly, they actively listen without judgment, aspiring to understand the other person's perspective without becoming aggressive, defensive, or manipulative.

Integrating the masculine and feminine means setting and honoring boundaries. Assertion rather than aggression frames all interactions and creates more balanced relationships. Consequently, self-awareness flows, contributing to progressive personal growth stages. Men and women become better able to nurture and care for themselves and others and create nourishing environments to sustain the web of life. The entire world, seen and unseen, benefits as a result. Teamwork, collaboration, and cooperation ensure a more inclusive planet where collective goals as opposed to individual power and control, sustain us.

Trauma brings low vibration density to our physicality. Normally, we resist clearing it. However, we can clear the low vibration low density with the 9 Steps in this book. Building prana via the Vortex clears the resistance in the Central Axis. It is a powerful technique—the Master Blaster. We can blast the trauma so the light can come through. Subsequently, our life force energy flows through to restore balance and to bring healing, awareness in the heart chakra and the intention to have gratitude and appreciate love.

The Vesica Pisces

In the ultimate Yin and Yang connection, Yin and Yang connect to make a third energy. In our biology, the first cell of our conception is created from the connection of male sperm and a female egg. The vesica piscis image depicts this act of creation.

Called the mandorla symbol, the vesica piscis is an ancient symbol known as the Vessel of the Fish in Christianity. In Hinduism this space is called the yoni, invoking the Great Mother's creative, life-giving fertility. Alchemists and Christian mystics defined the mandorla as the arcs of great circles, the left one for female matter and the right for male spirit. The overlapping space is the place of birth.

VESICA PISCIS

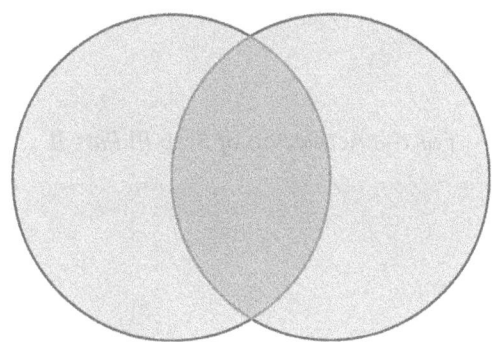

What is a fractal?

A fractal is a geometric shape that is self-similar across different scales. This means that when you zoom in on a fractal, you see the same basic pattern repeating itself over and over again. Fractals are often infinitely complex, and they can be found in nature, art, and mathematics.

- I am created by my mother's egg and my father's sperm.
- My mother was created from her mother's egg and her father's sperm
- My grandmother was created by her mother's egg and her father's sperm.

The Seven Generations Teachings and Sacred Geometry

What happens when the vesica piscis repeats itself endlessly?

This gets *really* interesting. Many of us have heard the belief that if you heal yourself, you heal seven generations back and seven generations forward—a Native American teaching. It is based on the idea that we are all interconnected, and that our actions have an impact on both our ancestors and our descendants. Think of the vesica piscis endlessly creating itself and having been created endlessly. The healing we bring to ourselves in this lifetime can flow through sacred geometry and heal generations.

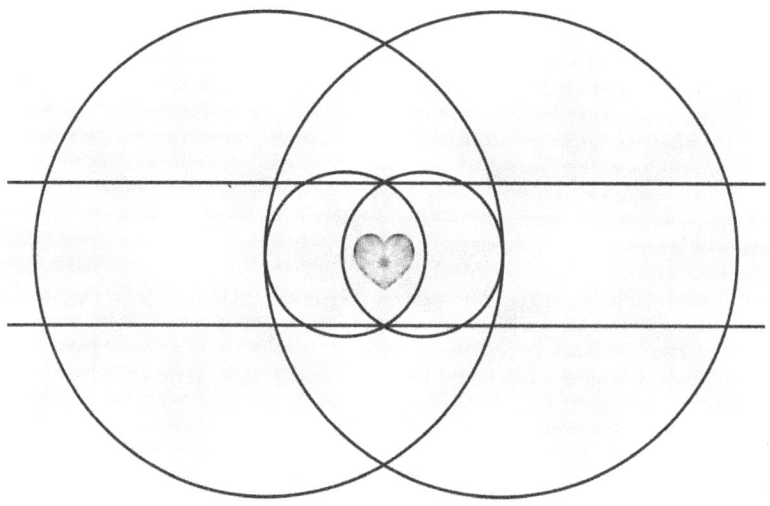

For the Activation of Step III Part II.

STEP IV: THE VORTEX
YOUR MOTOR
BACKGROUND ABOUT THIS STEP OF THE SEQUENCE

A key part of your energy body is a Vortex! It is your motor! Most importantly it carries a transmission and spark of Source.

Once the rotation of Yin and Yang gets strong enough, the energies combine, creating a Vortex—an ignition—that carries a spark of light, a transmission of life force prana from Source. Our energy body relies on the building of Vortexes made of both (-) Yin and (+) Yang currents of energy. If we don't have enough (-) Yin, our "ignition" becomes imbalanced and we won't be able to form a strong and balanced Vortex.

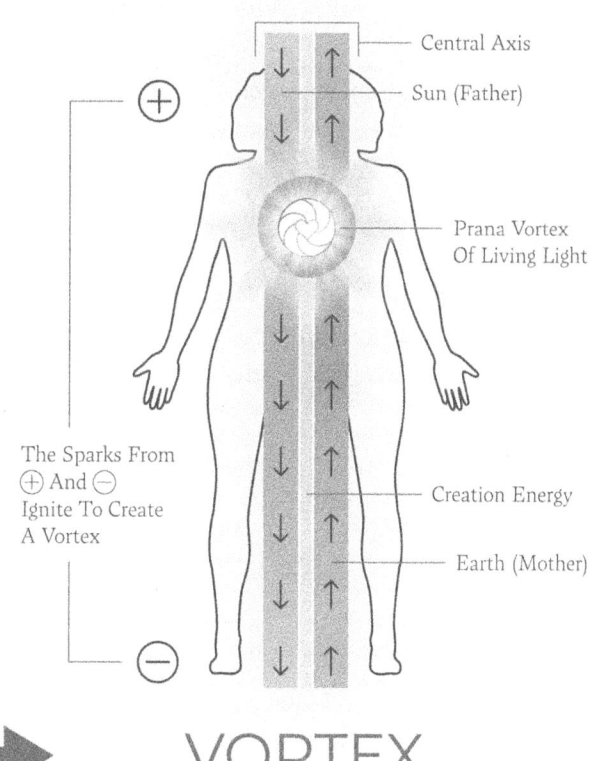

CREATING THE BIOELECTRIC VORTEX

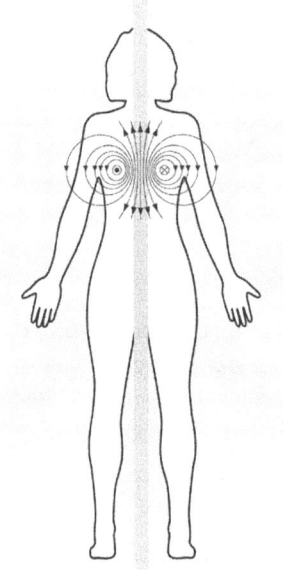

What and Why of the Vortexes

Vortexes convey enormous amounts of power for transformation. They are master blasters that push out the lower vibration density of suffering and trauma, to make way for prana from Source, the spark of light, our connection to the matrix of light from Source, to enter our physicality. They connect you directly to the flow from Source and help you drink that energy into your physicality.

The vortex master blaster pushes out the lower vibration density to make way for the spark of light of Source.

Balanced Yin and Yang connect and ignite the Creator spark, and the spark organizes a Vortex, the movement of Yin and Yang into a counter-rotating vortex. Our inner human Vortexes spinning vertically are made by the rotation of the Yin (-) and Yang (+) energies around the Central Axis. It is the rotation that makes the Vortex, and there needs to be enough rotation.

For there to be enough rotation, you need enough Yin and Yang.

The **Vortex** is primary; we need the **Vortex** because it carries the energy of flow. It pulls and moves energy. The Vortex creates movement. You have many Vortexes throughout your energy body, both large and small. The main horizontal one, located in your heart, pulls the energy from the Central Axis into your physical structure. The main vertical one, is your Pranic tube, and within it is the Central Axis.

We have two main Vortexes spinning vertically in our energy bodies, pulling in the prana from the Earth and Sun and from Source.

1. The Central Axis (Source)
2. Pranic Tube (Earth and Sun)

We have three main Vortexes spinning horizontally in our energy bodies.

1. The biggest Vortex is in your heart.
2. Another is in your navel point, and
3. The third is in your pineal gland.

These three points, known as your hara system, are huge storage areas of prana, and the Vortexes are there to draw the energy to them from the Pranic Tube. Smaller horizontal Vortexes include the chakras.

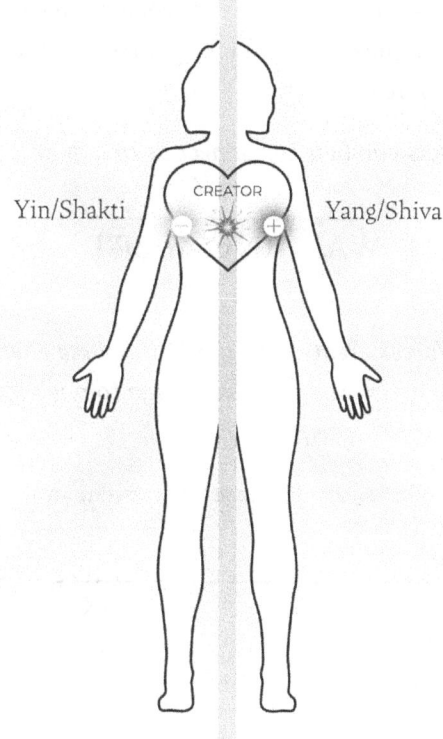

From physics we learn that a common denominator in all Vortexes is that they have a rotating motion around an axis. Another common denominator in all Vortexes is that they have a central core. The core of our energy bodies is our Central Axis (see diagram, above). A Vortex won't exist without this.

Importantly, the Vortexes in our energy bodies are **magnetic**. Magnetism is the force of attraction or repulsion between two magnetic poles. It is a fundamental force of nature, like gravity and electromagnetism. Only Vortexes that are created by magnetic fields have a (-) and (+) charge. The (-) and (+) is a force of attraction.

The magnetic field and the attraction of the two magnetic poles determine the Vortex's strength. We've discussed this earlier in regards to how strong both Yin and Yang need to be to make a strong Vortex, and they have to be moving, to be rotating, the attraction has to be strong.

I cannot emphasize this sentence enough:

Once the rotation of Yin and Yang gets strong enough, the energies combine, creating a Vortex—an ignition—that carries a spark of light, a transmission of life force prana from Source.

Once the rotation of Yin and Yang gets strong enough...
A transmission of life force prana from Source.

Here are the two key takeaways:

1. We need enough Yin and Yang energies in equal balance—so that when we get it,
2. We are able to create the spark that is the entry point for the transmission of life force prana from Source.

Both aspects combine to connect us to a matrix of light.

WARNING ALERT

Remember, the Vortex creates the spark of Source energy, so without a strong enough Vortex, one has less linkage to one's life force, as well as to Source.

"Stagnation is the Mother of all disease and movement is the Father of the cure." —**Lao Tzu**

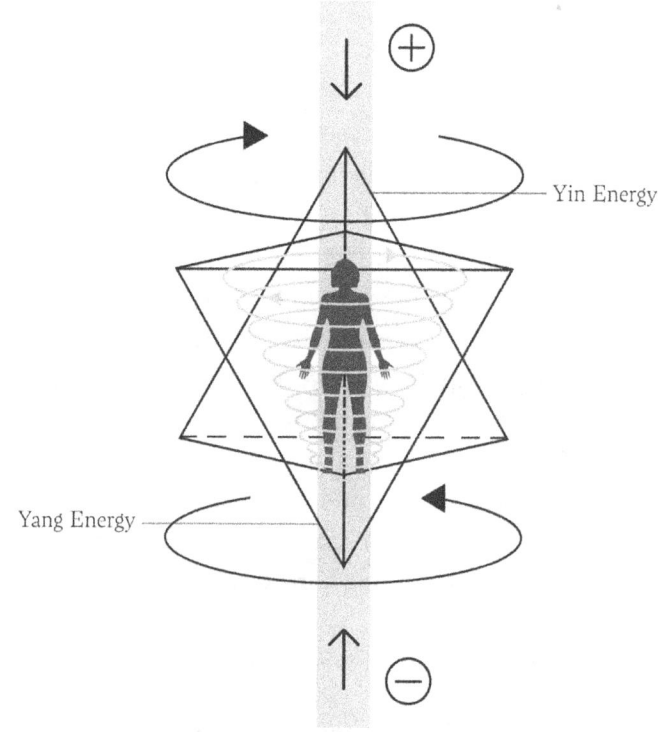

Sidebar: Note that in this diagram the upward (Yin) and downward (Yang) triangles form a merkabah. All bio-Vortexes are merkabahs, a spinning Vortex of energy that is made up of two interpenetrating tetrahedrons, one pointing upwards and one pointing downwards. These tetrahedrons represent the duality of existence, Yin and Yang, the body and the spirit. When they are spinning in perfect balance, they create a merkabah field that can transport the soul to higher dimensions. The word "merkabah" is a Hebrew word that means "chariot" or "vehicle."

Vortexes are created in nature by many things, including dolphins, tornadoes, hurricanes, and whirlpools. We find vortexes around an airplane's wings, in the wake of a boat, or in a rocket blast.

Powerful Vortexes on Earth exist in special spots on the Earth where energy is either entering into the Earth or projecting out of the Earth's plane. Vortexes or vortices are found at sacred sites throughout the world, such as the Great Pyramid in Egypt; Machu Picchu in Peru, Bali, Stonehenge, Sedona, Arizona; Glastonbury, England; and Mount Shasta, California or Irish Rock in Australia. Vortex energy moves in a spiral, traveling up and down. In the spiritual context, a Vortex is a place where energy is believed to be concentrated. People who experience Vortexes say they can positively affect the body and mind by promoting healing, increasing creativity, and enhancing spiritual awareness.

As discussed, the flow of our energy body relies on a balanced Vortex of negative and positive energy; so, it is critical to connect to the Earth for restoration. However, over the past 12,000 years, humanity's connection to the Earth and natural world has weakened, resulting in a shortage of negative Yin energy and a loss of connection to the universe. This depletion of shakti energy, the feminine power of Source, has led to a lack of health and disconnection from The All That Is. The evidence of depletion shows up in a number of different ways.

The Vortex: The Master Blaster

Think of the Vortex (and the Torus it creates) as purification systems. We need purification systems at many levels. When we feel a subtle block of energy, it does not feel comfortable, and gradually that discomfort turns into disease. Human systems short-circuit and malfunction when resources are not delivered where they are needed the most. Lack of reciprocity in any venue shuts our power Sources down. When we try to operate with a stagnant power Source, the current or voltage cannot move through us.

If you think about it, the body has its own purification system. It eliminates blood that's filtered through the kidneys and through bile that's filtered through the gallbladder and the liver. The subtle spiritual world of the energy body has its own filtration system so that it can filter out toxic energy that builds up and does not belong in the mind, body, or spirit.

BENEFITS

Releasing by asking the Sacred Elements to help is always beneficial: "I ask the Sacred Element Earth to magnetize down, Water to wash away, Fire to burn away, Air to blow away, and Ether to remove, that which I can release."

Water Vortex

Victor Schauberger (1885–1958) was a logger, forester, and visionary who grew up in Austria, where his father, too, was a logger by trade. Back then, loggers would float immense logs down the nearest river to the mills. Victor spent his childhood studying the river and watched as the logs followed its winding path. Schauberger noted, "From earliest childhood, it was my deepest wish to understand nature and come closer to the truth I could not find at school or church. I was repeatedly drawn to the forest where I could watch the flow of water for hours on end without getting tired or irritable." As expressed by the Chinese in the *I Ching*, Schauberger believed that water is the earth's lifeblood.

As a naturalist of unusual observational abilities and intuition, Schauberger concluded that water "must be allowed to follow its own course to keep its energy." He coined the term *living water* to describe water's vitality when it was allowed to follow its natural course of winding, vortexing, and spiraling. He noted that in undisturbed nature, river water flowed away from direct sunlight to be sheltered by the forests to keep a cool temperature and maintain its energy and vitality. He gained wide respect for the canal he designed that mimicked water's meandering sequences as it sent logs down Austrian mountains.

John Wilkes became a pioneer in water flow studies. Through his applied research into the flow and rhythm of water, Wilkes invented flowforms, a series of connected basins, where each basin is designed to cause a double Vortex in a figure eight. Flowforms incorporate Schauberger's wisdom—that water needs to move in a Vortex to stay clean and alive. Flowforms resuscitate "dead" water, bringing it back to life.

Half art and half technology, flowform sculptures allow water to cascade in a series of figure eights, replicating the path water takes in undisturbed flows found in nature. The natural movement of the water allows for better oxygenation, and it improves the water's capacity to support life-forms. Flowforms can regenerate water's natural power and are used worldwide in agricultural irrigation and sewage treatment systems.

The Vortex movement of the water provides rhythm and oxygenation and stimulates biological activity. Flowforms are now used worldwide for water and sewage treatment. King Charles of Great Britain uses Flowforms for the sewage system at Highgrove Castle. flowforms are also beautiful, sculptural designs, reflecting Wilkes's study of sculpture at the Royal College of Art.

For the Activation of Step IV see Part II

STEP V: RELEASE - EXHAUST
BACKGROUND ABOUT THIS STEP OF THE SEQUENCE

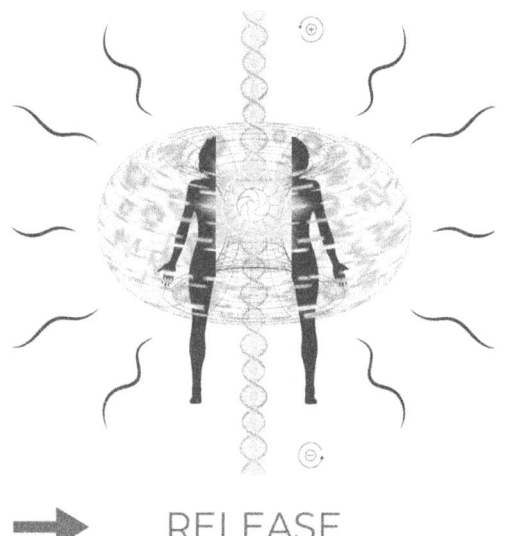

RELEASE

Although massively underutilized due to the depletion of our Yin and Yang and subsequent underperformance of our Vortex and Pranic Tube, our energy body does have its own exhaust system, just like a car, to remove lower vibration buildup.

The What and Why of Releasing

The Vortex acts like a pump to remove lower vibration density and release lower vibration energies. **It also brings in the spark of Source light, which is LOVE, and LOVE is an alchemy that also dissolves lower vibration density.**

Illness, trauma, stress, and required behaviors that run our lives, all create lower vibration density in our physicality (as a disease) and energy body (as a neurosis). We try to fit into old programming such as trying to fit into a culture where one isn't a perfect fit, or to please a parent.

It envelops us in a lower, darker, vibration. Some of it is so powerful it is solid, even hard. As a healer, I see this energy clairvoyantly. Sometimes I can even feel its strong resistant pushback. Energy that is entrenched and recalcitrant.

This is the lower vibration density discussed as being removed in the previous section (V) about the Vortex. As the Vortex, master blaster, removes lower vibration density so that light can enter, it hits against these hard layers of the mind. I say hard layers of the mind, because much of the wounding is from the wounded ego. But there is also terrible trauma that people suffer. And illness. All of this clogs the

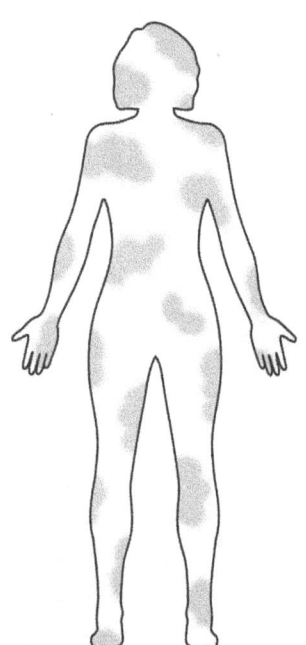

system and needs to be removed energetically so that we can better connect to the matrix of light.

It is worth mentioning that there are practices that we can do in our lives to reduce the amount of lower vibration density we carry in our systems, and to keep up with the practice so that we don't add any on! The first job is usually to work to remove childhood trauma, as we are generally not equipped to mitigate trauma at young ages.

Some of the ways to reduce lower vibration density with spiritual healing that will be covered elsewhere in the book, include:

- Positive thinking (and this is really remarkable, how the alchemy works);
- Clearing your auric fields (storage house of our trauma). The auric fields are the "pipeline" for intention.
- Self-love (talking about alchemy, self-love is magic for keeping from adding to the lower vibration density burden);
- Clearing our illusions with the help of the sacred element Ether;
- Working hard to come into equal balance of Yin and Yang energies in your body, mind, and spirit;
- Becoming a student of forgiveness.

As you remove lower vibration density from your energy body, you become lighter, more radiant, and more open to receiving higher frequencies of energy. You may also experience increased clarity, intuition, and creativity. When your energy body is clear and free-flowing, you are better able to manifest your desires and live a life of joy and abundance.

The importance of releasing lower vibration density in energy healing is that it allows for the body's natural healing mechanisms to be activated. When there are blockages in the body's energy field, it can lead to physical, emotional, and mental health problems. Releasing these blockages allows the energy to flow freely, which can help to improve overall health and well-being.

- Eckhart Tolle: "The more you are able to let go of the past, the more present you can be, and the more present you are, the more alive you are."
- Deepak Chopra: "The body is a storehouse of emotional energy. When we hold on to painful emotions, they can manifest as physical symptoms."
- Caroline Myss: "We are all energy beings, and when we hold on to negative energy, it can block our ability to receive and give love."
- Howard Wills, a spiritual teacher and author mentioned earlier who has written extensively on the importance of forgiveness and releasing, believes that when we hold on to anger, resentment, and other negative emotions, we are essentially poisoning ourselves!

In Awakening Prana!, releasing the lower vibration density is imperative so that we can open to and receive the life force energy from the matrix of light.

> ### DIARY OF A HEALER
>
> **Clearing Trauma**
>
> A few days before our last session Fred had put regular gas into his diesel fuel truck to the tune of $1,200 to repair the damage! On another recent day, he turned around quickly, forgetting he had placed an expensive and fragile gardening ingredient in an insecure place behind him, hit it, and broke it. The list went on. Fred came in complaining about his "crazy week." He found himself doing discombobulated things.
>
> He had been in a bad car crash a few years before that gave him a near-death experience (NDE) and caused a number of broken bones with a lot of pain. His recovery was long and arduous. Such an experience is a perfect setup for embedded trauma, and PTSD energy.
>
> I'd been working with Fred for over a month with two healings before he came in with this discombobulated energy. We'd worked through a few issues in his energy body that were out of balance due to the strong medicines he'd been on, and some depression he had developed from the process. The NDE had also changed him on a fundamental level and he was experiencing some challenges adjusting. Seeing the world as all love, as he experienced in his NDE, was diametrically opposed to the way his personality ran his career as a CEO of a large company.
>
> As soon as I scanned his energy body when he came in for his third healing complaining about his "crazy week," I saw dense energy around his left clavicle and throat. In the auric field coming off that area was a buzzy, spiraling energy about one inch wide, moving out to about a foot off of his body. Because I am clairvoyant, I see energy this way, but one could perceive it using any of the main clairs (clairsentience, claraudience, clairvoyance, claircognizance).
>
> The way these energies showed themselves—dark, dense energy around his throat chakra, and a spiraling, buzzy energy—are classic ways that PTSD and trauma energies show up energetically. They cause hyper stress and anxiety.
>
> In this case, the trauma was relatively recent, but it could well have piled onto an older, similar trauma. When we have a trauma, it anchors into our auric field, and if it isn't cleared, it shows up in our physicality in some way or another. For Fred the trauma hadn't cleared and was manifesting as a blocked energy in his throat chakra—and energy of lower vibration density—that also was giving off a very buzzy, hyper energy typical of PTSD.
>
> Using my healer tools, I first worked in his auric field, clearing the original trauma, and then moved into the way the trauma was manifesting in his energy body, removing

> the buzzy energy as well as the lower vibration density in his throat chakra. It is always wonderful when one can remove the buzzy energy as a client feels so much more peace.
>
> There is so much hope for a person knowing that trauma can be removed from their auric field, and that in turn removes how it is manifesting in their life. This simple healing has given him a good chance he won't suffer from the trauma anymore.

> ## WARNING ALERT
>
> *Is lower vibration density in your energy body blocking your connection to the matrix of light?*
>
> *Do we really create our own reality? If so, how?*

THE AURIC FIELDS

The essence of your mind is held in a vibrational pattern around your body. These patterns are called the auric fields. While affiliated with the chakras, they are the original source of experience. Do we really create our own reality? If so, how?

In response to life's trials, traumas, and tribulations, your mind creates formless thoughts, including words, imagery, emotions, and mental constructs. The more upsetting the topic, the more you can have patterns of repetitive overthinking—or "hamster wheeling." As these thoughts become more and more dense, they become thought forms and manifest as dis-ease, moving into your physical body and chakras from that formless field around you, dragging you down. These thought forms thus can then cause illness, emotional distress, stuck energy, and patterns of behavior that don't serve you.

It is in this way that our minds create our reality.

For example, if someone is beaten as a child the trauma will be held in the etheric body, the auric field closest to the body. Over time the trauma will fester emotionally and start bringing lower vibration density to the first chakra, its developmental partner. Unless the trauma is cleared in the auric field, that child will likely grow up with issues around safety, money, and security.

> *What is held and unresolved in our auric fields creates lower vibration density in our physicality.*

As we worry, mull, can't let go of, hamster-wheel about issues, they gain lower vibration density. They manifest in our physicality, chakras, and body as they gain lower vibration density, creating our reality.

We create thoughts—negative or positive—from our feelings. Are the thoughts positive or negative?

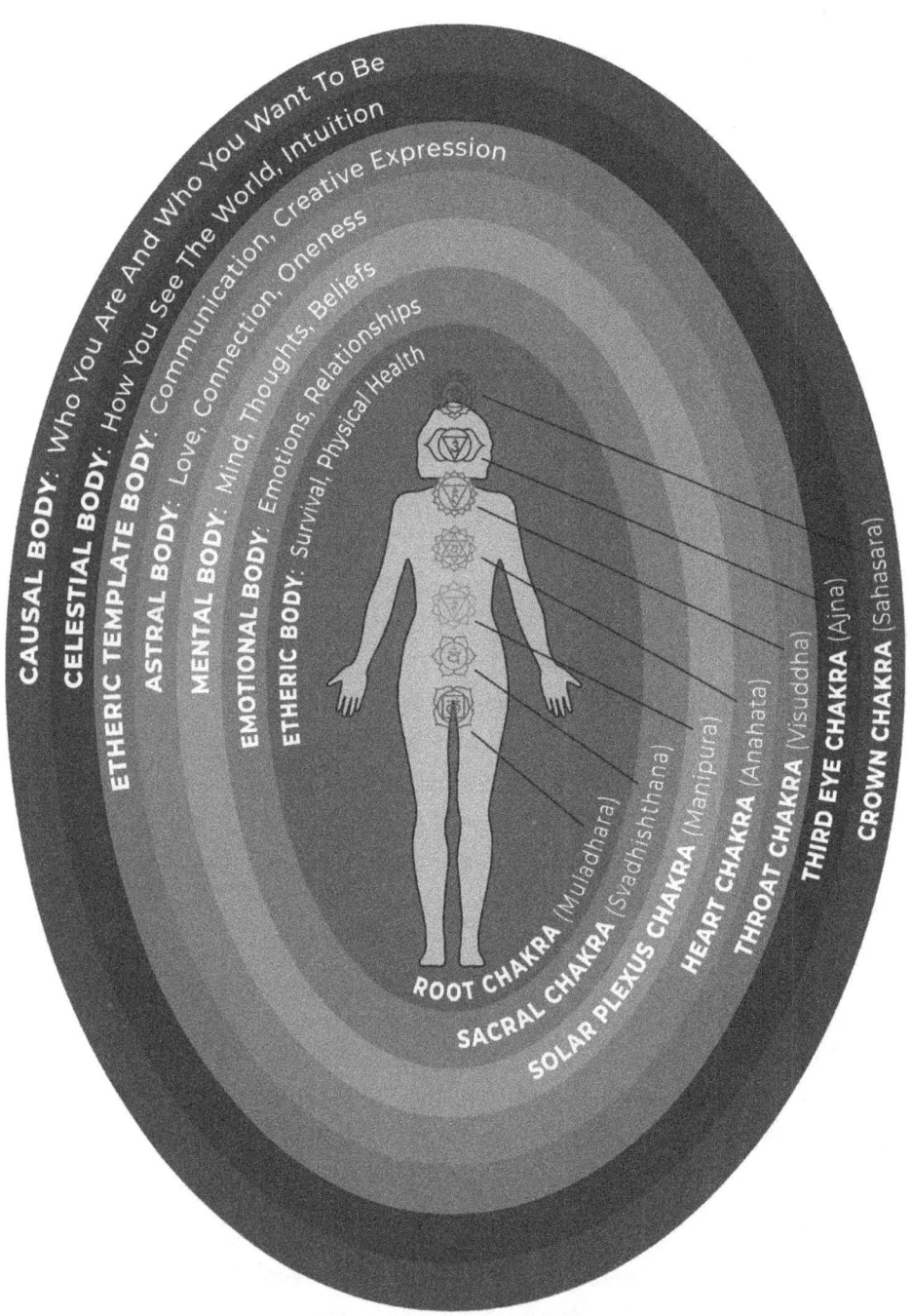

Trauma lodges in the aura and the resulting feelings produce (usually negative) thoughts. These thoughts ultimately can manifest in our lives, in our chakras, body and mind.

AURIC FIELDS

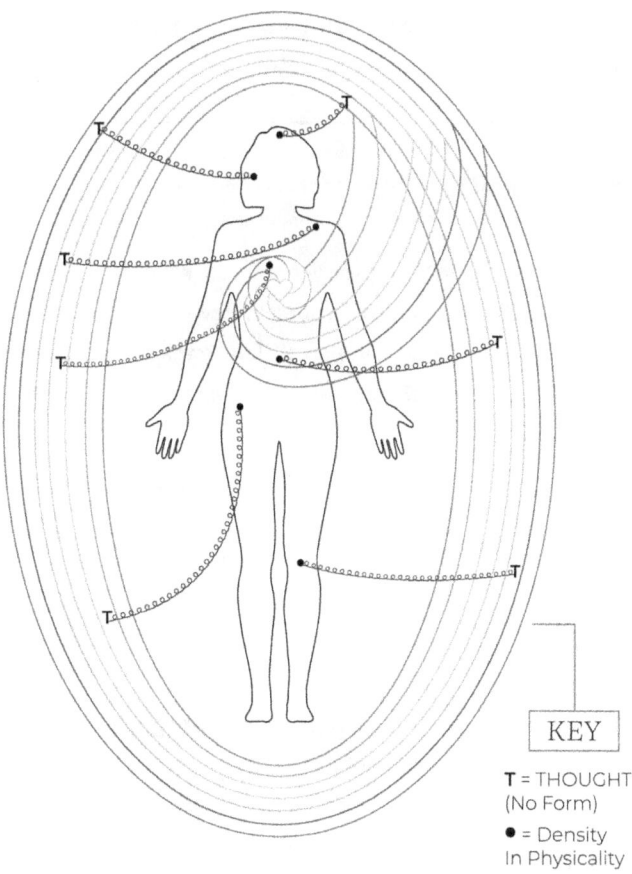

KEY

T = THOUGHT
(No Form)

● = Density
In Physicality

AURIC FIELD	TRAUMA-BASED THOUGHT
Etheric Body Survival, physical health	Example: Frequently hit by a parent. "Life is scary."
Emotional Body Emotions, relationships	Example: Parents divorced w/ tug of war for children "I'm not acknowledged."
Mental Body Mind, thoughts, beliefs	Example: Critical parent "I'm not good enough."
Astral Body Love, connection, oneness	Example: Strictly programmed upbringing. "I don't belong."
Etheric Body Template Communication, creative expression	Not believed, especially about trauma such as sexual abuse. "I am wrong."
Celestial Body Lens through which you see the world; intuition	As a young child, you saw a lot of trauma. "I am afraid of what I'll see."
Causal Body Who you are and who you want to be.	A feeling that life is hard and unfair. "I am separate from the Source."

Make Lemonade out of Lemons

We can help keep our experiences from manifesting in unhealthy ways in our 3D world by having positive thoughts in response to trauma instead of negative. By catching negative thoughts and turning them into positive thoughts.

EXPERIENTIAL EXERCISE

Explore some recent experiences you have had, what happened, how you felt, and what you told yourself. Rewrite the script!

Another way is to work on Step VII in Part II. The prana from the pranic tube can help clear the auric fields. The entire I-IX step sequence will bring color and sound healing to clear the auric fields.

DIARY OF A HEALER

Releasing with the Elements.

Every healing that I give begins with a long releasing prayer. I call in the Supreme being to vacuum out all that can be released. I work with each of the Elements to remove that which can be released (Air to magnetize it down, Water to wash it away, Fire to burn it away, Air to blow it away, and Ether to remove it). During this process I learn a lot about how well a person releases energy. If there is a lot of activity during this process I always recommend that the client work with the Elements for releasing on a daily basis (see Part II, Step I).

BENEFITS

Releasing creates invigoration, a fresh start, and initiates new life patterns!

For the Activation of Step V see Part II.

STEP VI: THE CENTRAL AXIS
THE MATRIX OF LIGHT
BACKGROUND ABOUT THIS STEP OF THE SEQUENCE

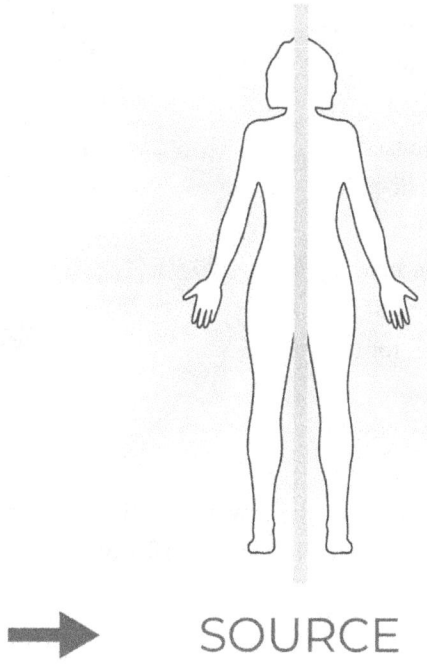

Your Central Axis is your connection to the currents of Source. The Central Axis carries this energy. The consciousness of the Universe. This energy is the essence of God/Source/ The All That Is. It is the ultimate consciousness of Source. An energy that is color/light/ sound. This is the energy of where we came from, the original Source. It carries our perfect blueprint, our Soul and Higher Self, our quantum DNA.

The Central Axis is in front of the spine and comes down to us into our crown and out through our root.

WHAT AND WHY OF THE CENTRAL AXIS

We are blocked from most of this living light because our mind's constructs, our suffering and personality's programming, all combine to make a dense barrier—a block—between us and this energy. Life force, and the sound of OM, is just on the other side of this lower vibration density.

Whatever you call this energy/sound/color/light—GOD, Source, Creator, Mother/Father God, etc.—for our purposes in this book we are talking about the vibration, not a personification of, say, "God the Father." We are focused on the experience. It is an important point because a person from any religious or spiritual tradition can access the healing technology in this book. Throughout the book I use the descriptor "Source" for this energy.

It is this Source energy that will be able to flow into your physicality to bring regeneration and renewal in Step IX, as the lower vibration density blocking it will be removed, and Source can then bring you all of the benefits of re.

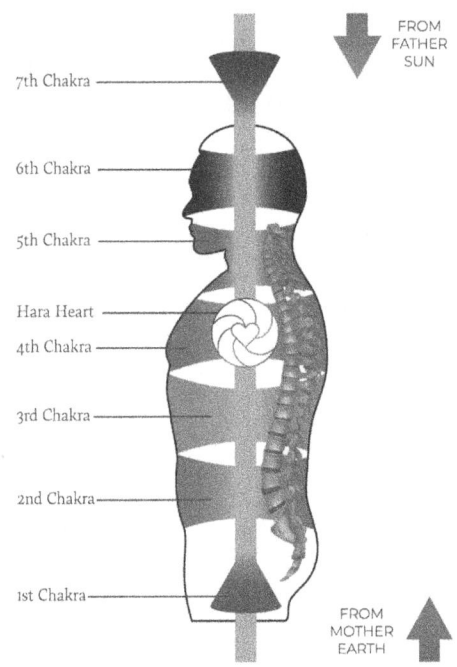

SIDEVIEW: CHAKRAS, CENTRAL AXIS, SPINE

7th Chakra
6th Chakra
5th Chakra
Hara Heart
4th Chakra
3rd Chakra
2nd Chakra
1st Chakra

FROM FATHER SUN
FROM MOTHER EARTH

The Central Axis Carries Life's Light Force:
Source Energy
- Quantum Energy, Quantum DNA
- The Akasha (eternal sum of our karmic records)
- Our perfect blueprint of our body/mind/spirit
- Consciousness
- LOVE
- Balanced Yin and Yang
- Soul and Higher Self energies
- Awakened prana
- Light
- Life Force

QUANTUM DNA IN THE CENTRAL AXIS

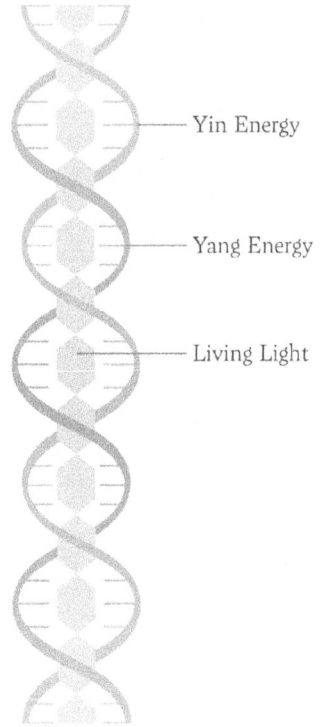

- Yin Energy
- Yang Energy
- Living Light

The Cherokee say that there is no name for this energy because it is so beyond our imagination that there aren't any words in the language to describe it. But all of us know it. Source energy—we know it when we see a whale breach, when we see a hummingbird drink the nectar from bee balm, when meeting a baby for the first time. The Source energy underlying the entire universe is the "one" that becomes the "many."

Life Force

Light Force Source energy is always available to you, it is always inside of you, and is in fact inside every single cell. Our Central Axis carries Source, the quantum field, life force, our perfect blueprint. We were designed to always have Source light flowing through us.

The purpose of the Step VI meditation in Part II is to entrain you to your Central Axis as much as possible so you can begin your relationship with this sacred part of yourself. The matrix of light. Luminosity.

Your Central Axis carries Source energy, including our life force energy, a quantum aspect of ourselves, and our interconnectedness with all that is. It is a universal, non-physical substance. It carries the perfect blueprint of all that constitutes you. It is perfect. It is the energy of love, it is the Akasha, the storehouse of all knowledge and experiences about you, both past and present, and throughout lifetimes. It is carried by the sacred element Ether and therefore has no lower vibration density. Hence, connecting to the Ether element is essential.

Life force energy is often referred to by different names, such as prana in Hinduism, chi or qi in traditional Chinese medicine, and ki in Japanese martial arts. It is what sustains and nourishes our physical, emotional, and spiritual well-being. We want to help it flow through our bodies along its natural energy channels, so it can release blocks and flow and return us to harmony. Unimpeded flow means generating health, vitality, and spiritual growth.

The Central Axis provides life's Life Force in Yin and Yang Balance

The Central Axis consists of perfectly balanced (-) Yin and the sacred masculine (+) Yang currents from Source. As bio-electric beings we require both, and it is the connection between these sacred feminine (-) and sacred masculine (+) currents of Source that formed us all.

Read the following excerpt from the epic fantasy novel *Fourth Wing*, by Rebecca Yarros. Twenty-year-old Violet Sorrengail describes how it felt as the dragon who chose her as a rider during an epic trial, channels his energy to her. Her description is an advanced version of what happens to us when we open to allowing the Life Force Current from the Central Axis to flow through us.

> I pause mid-brushstroke when a rush of energy races down my spine, dissipating in a heartbeat.
>
> Well, that's . . . weird.
>
> Maybe it's. . . . No. It can't be . . .
>
> Another wave ripples through me, stronger this time, and I drop the brush, clutching the edge of the dresser so I don't fall as my knees threaten to buckle. The energy doesn't dissipate this time; it sticks around, humming under my skin, ringing in my ears, overwhelming every sense.
>
> Something in me expands, somehow too big for my own body, too vast to be contained, and pain sears every nerve as I crack open, the sound reverberating through my skull like bones shattering. It's as though I've been split at the very seams of the fabric of my being.
>
> Energy pours in—a deluge of raw, endless power—eroding everything I was and forging something completely new as it fills every pore, every organ, every bone.
>
> … I stare at my brush, the hardwood floor biting into my cheek, and breathe.
>
> In and then out.
>
> In…and then out…surrendering to the onslaught.
>
> Finally, the pain ebbs, but the energy—the power—doesn't. It's simply…there, prowling through my veins, saturating every cell in my body. It is everything I am and everything I can be all at once.

In other words, Violet describes what it feels like to embody Source Energy, All That Is, radiant awakening.

Radiance through Experiencing OM

The sound of OM is essence. The essence of Source. The sound of OM has a vibration—and the vibration is resonant in every cell. In the experiential meditation in Step VI Part II you'll remove the barrier between you and the sound of OM, the sound of the universe, the primordial sound, and the greatest healer of all time.

The sound of OM is the highest of the high vibrations. High vibrations eclipse lower vibration density, hence the more you can embody and entrain to the sound of OM, and that OM can expand within you from your Central Axis, the more healing is revealed and manifested.

The more you release lower vibration density in this 9 Step practice, the more your physicality can handle this highest of the high vibrations. It has a ring to it, a zing, a bedazzling quality. It takes time to adjust but once you have adjusted, you'll have a song in your heart and in your energy. OM can expand in you, connecting you more and more to the matrix of Source light.

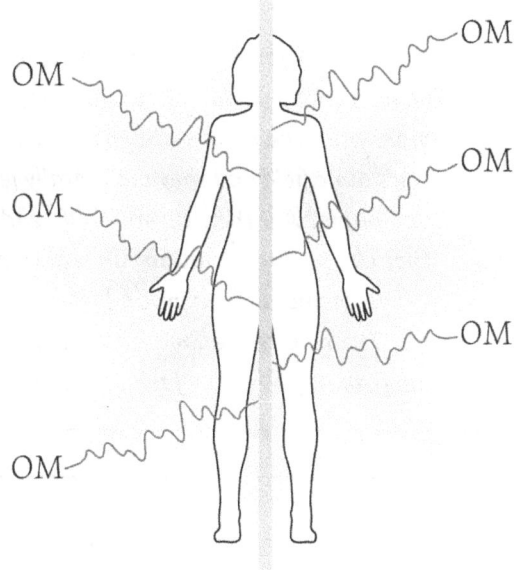

OM the Eternal HUM as a Sound Healer

The technology of healing in this book features sound healing as a profound transformation technique. Once the Vortex is activated and continues to clear lower vibration density, one can detect a universal sound vibration, a Hum. The Hum is the sound of OM—the primordial sound vibration encompassing Source, preservation, and destruction.

The experiential meditations, sound healings, and self-observation recommended in this book provide the foundation to hear and *experience transformation from* the eternal sound. By repeatedly applying the tools of the healing technology unity is within our grasp. One of the most ancient texts from Indian philosophy, the Rig Veda (4.58.3), confirms that Brahman, the Source, and the Hum are inextricably linked. It states that:

> Vrishabho roravitti
> Brahman is humming.
> —Rig Veda (4.58.3)

The OM syllable is said to be the most perfect sound, and it is believed to contain all the other sounds in the universe. When OM is chanted, it is said to create a vibration that resonates with the entire cosmos.

When we connect at last to our Central Axis we also connect to all its radiance, including the sound of OM.

> ## WARNING ALERT
>
> *There are a few dire situations that have shown me what happens when a person is drained of their life force energy, and is disconnected more from the matrix of light. One is when there is a big rip in a person's auric field and they are literally leaking out that critically important prana. Another, as you will read in Diary of a Healer below, is that chemo and radiation can reduce prana by extraordinary amounts. While chemo and radiation blessedly save lives, the experience is brutal. The results are lack of vitality, and lack of connection to body, mind, and spirit—one feels spent on all levels.*

> ### DIARY OF A HEALER
>
> **What Happens When We Disconnect from Life Force**
>
> If you have witnessed or experienced the suffering chemotherapy causes, you know the horror of a treatment that all but kills, even as it saves. Among other challenges, with chemotherapy the immune system can become so fully depleted that it can't fight against its own pathogens. Yet, without chemotherapy, called "chemo" for short, loved ones would no longer be with us. There wouldn't be the same number of survivors reading these words. We can only feel grateful. But I am sure that in 50 years we'll look back at chemo as a barbaric act. Given the suffering the treatment entails, it is upon us to find ways to ease its side effects where we can.
>
> I've seen a consistent and surprising need in chemotherapy and radiation survivors: their chakras need a pranic reboot.
>
> **Restoring Pranic Energy**
>
> A sobering find of my experience with chemotherapy and radiation patients is that the amount of prana left in their chakras is down to wisps. A great gift to help them is to "relight" the chakras with prana so that it can flow abundantly. In so doing, the pranic energy begins to spread out through organs and permeate bodily systems, bringing with it a rejuvenating life force.
>
> My most intimate and first experience facilitating such a healing with a cancer survivor happened when working with a close family member who had acute myeloid leukemia. He had been through three harrowing rounds of chemotherapy to enable him to have a stem cell transplant using his own stem cells. After the stem cell transplant, it was clear to me that he was too weak for healing. Not only was he exceptionally frail, he was also

suffering from withdrawing cold turkey from morphine that had been given for the pain caused by dental complications. His body was spent and every ounce of energy he had was being used to keep himself stable during the drug withdrawal.

Re-lighting the Energy Body
Within about fifteen days of his final hospital release date I felt he was strong enough for receiving the energy of a healing. I entered the healing state that enabled my clairvoyant intuition to be the clearest. It quickly became apparent that the healing would be about his energy body. I started using the singing bowls and getting into the still point so as to let healing generate. The best way that I can describe what I saw with my third eye is that a giant candelabra with candles of prana came to light each chakra to replenish them.

This "chemo healing" was simple and powerful. I have seen the exact same healing happen in other cancer survivors I have worked with. Once the energy body is "relit," there is a renewed sense of harmony and flow in the body. One wonders how slow recovery would proceed without fundamental energetic replenishing.

Restoring Harmony to the Body
My family member said, "As a leukemia patient I've spent months in the hospital treated with powerful chemicals and drugs, feeling my body had become shrunken and foreign. I'm grateful for what the oncologists have done for me. But it was the sound/energy healings that restored me mentally and emotionally to my body and to my sense of harmony with myself."

Mitchell L. Gaynor, M.D. is an oncologist and the author of *The Healing Power of Sound*. He writes that "The crystal singing bowls demonstrate the truly manifold possibilities for healing through vibratory sound. Our body-mind systems are 'returned' by the bowl sounds, and the effects can be physical, psychological, spiritual, or all three at once."

"Love is the breathing of the soul." — **Sri Mata Amritanandamayi Devi**

The heart chakra is a huge access point to our Central Axis.
The point of your strongest connection to the Central Axis is in your physical heart. The vibration of your—anyone's—heart is very high and it alone uplevels you to closer resonance with the Central Axis. There is flow, constant flow of information between your body and mind in your physicality, and your spirit, and the Central Axis. A push and pull. A give and take. A pathway.

The heart chakra carries a unique role of being the Vortex of energy—the power of the pulsing heart—the strongest of them all. It connects to the Central Axis between the front and the back Vortexes of the chakra, the front being the way you show your life force to the world and the back bringing the quantum DNA and all the information about our master cell into our physicality.

> ### DIARY OF A HEALER
>
> **Entraining to the Quantum Self**
>
> Given a lifetime of "fight or flight" coping mechanisms, a physiological reaction to trauma he had, Sam developed AFib, an irregular and often very rapid heart beat. He followed a number of holistic protocols, including gamma-aminobutyric acid (GABA) for adrenal exhaustion, and a medication to keep his heart from racing too fast. His AFib became much less frequent, a few times every few months, but it was something on his mind. How to heal this? Becoming increasingly adept at the steps of this book, he began to do what you will learn to do in Part II Step VI, entraining to his Central Axis, his Quantum Self, and the matrix of light. Our "quantum self" is the mirror of our physicality, yet as the original perfect blueprint of who we really are. I asked his physical heart to entrain to his Quantum Self's heart—his heart's perfect blueprint—for healing. I asked for the physical cause of AFib to entrain to his Quantum Self's healed mirror, for healing. I urged him to do the meditations in Part II for this step every week and of course continue with his cardiologist.

> ### BENEFITS
>
> When a person comes into a deep integration with their Central Axis—the matrix of light—they develop radiance, flow, clarity, are grounded, and become their own lighthouse.

What are the benefits of meditation?
Our invisible thoughts travel and convey energy. They govern our nervous system, endocrine system, immune system, and every other system in the body. Stress causes elevated cortisol levels. Cortisol is a stress hormone, and when its levels remain high, inflammatory, immune, and cardiovascular disease markers increase. Neurological imbalance encodes in our cellular memory system. A vast body of evidence shows that patients exposed to trauma-induced stress during their childhood years are far more likely to develop mood disorders, post-traumatic stress disorder, type 2 diabetes, high blood pressure, and heart disease. Conversely, meditation and laughter reduce stress hormones, inflammation, mental illness, and heart disease. (Dr. Drobot, Dr. Thom, 2018) We may suppress our emotions, yet our bodies express them physically to heal. We have to see to them.

Our nervous system is the control center for the rest of the body. Many top-level alternative medical physicians recognize that the nervous system must heal first before any other disease can heal. (Dr. Drobot and Dr. Thom, 2018; Yance, 2014) Our bodies naturally work with our emotions so that healing occurs, but we have to allow the process. Emotional tears contain endorphins that reduce pain and elevate mood. Reflexive tears that come from peeling an onion or smelling a strong chemical do not contain these endorphins. Our bodies know the difference between having a good cathartic cry and efficiently flushing out the eyes. (Dr. Drobot and Dr. Thom, 2018)

Our sympathetic nervous system responds to stress like an airplane taking off that never comes in for a landing. If the aircraft never lands, eventually, the plane will run out of fuel. However, if the plane arrives for a landing or has a stopover, it can refuel and get repairs or new parts. Humans can only handle sympathetic nervous system stimulation 40% of the time. Yet, physicians, practitioners, and therapists report that most of us far exceed that limit; we are in a sympathetic mode close to 80% of the time. We do not rest, do not recover, and become burnt out. Meditation practice is essential for repairing the nervous system to experience the repair and regeneration from practices in this book! We must make the time to restore.

Eckhart Tolle, the meditation teacher, points out that meditation has substantial advantages compared to mindfulness steps that we can practice at any time. Becoming aware of the timeless quality meditation induces fills us with power, even if it is only for a short period. Seconds or even one or two minutes of shifting your perception of time allows you to go beyond the 3D self. In meditation, one moves back and forth from timelessness to the 3D state. However, even a short period of the timeless state reminds a person of what is always possible. (Tolle, 1999, p.44)

Meditative states are measured by tracking brainwave patterns. For instance, slow brain waves show a person has fatigue, is sluggish, or lacks focus. Faster brainwaves match alert to face-paced behavior and even correlate to more extreme mood changes and hyperactivity as the brainwaves increase.

Brain waves fall into four categories:
Delta waves have a low frequency. They reside in the deepest layers of the brain during sleep, meditation, and the dreamless sleep state. In this state, awareness of the external is minimal or, in rare cases, nonexistent.

Theta waves materialize during our dream state and also in deep meditation. When we receive and process information, try to memorize something, have intuitive awareness, or engage in creative activity, theta waves are dominant.

Alpha waves occur during the mindful state as we tune into the present moment. It is a meditative state. Rest, contemplation, or walking in silence is also a healthy state.

Beta waves transpire during waking when one is alert and engaged in mental activity. It is a conservative state where the brain waves become more active.

The four states work with one another. However, one usually dominates while the others recede. Regardless, meditative states occur during the delta and theta levels.

Signs that one is entering a meditative state include:

- Loss of self-consciousness
- Losing a sense of time
- Losing the sensation of desires and cravings
- Gaining an understanding of internal reward unattached to any particular outcome
- Increased clarity and confidence in handling outcomes
- Experience of emotional neutrality
- Ability to witness emotional states or memories without reaction

It is worth noting that your sleep quality and meditation quality go hand in hand. Meditating for a few minutes before sleep will help you release stress and exhaustion. Emotions of the day, both positive and negative, clear the mind for deep sleep. If you develop this step, you will wake up less during the night. Your deep sleep cycle will become more profound. Deep sleep becomes a long and refreshing meditative state. (Satyamayananda, 2021)

Your Quantum Self! DNA, Your Perfect Blueprint
This is your Ka body. Your perfect blueprint. Light as air, dense as water, filled with prana and intentionality. This is the quantum field. It is inside of your Central Axis.

For the Activation Of Step VI see Part II.

STEP VII: THE PRANIC TUBE: UP YOUR VOLTAGE!
BECOMING PHYSICAL
CHAKRAS, NADIS, ETC.
BACKGROUND ABOUT THIS STEP OF THE SEQUENCE

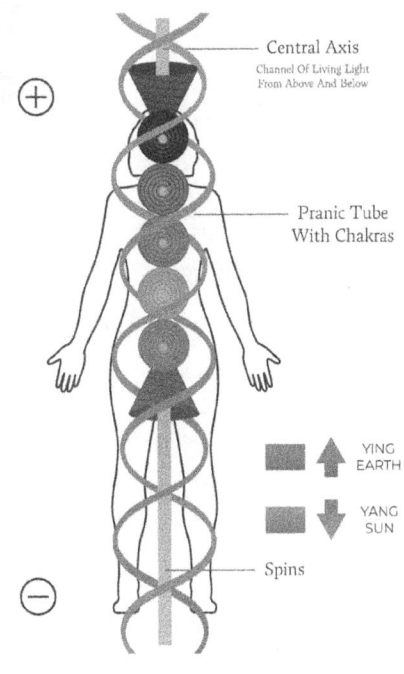

The Pranic Tube, also known as the central channel, is an energy channel that runs along in front of the spine and around the Central Axis from the base to the crown, and it creates the Torus. The Pranic Tube is the hole in the middle of the Torus donut shape.

What and Why of the Pranic Tube Perfect Blueprint

The Pranic Tube is the Prana Receiver

The Pranic Tube is formed around the Central Axis, and it is hooked into physicality. Polarity. The Earth below and the Sun above. It was created by the Vortex from Yin (Earth) and Yang (Sun).

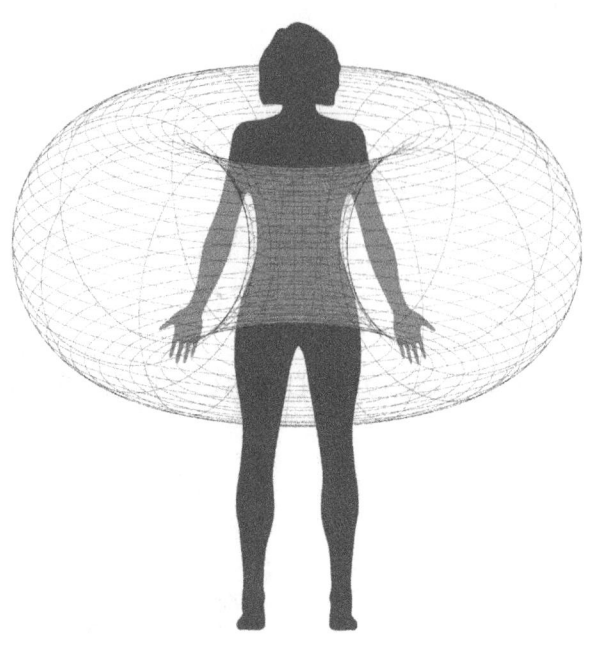

The Pranic Tube continually flows with (-) Yin and (+) Yang *polarity*, counter-rotating around each other and the Central Axis, creating the Torus (see Step VII). Energy from the Earth and Sun. The Pranic Tube is the inside sleeve of that Torus. It continually flows with polarity energies that support the Torus and is always strengthened by the blasting away of lower vibration density from the Vortex. The more energy it draws in, the higher the voltage.

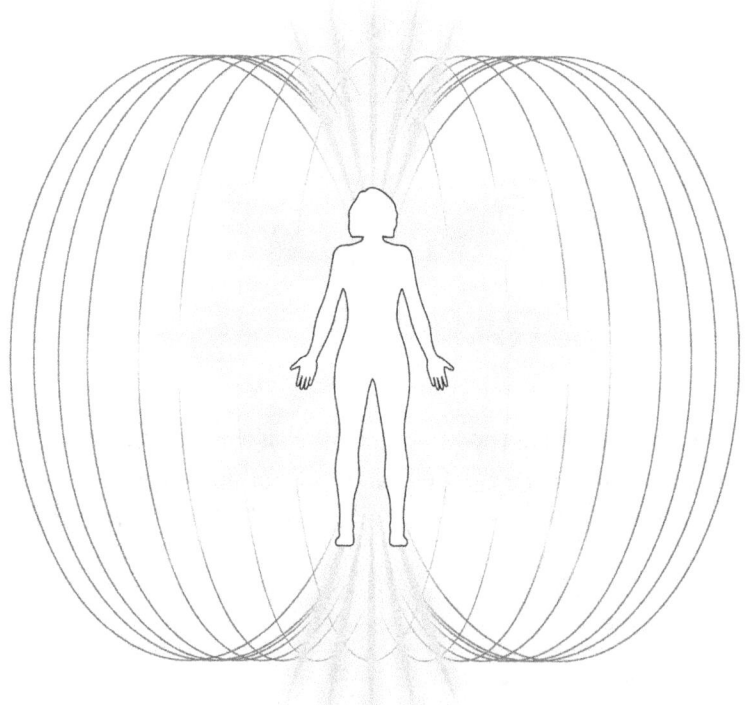

Voltage in the Pranic Tube happens by drawing the prana into it from above and below as well as from the Central Axis. **Your Pranic Tube is the receiver of prana.** It is your personal lifeline to the universal Source of energy. **The more prana you have, the more voltage.** Since the Pranic Tube also creates a Torus, the more prana you have, the stronger the Torus.

How much voltage do you have to make a super strong energy body?

Up the Voltage in Your Pranic Tube!

BENEFITS

Drink up prana!

Something I love to do is to imagine straws coming out of my Pranic Tube and drinking in the prana! A straw down into the Earth and drinking up, a straw up towards the Sun and drinking down. With intention I ask the straws to draw in the light. I can feel the prana be pulled to where it is needed in my physical body. It feels so good! This alone is a beneficial daily practice.

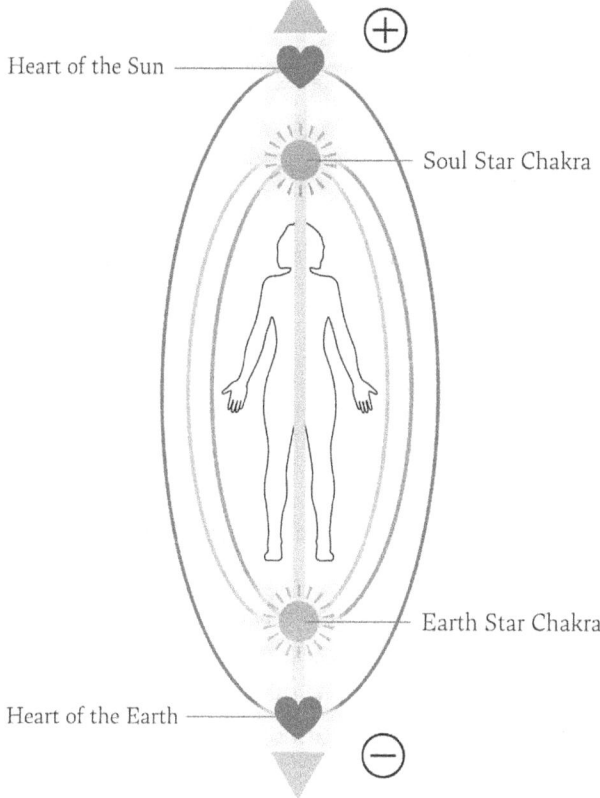

Voltage

In simple terms, voltage can be understood as the force that drives electric charges to flow in a **circuit**. It represents the potential energy difference between two points in the **circuit**, creating an electric field that causes electrons to move from areas of high potential to areas of low potential. The energies we work with mostly in the Pranic Tube are part of a circuit.

Because of its physicality, the Pranic Tube is the axis of being human. The healing and transformation of your life, your day-to-day, happens in this arena, because of prana, and by awakening prana, especially. As you are more and more connected to the matrix of light you have more prana.

The Pranic Tube holds the joy and sorrow of life.

The Elements help integrate your Pranic Tube with your physicality. Earth, Fire, Water, and Air. (Ether doesn't not have any lower vibration density.)

A person or animal comes into duality because of the Pranic Tube's polarity.

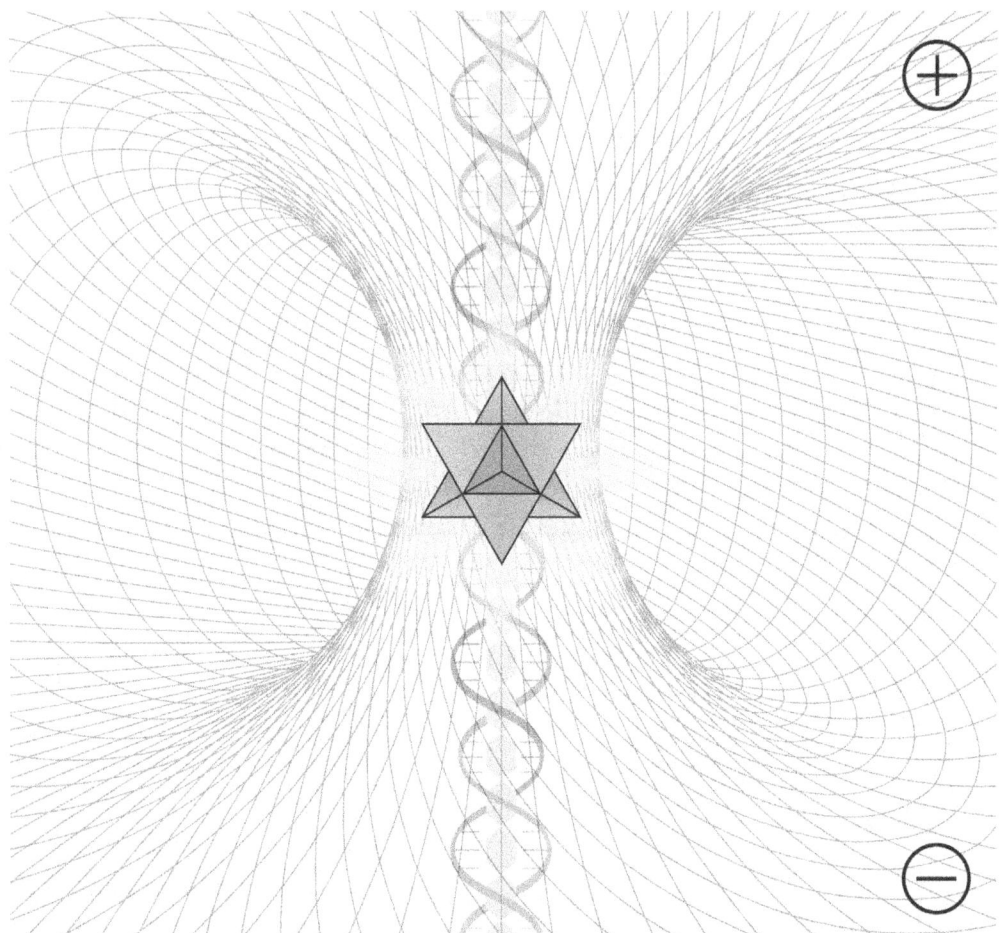

Description of this Diagram

In the above diagram you can almost feel how the Pranic Tube pulls energy up and down, powerfully, to create the Torus. In this instance the merkabah represents the Vortex spark from the connection of Yin and Yang.

The Vortex is the master blaster that clears the way for the matrix of light to reach us in our Pranic Tube. We want to receive that prana into our Pranic Tubes, to help us recover from the lower vibration of duality in our lives, such as with illness and trauma.

When the Pranic Tube is clear and open, and the energy is strong, the Torus, which it creates, spins freely and evenly, distributing prana throughout the body.

The Pranic Tube never leaves our physicality. It carries all about our 3D world including our aspirations. The All That Is, both good and bad.

CHAKRAS; IDA AND PINGALA

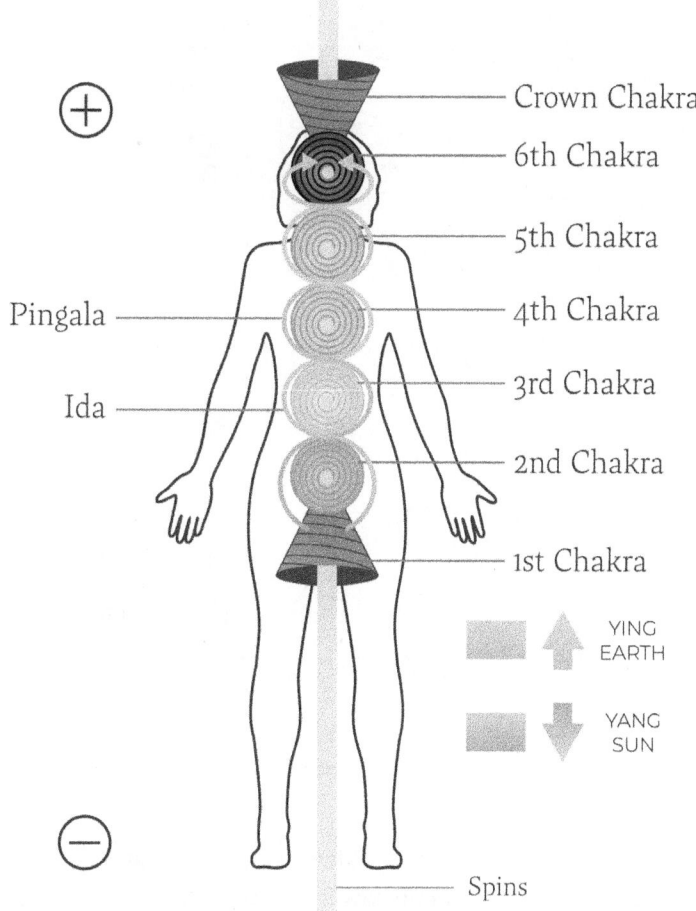

Whereas for the Vortex connecting to Yin and Yang was everything, for the Pranic Tube, connecting to the flow of POLARITY from the Earth and Sun is everything.

Polarity is what grounds the light into physicality and that is in the Pranic Tube. Without polarity, we wouldn't exist.

The Hara System Fed by the Pranic Tube

In simple terms, the Hara System is called the gas tank of the energy body. If you think of the Pranic Tube as a receiver of prana, this makes sense as the prana flows into the hara system from the pranic tube. For the Hara System there are three main receptacles:

- Pineal – in the third eye – covers the glands
- Heart – in the heart chakra – covers our Source
- Navel – in the navel point – covers the spine and organs, and the nadis

THE MASTER GRIDS
The Hara System

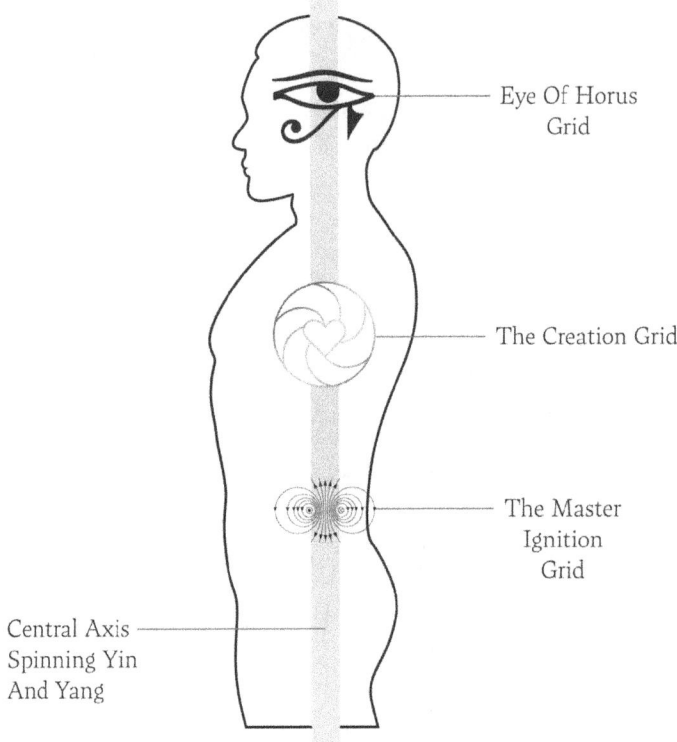

In martial arts, the hara system is known as the dantian. The dantian is comprised of three energy centers in the body, located in the lower abdomen, the chest, and the head.

- The lower dantian is located three finger widths below the navel. It is considered to be the root of the body and the Source of qi (vital energy). It is associated with strength, stability, and grounding.
- The middle dantian is located in the center of the chest, slightly below the sternum. It is associated with the heart and lungs, and is believed to be the center of emotional balance.
- The upper dantian is located in the center of the head, between the eyebrows, in the "Eye of Horus" area that includes the pineal, hypothalamus, and pituitary. It is associated with the mind and spirit, and is believed to be the center of wisdom and intuition.

In martial arts, the dantian is used to cultivate qi, focus the mind, and generate power. By cultivating qi in the lower dantian, martial artists can develop a strong and stable foundation. By focusing the mind on the middle dantian, they can achieve emotional balance and clarity. And by cultivating qi in the upper dantian, they can develop wisdom and intuition.

The Nadis - Channels of Prana

We have an incredible network of energy channels within us that carry the prana we gather in our Pranic Tube into our physicality. They are called nadis. Ancient texts have revealed more than 72,000 nadis existing within us.

Once again, we come to the same teaching: The key to the flow of the nadis is the balancing of the sacred feminine and sacred masculine principles. When our lives aren't balanced in the Yin and Yang arenas, it really affects the health of our nadis.

The nadis transport life energy to every part of the body. They suffuse the body with prana as they run from the soles of the feet to the crown chakra. Not only do they contain prana or the breath of life, but they also hold the vehicle of the soul from the Central Axis, where Shakti and Shiva, the sacred power of Mother /Father energy, reside.

We want our nadis flowing with prana!

The three main nadis are called the Ida (feminine), Pingala (masculine), and Sushumna (carries kundalini). The Ida and Pingala flow around the chakras, the Sushumna flows up the spine.

> **DIARY OF A HEALER**
>
> Every meditation I share with my students begins with a connection to the polarity of the Pranic Tube. This connection is fundamental to all of the steps in this book. Be here now—be embodied. First, I send love and gratitude to the heart of the Earth, and ask Mother Earth energy to come up our Pranic Tube and the energy goes where it needs to go. Next I send love and gratitude to Father Sun and ask Father Sun to send his beautiful energy down our Pranic Tube and go where it needs to go.
>
> I'll also finalize healings with clients with it, only to see their chakras (see below) vibrate at a higher vibration, and their whole energy field comes into coherence.

Chakra System Fed by the Pranic Tube and Central Axis
The Chakras are Fields of Consciousness.

The chakras are created by the spark of light from Source, when the structure of our energy bodies are formed, but the flow of prana to the chakras comes from the Central Axis and the Pranic Tube. That system feeds the chakras.

The Nadis also feed the chakras from the navel point Hara system, but all three hara points feed the chakras, as the chakras are a rainbow bridge of spiritual growth and encompass all phases of our evolution.

Chakra means wheel in Sanskrit because most mystics see the chakra as a Vortex of energy that resembles a wheel. However, there are some who see chakras differently, such as those who see them as flowers.

I like to think of the chakras as fields of consciousness that hold developmental spiritual lessons and growth. As you read the following description of each chakra, think of your own spiritual development and how chakra healing might support you.

First Chakra
Issues: Safety, security, grounding. The Earth is our mother, our body is our home.

Second Chakra
Issues: Emotions, feelings, family, creativity, pleasure, sensuality, sexuality, dwelling of the self.

Third Chakra
Issues: Ego, personal power in the world, self-esteem, achievement, able to meet challenges.

Fourth Chakra
Issues: Unconditional love for self and others, serving self and others, the center of love and friendship.

Fifth Chakra
Issues: Singing the song of the self, resonance, truth of self, purification—the communicator.

Sixth Chakra
Issues: "The third eye," the visionary, intuition, having vision. Who am I?

Seventh Chakra
Issues: Consciousness, cognitive and transcendent, attachment versus letting go of control—the seat of spirituality.

Chakras - Masculine and Feminine Aspects

The two different energies of masculine and feminine are harnessed through the body, with the feminine on the left side and the masculine on the right. This is how the system is structured for the first through fifth chakras. However, after the fifth chakra, or above the ear's, the energies switch, or cross over, to the opposite side. So, for the sixth and seventh chakras, the feminine is on the right side of the head, and the masculine on the left.

First – Fifth chakras: Left side feminine / right side masculine
Sixth – Seventh chakras: Left side masculine / right side feminine

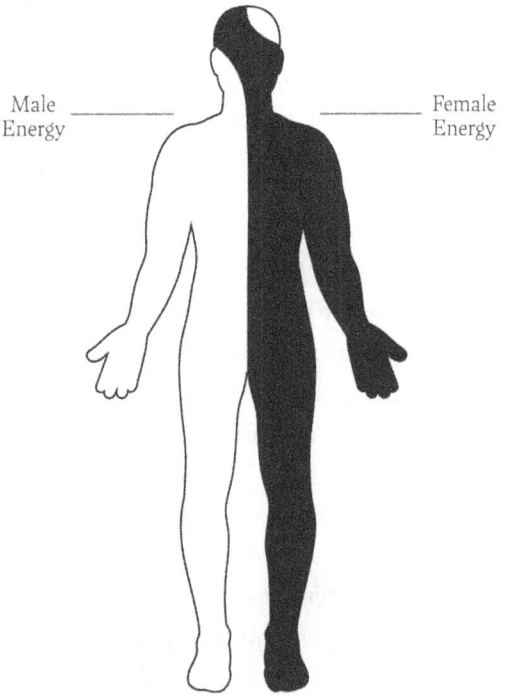

THE CHAKRAS
SIDE VIEW WITH NERVES

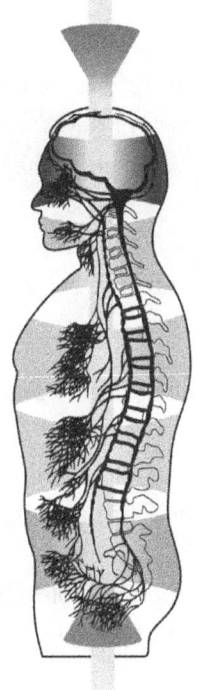

The light from the Central Axis is pulled into the chakras

THE CHAKRAS

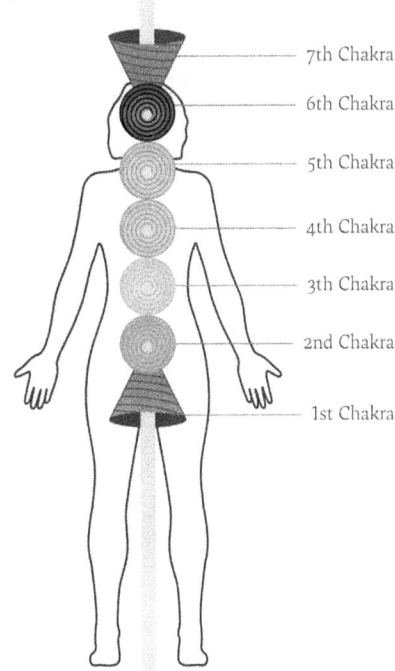

- 7th Chakra
- 6th Chakra
- 5th Chakra
- 4th Chakra
- 3th Chakra
- 2nd Chakra
- 1st Chakra

>  **BENEFITS**
>
> Continually increasing the voltage of your Pranic Tube will bring untold joys of health and well-being. Your physicality will be receiving more prana because the Torus (see below) will flow strongly, and that will bring the Source lines of living light to you on all levels. Welcome to the joy of spiritual growth.
>
> *I felt my body drinking in life force energy, just drinking as if dying of thirst. It felt radiant and still does a week later. I can't wait to learn to do this myself so I always have access. - AS*

Polarity is what grounds the light into physicality and that is in the Pranic Tube. Without polarity we wouldn't exist.

We are Earth-bound, and the key to our reincarnation is the Earth-bound POLARITY We must be connected to the two poles, the Earth and the Sun. Polarity is what grounds the light into physicality and that is in the Pranic Tube.

Polarity is the property of having two opposite poles. In the context of magnets, the two poles are the north pole and the south pole. Like poles repel each other, while opposite poles attract each other

The Pranic Tube supports the Vortex's pushing out of low vibration density with the help of the Elements. There is an exhaust.

For the Activation of Step VII see Part II

STEP VIII: THE TORUS – THE CONDUCTOR

BACKGROUND ABOUT THIS STEP OF THE SEQUENCE

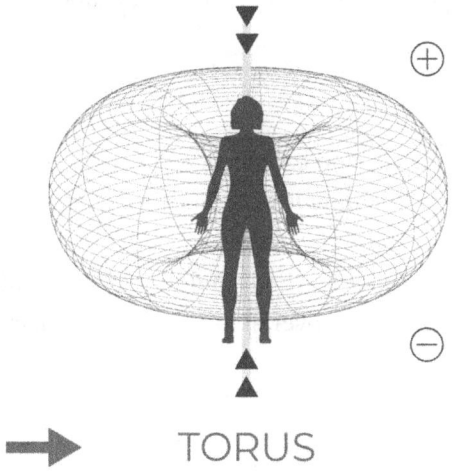

Torus Is Created From The Yin And Yang Vortex

TORUS

The concept of the energy body as a toroidal system is a way of understanding the human energy field as a dynamic, interconnected whole. A Torus is a three-dimensional shape that has a continuous flow of energy. In the context of the energy body, the Torus represents the flow of energy through the physical, emotional, mental, and spiritual aspects of ourselves.

Many people believe that there is a torus, or doughnut-shaped energy field, around all living things. This torus is thought to be responsible for the flow of life-force energy through the body, and it is also believed to connect us to the energy of the universe. The Torus flows around and through us, bringing Source energy to our physicality.

Here are some of the benefits of strengthening a Torus of pranic energy:

- Increased energy and vitality
- Improved circulation
- Reduced stress and anxiety
- Enhanced immune function
- Improved sleep
- Increased creativity and intuition
- Deeper spiritual connection

WE ARE CRADLED IN THE TORUS

The Torus cradles us in an energy system of unimaginable light and love, that of our soul, of our consciousness, of the Source. The stronger our connection to our Torus becomes, the more cradled we become, the more of this light we receive, and the more in flow with our lives.

What and Why of the Torus

The Torus System
The Torus is a structure and it carries our life force and soul as well as much more. A supplier of energy, of powerful prana—or chi—and consciousness. It envelops and interpenetrates the more commonly known chakra system and our spine.

The Torus is a donut-shaped Vortex of energy that is said to be the basic shape of our energy body.

Energetically the Torus:

- Channels prana, helping keep the body healthy and balanced.
- Acts as a protective field around the body, shielding it from negative energy. It is exceedingly strong in this.
- Is a channel for communication between the physical body and the spiritual body.
- Clears blockages in the energy body and promotes overall health and well-being.
- Carries our consciousness.
- Cradles our Pranic Tube.

The 3D self is either healthy or unhealthy due to how effectively the Prana Vortex boosts the Torus. Remember: The Vortex is created from the counter-rotation of Yin and Yang around the Central Axis, creating the spark of Source prana that builds the Torus by creating the powerful Pranic Tube.

Take a moment and notice from the diagram, below, how the Torus envelops and simultaneously expands our energetic body.

The Torus carries the flow of Source prana to the physical body. The sacred element Air resides at home in the Torus. It provides just enough form without lower vibration density, *to flow and push out* lower vibration density. Air helps clear and cleanse the Torus. The sacred element Air flows through the Torus, bringing and supporting the flow of living light to the physicality.

The Torus also carries the flow to our energetic centers. The Light Force channels, the ancient energy lines, even lifelines, are our sacred heritage from Source. The Torus strengthens as lower vibration density releases. As it becomes fortified, the Source transmits Light Force to the receptor Energy Centers.

STEP VIII: THE TORUS – THE CONDUCTOR

> **WARNING ALERT**
>
> *If the Torus isn't strong enough, then less Source Energy reaches our physicality. Lower vibration density builds. Consequently, traumas are not cleared.*

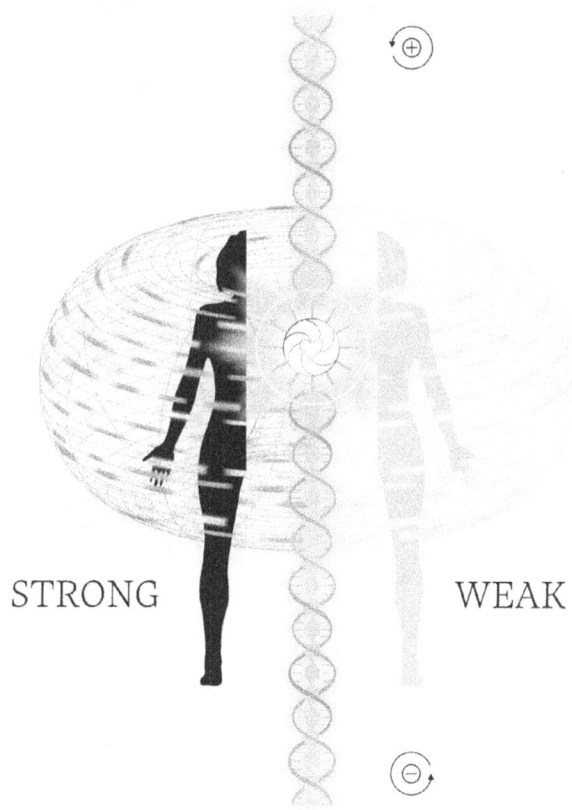

STRONG   WEAK

DIARY OF A HEALER

When the Torus is weak and dim a person often has chronic illnesses and poor emotional boundaries. I think of a woman who came to me who was 90% deficient of the divine masculine energy in her Torus. Her father had invaded her boundaries from his neediness, hence the severe depletion of healed father energy. She had been sick for years. She had murky relationships with her immediate and extended family members.

Once the masculine energy was restored to her torus her health and relationships improved dramatically. Within just a year she was navigating her life with purpose and vibrancy.

> See the diagram, below where the receptor sites in our Torus convey these Source lines of light. These energy centers receive the Light Force data transmissions from Source for regeneration assuming your Vortex and Pranic Tube have been at full functioning and the lower vibration density has been removed so that the Source lines flow unimpeded into our physicality.

AXIATONAL GRIDS

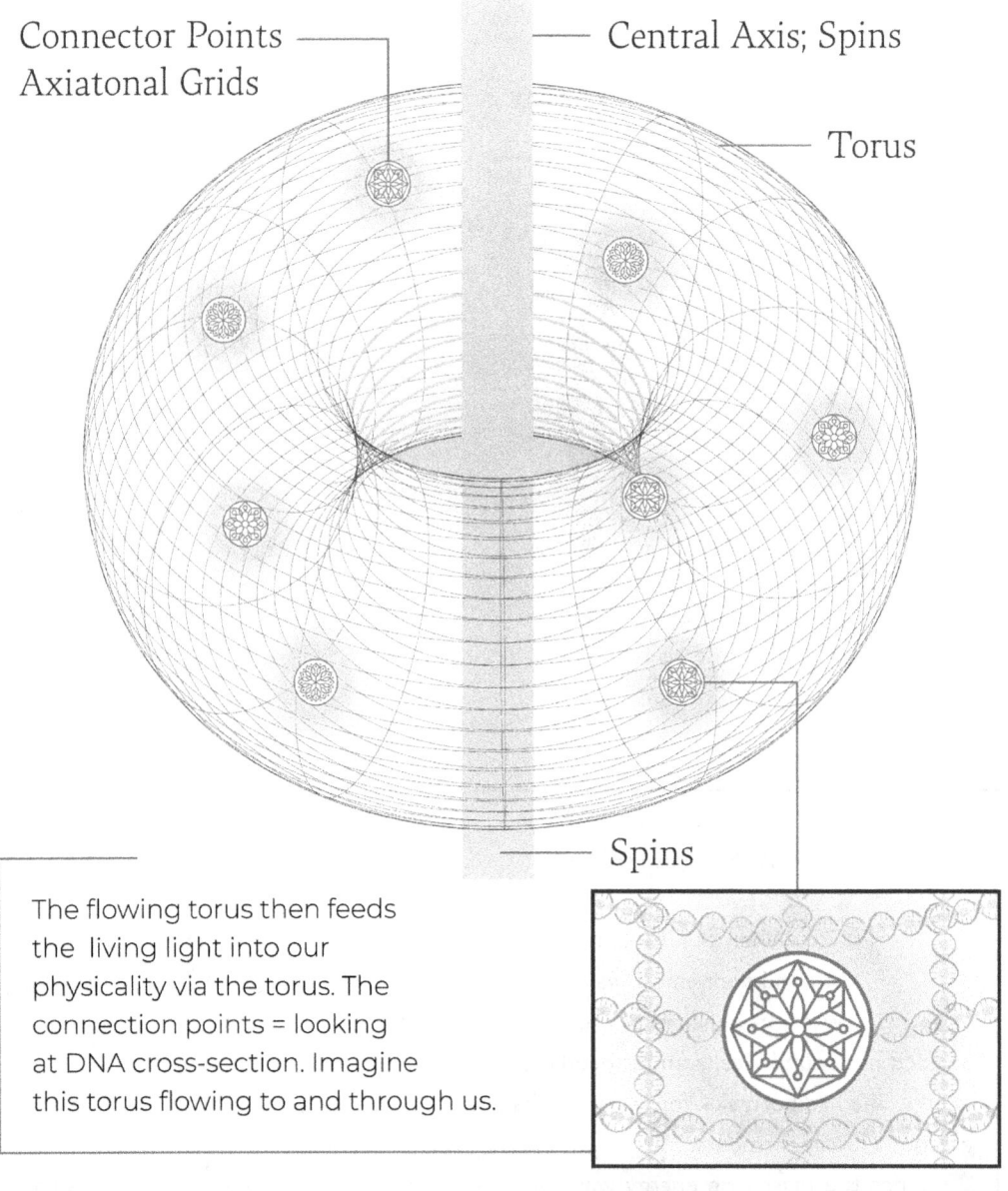

The flowing torus then feeds the living light into our physicality via the torus. The connection points = looking at DNA cross-section. Imagine this torus flowing to and through us.

Once the Source lines can make it through the receptor sites (and yes, these receptor sites are like mandalas), the light enters the cells of our physicality and they direct the currents of light used in regeneration.

>  **BENEFITS**
>
> One of the aspects of a strong Torus that I especially love is how it feeds the spine with life force. Our spines are our circuit boards that guide healing to our organs, among other jobs.
>
> Another is that the Torus provides a boundary between us and the world around us.

Your relationship with your Torus

It is the conductor of the Source Light flowing into your body, mind, and spirit.

You want it to be in full flow, unimpeded by low vibration density. You especially want to pay attention if you have health issues or are feeling stuck in any way. You always want this to flow. It is important to recognize that Steps I-VII leads you to this flow.

Ground. Connect to Source. Learn who you are. Stabilize your duality. Magnetize yourself. Strengthen your polarity. The Torus will only flow as strongly as the voltage of your pranic tube.

For the Activation of Step VIII see Part II

STEP IX: AWAKENING PRANA! - CONNECTING TO THE MATRIX OF LIGHT
AWAKEN YOUR ENERGY BODY
BACKGROUND ABOUT THIS STEP OF THE SEQUENCE

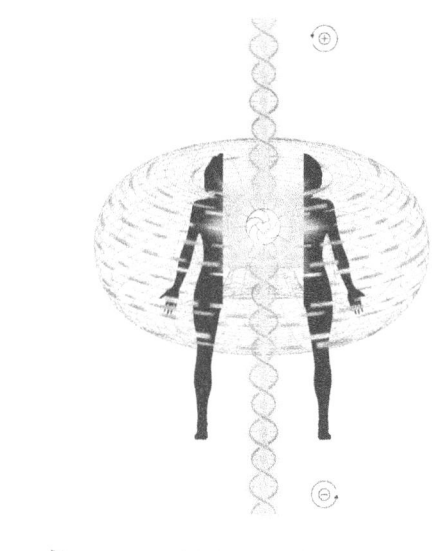

➡ AWAKEN

"When you connect to your light body, you are connecting to the Source of all Source. You are aligning yourself with the highest frequencies of love, light, and peace." —**Doreen Virtue**

Now you come home at last. Heaven is on Earth. Your energy body flows, you are embodied in your physicality, and you have the tools to find your way back to this point of harmony and perfection.

Connecting to the Matrix of the Light

We have come to the fruition of the work, the point of radiation, regeneration, renewal. Here and now, light can reach us from our Central Axis and remove that which no longer serves our higher purpose and physical well-being. When we are grounded and present, we can receive the light streams, the true vibration of our being and regenerate into our perfect blueprint. We renew every cell from the dim aspects of ourselves that have awaited lumination. We have come home.

Light Force carries our quantum DNA; it is a data transmission system outside the control of physical laws. It is connected to our 5D circulatory system made of light transmissions and high sound frequencies. such as OM. Transmission and frequencies flow to the receptor energy centers of our physicality. Using the Vortex, we have cleared all lower vibration density blocking this flow.

Now we embody:

- Flow

- Resonance
- Authenticity
- Self Love
- Vibrant Health

We celebrate as we are:

- Cradled by our energy body
- Connected to the All That Is
- Living from our Soul's Higher Frequency
- Awakening Radiantly to Care for the Planet, Ourselves and Each Other.

Now we have reached the point of renewal, regeneration, radiance. The light of the Source can reach us and transmute that which no longer serves our well-being and higher purpose into a regeneration of our perfect blueprint.

RECOVER

The 12 R's of regenerative healing are:
Remember | Return | Re-experience
Re-connect | Reactivate | Rejuvenate
Restore | Refresh | Repair
Radiate | Regenerate | Renew

Connecting us to the light lines
Light Force comes to us on ancient energy lines—light lines—
connecting us to the Source.

AWAKENING PRANA TRINITY

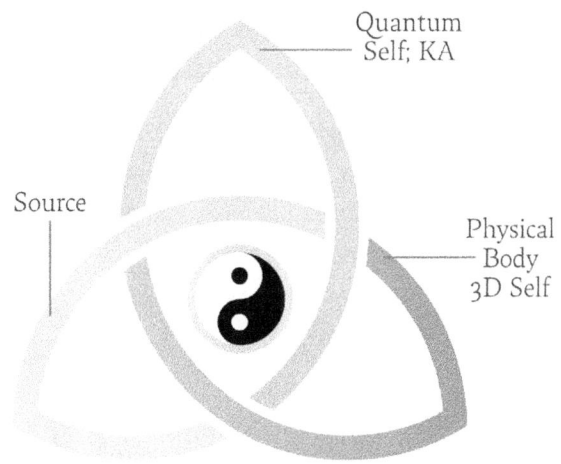

> **DIARY OF A HEALER**
>
> It was pouring this morning, and I woke up early, at 4:30 am. My dogs were unsettled by the thunder and their pacing woke me. The sound of the rain was meditative. Given I was very awake, I put I put on the long 42-minute version of The 7 Keys of Awakening Prana, the sound healing or transmission from Stoneman—the full awakening of the energy body for Step IX.
>
> Inspired by a friend, I added her suggestion, done when she listens to The 7 Keys of Awakening Prana, and laid a twenty-inch selenite wand vertically from my belly button to my neck. At first I felt very agitated, which was odd given I had felt calm lying there listening to the rain. Soon enough, a deep peace and coherence came over me. I experienced extraordinary serenity, and I still feel the effects. The sound healing activated my entire energy body, and brought it all into a feeling of full agency.

"From our perspective, the sounds of OM and humming have the same effect on the body." —**Jonathan Goldman and Andi Goldman**

For more about the sound healing in this book, see the meditations for each step in Part II.

> **BENEFITS**
>
> Prana is the lifeline from the Sun and to the Earth. Without prana you would die. Your prana is your lifeline to your heart and also the answer to all of your sorrows.
>
> *I felt my body drinking in life force energy, just drinking as if dying of thirst. It felt radiant and still does a week later. I can't wait to learn to do this myself so I always have access. - AS*

The mind, its constructs, and our identification with our egos and suffering, has generally prevented us from connecting to universal energy. The mind leaves the present moment, from "being here now", as we try to change in Step I. As a result, we think in a linear way. According to Eckhart Tolle our mind leaves when our ego is grasping at the future or evaluating the past. It won't allow us to be here now.

What Does "Being Here Now" Mean?

One of the most ancient spiritual traditions is Vedanta. Although based on Indian scripture, Vedanta combines two words, *Veda*, meaning knowledge, and *Anta*, meaning "the goal of." The goal of knowledge is oneness. We can apply Vedanta universally because it is relevant to all cultures, countries, and religions. When we go beyond books and tap into experience, it is possible to understand our sacred nature, our Higher Self, or the essence of oneness. Specifically, oneness means the following:

- Understanding the divinity of all souls
- Perceiving the oneness of existence
- Expressing the harmony of all religions
- Seeing the same vibration, in everything.

As we advance and grow, discovering how to quiet the mind, the goal of realizing our divinity, becomes clearer. Infinite existence, consciousness, and bliss never die. A person might perceive these aspects within a personal or deified form or incarnation like Buddha or Jesus. It can also take an impersonal form. However, most importantly, the greatest temple of the sacred resides in each and every heart. It is never born and can never die. Thousands of years ago, the Rig Veda declared, "Truth is one; the sages call it by various names."

All religions teach the same foundational truths about "God," the world, and our relationship to one another. The world's religions offer varying approaches to "God," each true and valid, each offering the world a unique and irreplaceable path to "God"-realization. Conflicting messages found in various religions arise from doctrine and dogma rather than spiritual experience. While dissimilarities exist when looking at external observances in world religions external observances, the internal similarities are astounding. Each approach has the potential to lead to the ultimate awareness of being perfect, pure, and free from limitations.

> Watching you merge with your light
> Watching you go through the veil
> Watching you experience yourself as nothingness, as love, as light, as this boundaryless ocean of consciousness as you, is a sublime joy to your soul.
> —SAI MA

Uplifting the mind through sound healing with higher vibrations will transform your thought processes daily. Choosing to repeat "OM" is an easy practice with incredible benefits. The following section describes the science behind repeating OM as a spiritual step.

What Does "Being Here Now" Mean?

The first sound ever experienced by the Universe was the sound of the Big Bang. Just as the Big Bang created the universe, sound can be seen as a creative force that can help to heal and transform us. The sound of the Big Bang is often seen as a metaphor for the spiritual potential of sound.

Neuroscientist and yoga teacher Mark Changizi has studied the patterns of nature that exist in the Sanskrit language, in code form. Its syllables represent the way nature works. OM, the universal mantra is perhaps the most profoundly transformative. Mantras hold the key to the universe. When one becomes engrossed in music it is quite similar to the response mantras evoke. A mantra stimulates the nervous system creating movement in physical and emotional energy. From movement, new memories are created as one forms a new narrative and embodies a new being. (US News, Axel, June 29, 2013)

When we remove low vibration or density, OM delivers physical healing. It comes from supreme stillness and subtle ultrasonic vibrations. We translate it into form. Then according to cymatics, it shapes reality. When we practice a mantra, we dive deeply into the power of manifestation at the universal level. It is important to recognize that we drive our awareness into our cells, bones, muscles, and tissues. OM amplifies the perfect blueprint of our kinetic form. Every time the syllable is heard or uttered it brings us closer and closer to a stature of wholeness. (US News, Axel)

Scientific studies have verified that OM, along with other yogic mantras and prayers, benefit psychological and physiological functions. One study tested whether or not OM recitation improved cognition, cardiovascular rhythm, and an overall sense of wellbeing in 23 volunteers. Repeating OM six times a minute reduced cardiovascular rhythms and elevated mental alertness and overall cognition plus baroreflex sensitivity. So, when scientifically measured, the OM frequency repetition produced very favorable results. (Kumar, et. al 2010)

The expansive quality of consciousness with its foundation of pure intelligence emanates from OM, the primordial vibration. If it were not for this expansive quality, consciousness would simply refer to unity with the Atman, and would remain an ocean of Consciousness eternally silent and peaceful. Nothing diverse would arise from it. (Sands, 2023) Think of it this way, during one stage when a tree produces sap it is neither green nor white. It is clear. However, the sap begins thinking, "I want to become green, I want to become white." Then, different sap colors manifest. (Sands, 2023, p.27)

When we chant OM we are manifesting the transformation of our consciousness, consciously. We are deepening our connection with All That Is. Science has verified the existence of OM, as the hum of the universe.

Science Verifies the Universal Hum

At MIT researchers have translated spiders creating webs into music. A sound vibration accompanies each web-making action. Scientists converted laser scans of a spider web into a mathematical formation recreating the spider web in a 3D formation. It allowed them to record a subtle musical instrument algorithm of the spider making a web. Its sound vibration accompanied, and coordinated every movement. (Courtesy of: Tech It Out, YouTube, 2021) The spider world as the microcosm of the macrocosm. What is the macrocosm according to science? See YouTube for how MIT scientists translated spider webs into music.

Image courtesy: Why Do Spiders Weave Webs?

The study of cymatics and the sound "Om" suggests that there is a deep connection between sound, vibration, and the natural world. This connection has been explored by many cultures throughout history, and it continues to be a Source of fascination and inspiration today.

Here are some of the cymatics experiments that have been done with the sound "Om":

- In 1972, Dr. Hans Jenny, a Swiss scientist, conducted an experiment in which he played the sound "Om" on a plate of sand. The sand vibrated in response to the sound waves, and it formed a beautiful pattern that resembled a lotus flower.
- In 2008, Steven Halpern, an American composer, recorded the sound "Om" inside the Great Pyramid of Giza. When he played the recording back, it created a complex pattern of sound waves that were visible on a tonoscope.
- In 2016, a team of researchers from the University of Vienna conducted an experiment in which they played the sound "Om" on a water surface. The water vibrated in response to the sound waves, and it created a series of concentric circles.

These are just a few examples of the many cymatics experiments that have been done with the sound "Om". These experiments suggest that there is a deep connection between sound, vibration, and the natural world. This connection is still being explored by scientists and artists today.

Sound is at the Heart of the Universe

Science is verifying what metaphysical practitioners, energy healers, saints, and sages have known for thousands of years. Sound operates at the heart of the universe and defines its structure. Astronomers across the world recently announced that they have found the first evidence of a long-theorized form of gravitational waves that create a "background hum" rumbling throughout the universe. (Hindustan Times, June 29, 2023, New York Times, June 29, 2023) This scientific breakthrough confirms the inner tuning of the universe.

Hundreds of scientists working with radio telescopes in North America, Europe, China, and Australia confirmed the existence of the universal HUM, following years of research. Albert Einstein spoke of this phenomenon more than a hundred years ago. He knew that gravitational waves ripple through the coherent grid of the universe at the speed of light without interruption. It is a unified force. (Hindustan Times, June 29, 2023)

The scientists under the banner of the International Pulsar Timing Array consortium, who have detected this background HUM have worked with gravitational wave detectors on several different continents. "We now know that the universe is awash with gravitational waves," Michael Keith of the European Pulsar Timing Array told AFP. As the gravitational waves move through space, they "gently squeeze" everything they touch. With a spinning motion, some of the waves flash, like beams coming from a radio, at regular intervals like a searchlight at the top of a tower.

French astrophysicist Antoine Petiteau said they were able to "detect changes of less than one-millionth of a second across more than 20 years." Recent scientific revelations verify Einstein's theory of relativity. Currently, scientists detect the waves emanating from pairs of supermassive black holes sitting at the center of galaxies that are slowly merging. The black holes are incomprehensibly enormous, billions of times larger than the Sun. (Hindustan Times, June 29, 2023)

In many spiritual traditions, sound is seen as a sacred force that can connect us to the sacred. In Hinduism, for example, the sound of OM is seen as the primordial vibration that created the universe. In Buddhism, mantras are used to focus the mind and to connect with the Buddha nature.

Transformation from the Vibration of Life Force

Holy sounds, names, and mantras help us hear and feel the vibration of Source. For instance, the sound of OM is the vibration of oneness. The sound of OM is the hum of the universe, the primordial sound. The sound of OM is the essence of Source. The sound of OM has a vibration—and one can feel that the vibration resonates in every cell.

The heart generates a bioelectromagnetic field, which can be used to activate or energize an energy field around the body, often associated with ascension or spiritual enlightenment. The field, emanating from the heart, creates a powerful electromagnetic field, extending several feet beyond the body. Sensitive instruments can measure it.

Sound Healing: Why Does Sound Heal?
Sound vibration is a universal healer. Chanting, toning, and music have always been an important part of all cultures, past and present. Music has been referred to as "the universal language" and once called "the greatest good that mortals know," it has played a key role in expressing unspoken emotions commonly served to "solace the sick and weary" (Stevenson, 1967). Scholars from diverse disciplines, including anthropology, psychology, musicology, and physiology, have asked why music has played an integral role in society and culture for thousands of years.

The human body may have produced the first sounds interpreted as music. "Motherese," the vocal or gestural communication between mothers and infants, was a simple yet powerful form of music as medicine. A teaching tool, it involved melodic patterns and rhythmic patterns and helped the infant acquire language skills. These skills would, in turn, help that child grow up and function in the tribe. So, it added another resource for survival during the process of natural selection. (Mongush, 2023)

The infant is always attuned to its mother's sounds, footsteps, breathing, and heartbeat. Likewise, the mother waits for sounds the baby makes that indicate its cry for food, sleep, and discomfort in general. Historically, one example of this comes from the Inuit, the indigenous peoples of northern Canada. This rhythmic form of throat singing is done almost exclusively by Inuit women. It is also a more communal form of singing, usually performed in groups of two or more women. Their technique relies on short, sharp, rhythmic inhalations and exhalations of breath. In prehistoric times Motherese across all cultures was traditionally used to sing babies to sleep, or during games, women played throughout the long winter nights while the men were away hunting. (Mongush, 2023)

Babies learn their cues for survival through sound. Consequently, in all of us, from our very birth, music is interwoven in our very being. After all, the human fetus can hear music 20 weeks before birth. The relationship between the sounds and the patterns of daily life determines the visceral connection we have with music. It may explain the connection between rhythm and music. It may account for the changes in consciousness that music evokes, often when nothing else can.

The beauty of sound healing is that it works in many ways rather than one specific way. Scholars have pointed out that memory itself has ten different categories of function. Music stimulates all of them. This is the reason why it can alter symptoms from the emotional to the physical to the social. These types of memory include arousal or readiness to respond by mobilizing the endocrine system and the immune system, associative memory, meaning that one form of memory information is linked to another form through association, emotional conduct, or the degree of attraction or repulsion that a person feels towards a person or event.

Psychologically, music evokes strong emotions and, at the same time, expresses distinct emotions. When emotions are facilitated through sound healing, their expression takes place with less effort and allows better social communication. Historically, group rituals have depended on music because it restores wider and deeper connections. Sound healing and music have always allowed individuals to identify with a group.

Professor Emeritus from the Berklee College of Music, Dr. Suzanne Hanzer, points out that music takes our mind away from hardship and helps us see how to resolve that hardship instead. Rhythm provides an underlying supportive structure to synchronize our breathing patterns, slow them down, and relax. Memories of music help us envision happier moments. Those moments occur when we listen to music, and our current challenges become enveloped by the essence of a song. Music gives us a particular depth of relaxation that is transformative.

Ancient sound practices in this text are particularly important for communicating with the sacred. Hanzer reminds us that a singular sound vibration, or repetitive mantra, gives a person a continual affirmation of who they are, what they can be, and why staying present matters. Repetitive sound vibration is an indispensable antidote, she says, for anxiety, depression, chronic and acute ailments. Simply put, it is positive, and anyone can remember a repetitive sound vibration for healing anytime. They can even link sound to their breathing pattern. (Hanzer, 2023)

Sound of the Spheres - Our Place in the Cosmos

At the heart of the Pranic Tube work is embodying polarity by connecting to the Earth and Sun. Being here now includes integrating with the Schuman resonance, the earth resonance—earth's connection to magnetism. Hearing the "sound of the spheres" around us.

The music of the spheres is a philosophical concept that regards the proportions in the movements of celestial bodies—the Sun, Moon, and planets—as a form of music. The theory, originating in ancient Greece, was a tenet of Pythagoreanism and was later developed by 16th-century astronomer Johannes Kepler.

According to Pythagorean philosophy, the planets and stars are all made up of perfect spheres, and their movements through space create a harmony of sound. The pitch of this music is said to be determined by the distance of each planet from Earth, with the Sun being the lowest and the outermost planets being the highest.

The frequencies of the notes are said to be far too high for the human ear to perceive. However, some people believe it is possible to hear the music of the spheres with the inner ear of our souls.

Understanding the sound of the spheres, you place yourself in coherence with the cosmos. You ask the sound of spheres to ground you. You ask the sound of the spheres to bring coherence to your Pranic Tube. You become one with the All That Is.

For the Activation of Step IX see Part II

PART II

ACTIVATING THE NINE SEQUENTIAL STEPS OF THE AWAKENING PRANA! KRIYA
ESTABLISH YOUR DYNAMIC ENERGY BODYFLOW

> "To understand the concept of medicine in the Native American way, one must redefine 'medicine'. The way medicine is defined [...] is anything that improves one's connection to the Great Mystery and to all life. This would include the healing of body, mind, and spirit. This medicine is also anything that brings personal power, strength, and understanding. It is the constant living of life in a way that brings healing to the Earth Mother and to all of our associates, family, friends, and fellow creatures. Native American medicine is an all-encompassing 'way of life,' for it involves walking on the Earth Mother in perfect harmony with the Universe." —**Medicine Cards, by Jamie Sams and David Carson (p. 13)**

Awakening Prana! is a self-help manual to bring your energy body into balance and harmony. There are nine sequential steps to mastery of the system, and each step develops a key skill. An overview of each step was discussed in Part I.

Once you have experienced each sequential step you can in the future just jump to Step IX for the full "activation" of your energy body. I try to do the full 9 Steps every day, but there are often times when I need to linger on different step components that make up the complete activation, and having spent time on each step has enabled me to do so fluidly.

You'll receive the flow of life-force energy through your energy body with this system! It will assist with releasing dense energy forms that prevent us from connecting to Source as we are designed to, and from which we can regenerate. This energy will support your leading a vital, harmonious and peaceful life.

Let's begin the journey of embodying the technology of healing by reviewing the steps, before we review the "mechanics" underlying the healing technology.

THE JOURNEY: HEALING TECHNOLOGY SUMMARY

Each step in the book creates space for you to:

1. Set an Intention
2. Complete a meditation. The meditations for each step are designed to help you put regenerative energy healing into practice for yourself and others. Each meditation has a link to an associated sound healing. Many offer an audio link for a guided meditation. I also provide a version with written prompts.
3. Complete a sound healing transmission.
4. Engage in Action Steps to fully Embody the material as discussed in more detail in Part II.

Regeneration Occurs As We:

- Open our Life Force flow
- Balance our Yin and Yang energies
- Increase our Life Force Energy

BENEFITS

As the practice has unfolded I have found incredible and profound **benefits:**

- Continuous Transformation Through Connection With My Higher Self;
- Freedom from Trauma
- Embodying Radiant Awakening
- Physical Well-being - Youthful Energy
- Wholeness From Returning To My Perfect Blueprint of Mind/Body/Spirit
- Daily Opportunities For Regeneration And Renewal

THE POWER OF INTENTION

Transformation is a process of being and becoming. In order to become our Higher Self we must make a commitment through intention. Intention is powerful because it is a statement that thinks forward and creates momentum. We know what we want. We declare our intention to heal and then, we are automatically met by that which heals us. Setting an intention is a one line statement. When uttered, it activates Source to clear our auric fields, allowing renewal, and clearing dense energy forms.

You will set intentions throughout these steps. Intention becomes an important foundation for meditation, in fact, the most productive meditations occur through intention. Intention is like the road map we carry in our car, navigating the way for our travels as we "tune up" our bioelectric being.

When I set an intention for any of the meditations in the following steps, I generally ask for a healing, whatever is in the highest good. Sometimes, however, I will request help for a specific issue, such as a health problem, emotional block, or even for something I want to manifest.

The "asking" becomes a prayer. An invocation.

The key to removing the lower vibration density of trauma, etc., to receive Source energy for healing and regeneration, is to support and strengthen our bioelectric engine. The "repair shop" for this engine comes in Steps III-IV, the essential steps for empowering yourself.

ABOUT MEDITATION

My belief is that one of the reasons—if not the reason—meditation is so rejuvenating is that it helps us access a power beyond the emotional and physical body. In this book, through guided meditation, we learn to sink into an existing spiritual energy system designed for our well-being such as the energy system and technology described in Awakening Prana! It is the heavy energy of trauma and stress that normally separates us from this vibrancy, and a culture that hasn't included working with this energy system in our upbringing, to help clear it out. We tend to suffer, until we clear out the dense energies.

Eckhart Tolle reminds us of the fundamentals we must repeatedly apply during meditation practice.

1. Withdraw attention from the past and the future unless necessary.
2. Use your senses fully from awareness and observation while remaining disengaged.
3. Break the habit of not focusing on the present.
4. Be present with your mind, and observe, but do not judge your thoughts.
5. When discontent arises, know that it is normal and try to understand its source. Let the start of the problem dissolve into the inner space of now, outside of psychological time.
6. Remember that psychological time repeats old thought patterns. Infinite creative time lies outside of psychological time. (Tolle, pp. 33-46)

However, every moment of the day creates impressions in the mind that resurface during our practice. Swami Tyagananda, Chaplain at Harvard University and MIT, a Vedanta teacher and monk of the Ramakrishna Order, teaches students that our meditation practice consists of every thought we have. The more we cultivate positive thoughts and strengthen ourselves, the stronger our practice.

We find our way back to wholeness by reestablishing the basic tenets of meditation, and prayer mastery: first, we humbly ask for help. It is important to ask for restoration to the love of the universe, to the love of the Earth—our home—and the love of our Soul. Asking for help prepares us to learn how to restore the flow.

THE SOUND HEALINGS

The sound healing in each of the 9 Steps is the spiritual transmission of that Step. All you do is sit back and receive.

Sound healing is an integral part of the 9 Steps.

The sound healings in Awakening Prana! are transmissions, created by Hz and musical notes given to me from Stoneman and then given to my wonderful Masters student, Nick Raineri, who produced the music.

The entire 9 Step practice can be done with sound alone. The full step is called The Awakener, a 47-minute sound healing.

All the components of the 9 Steps are available one-by-one as well, including self-love, releasing, building a Vortex, and balancing Yin and Yang.

In recent years, there has been a growing interest in the use of sound for healing purposes. Sound healing helps us entrain, or synchronize more effectively and more efficiently with the power potential in the Central Axis. The healing technology presented in this book is designed to solidify your relationship to sound healing, so you can utilize it all day! Our connection to sound is innate, prior to our human birth; it is our primordial connection to the eternal Source.

Many of my clients and students listen to these sound healings every single day, and some multiple times. For months I listened to the long 42-minute version of the 7 Keys of Awakening Prana (Step VI) before going to sleep at night and on awakening, before getting out of bed. The experience changed me. In all the best ways. I am clearer, more in flow, and carry an agency I've never carried before. https://soundcloud.com/awakening-prana/7-keys-awakening-prana-long

Sound healing is the way of transformation and healing in the future. Here is an entry point!

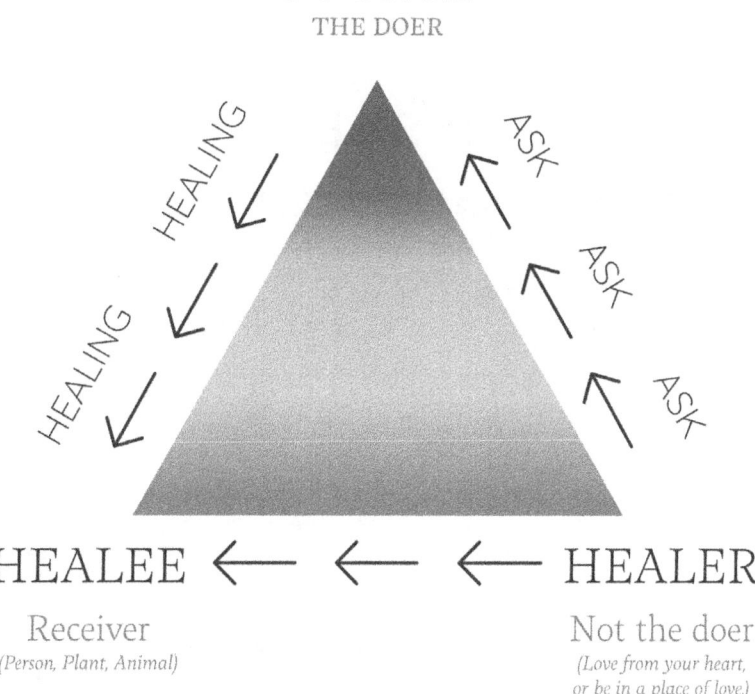

The Sacred Triangle

It wasn't until I fully understood the Sacred Triangle that I could hang a shingle out as a healer. I always felt uneasy being the "doer" when facilitating a healing. Instead, when I asked a person's soul—or Source, an archangel, an Element—to give the healing, the healee received the high wisdom that came from those benevolent energies.

It is the same when you meditate with the steps, below. You'll be asking the Elements, your Higher Self, etc., to bring the energy. You'll be in the Sacred Triangle when you do so.

STEP 1: EMBODY
THE FIVE SACRED ELEMENTS

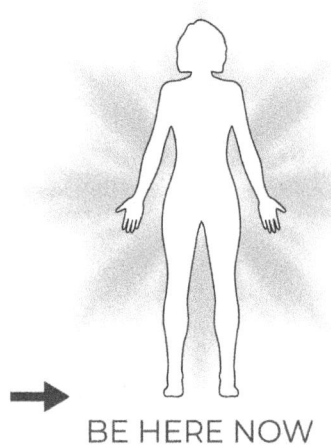

BE HERE NOW

"The simplest thing you can do to change the health and fundamental structure of your body is to treat the five Elements with devotion and respect."
—**Sadhguru, Inner Engineering**

The Purpose of Step 1

"Your conscious relationship with the Sacred Elements that make up the world in which you live . . . makes up one of the four [crucial] cornerstones of your existence." —**The Hathor Material, by Tom Kenyon**

Step 1 is designed to help you connect to the Sacred Elements Earth, Fire, Water, Air, and Ether, of which we are created. The Sacred Elements create all things, all matter.

The Energy of Step 1

1. Grounding
2. Experiencing the Sacred Elements moving, healing, supporting your body, mind, and spirit. You learn to feel their movement in your physical and energy body. By supporting the Elements coming into their highest possible relationship, harmony, balance, and vibration in the All That Is About You, you strengthen how they bring dynamism to your energy body.

Putting Step I into Practice

Set Intention
- I intend to love the planet as much as myself, as I am nature.
- I intend to choose natural and organic tools with which to live my life: whole foods, natural and organic products for cleaning and lifestyle choices; conserve water, heat, electricity, building materials, etc.
- I intend to be grounded.
- I intend to connect to the Earth, Sun, and the Elements in my daily life.

Daily Life Tip
Make sure to be grounded, whenever you think of it.

Step I Healing Meditation

Short Version
A Powerful Elements Embodiment Walking Meditation
It is interesting to feel where the energy goes. You learn about your personal energy body from feeling it. You will return from this meditation cleansed, with a feeling of purification.

Besides providing you with a moment to tune into each element, this step invokes the Law of Reciprocity. When you send love and gratitude to the Elements they will send healing back.

Directions: You'll work with one element at a time. As you feel prompted, repeat each step with an element a few times.

Repeat for each Element Earth, Water, Fire, Air, and Ether (consider Ether "space" for this exercise.)

I send my love and gratitude to the Sacred Element _____. I thank the Sacred Element _____ for being with me. I invite the Sacred Element _____ to bring me healing. I thank the Sacred Element _____.

Wait a full 30 seconds or more before moving onto the next element.

Finish by thanking the Sacred Elements and ending with
a'ho mitakuye oyasin
(Lakota prayer meaning "All my relations. I honor you in this circle of life with me today. I am grateful for this opportunity to acknowledge you in this prayer . . .")

Short Version 2
Get Grounded

Imagine yourself a tree with deep roots, but the roots not only go down deep into the Earth but they also drink up the Earth's nutrients. Your branches reach up to the sun and draw down the sunlight. Repeat whenever you feel you could use being more embodied.

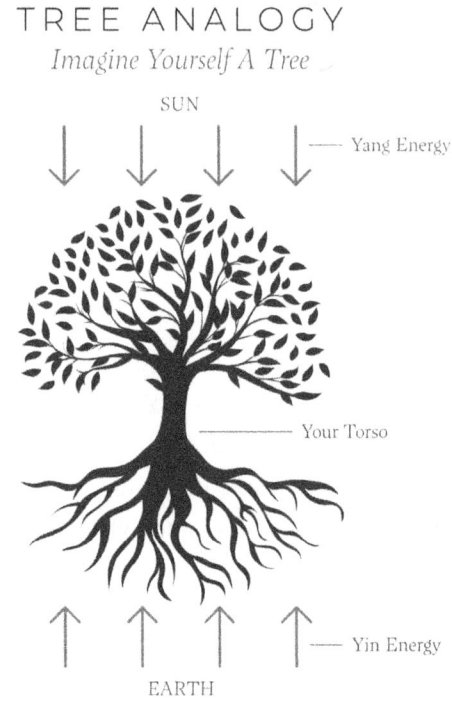

Long Version and Part I of the Complete 9 Steps Meditation

- I send love and gratitude to the heart of the Earth. I ask Mother Earth to send her beautiful energy up to my earth star chakra, about eight inches below the ground, and from my earth star chakra, up my Pranic Tube, along my Central Axis, and the energy goes where it needs to go.
- I ask the Sacred Elements Earth, Fire, and Water to help support my connection to Mother Earth.
- I send love and gratitude to the heart of the Sun. I ask Father Sun to send his beautiful energy down to my soul star chakra, about eight inches above my head, and from my soul star chakra, down my Pranic Tube, along my Central Axis, and the energy goes where it needs to go.
- I ask the Sacred Elements Air and Ether to help support my connection to Father Sun.
- I send love and gratitude to the Sacred Elements: Earth, Fire, Water, Air, and Ether.

(Connect to our Higher Self)

- I ask my Higher Self to clear our connection, to be with me.
- I drop into my heart chakra and tune into a feeling of gratitude, for Source. I tune into something that puts a song in my heart.
- I invite the Sacred Element Ether to bathe any illusions I have that I am separate from Source in Eternal Love"

repeat

A'ho Mitakuye Oyasin

THE TRANSMISSION

Audio Version
Audio Meditation Step 1

Sound Healing
The Elements

Crystals
Reciprocity of the Elements

STEP 1 ELEMENTS WORKBOOK

Stoneman insight

Remind ourselves that we are whole because of the Elements and if we feel fragmented, we are fragmented with one or more of the Elements.

Assess Yourself and the Elements

What is your relationship to the Elements?

Outside, nature, how much do you have nature in your life. Do you drink enough water, do you swim, do you revel in its delight.

> *Annie's Example:* I keep seeing an hourglass. I am measured with them, the Elements. I have my outdoor time, I think of a bath, etc. I don't realize that they are everything. Instead, I need to come into coherence with them, not compartmentalize my relationship with them.

What is your relationship to the Elements?

How do you know where you are at with the Elements?

> *Annie's Example:* I asked my Higher Self and this was the answer: How often do I remember them?

STEP II: CONNECT

"The noblest foundation for medicine is love. It is love which teaches the art of healing. Without love true healing cannot be born." —**Paracelsus**

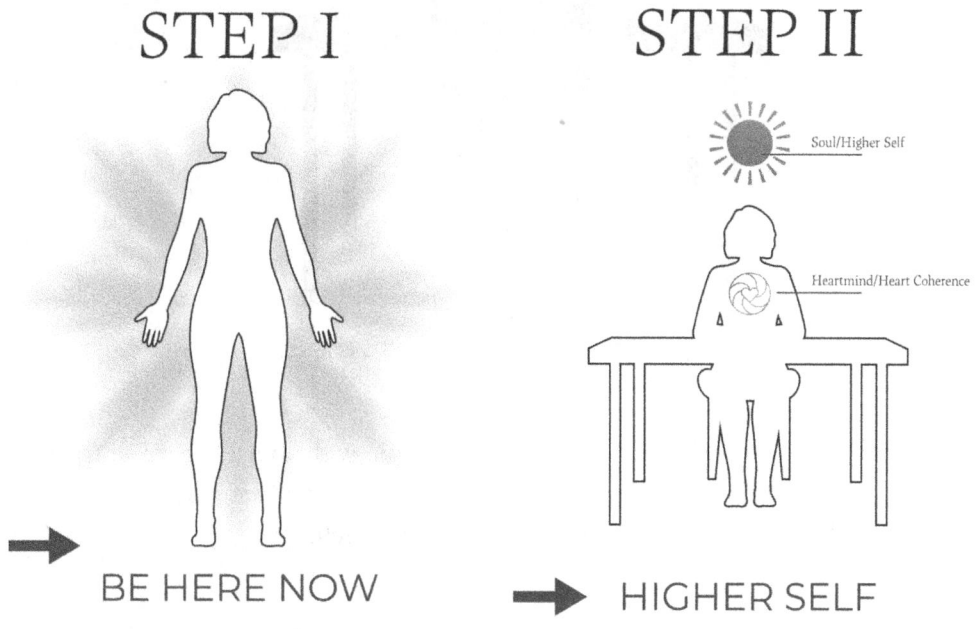

Before we meet the Higher Self let's revisit the steps and orient our journey. We have been through a lot of food for thought and context of the technology of healing. Here it is again in a nutshell:

Step I - Embody (the Sacred Elements)
>>>>>>>>>> You are here: **Step II - Connect [Higher Self/Soul]** <<<<<<<<<<
Step III Charge - Replenish Yin and Yang
Step IV - Power Up (Ignite the Vortex)
Step V - Release (Remove lower vibration density)
Step VI - Meet (Source/Source)
Step VII - Increase Voltage (Pranic Tube Draws Prana)

Step VIII - Conduct Energy (All Systems Go, Toroidal Flow)
Step IX - Awaken (Come into Complete Flow with Source)

Meeting Your Higher Self

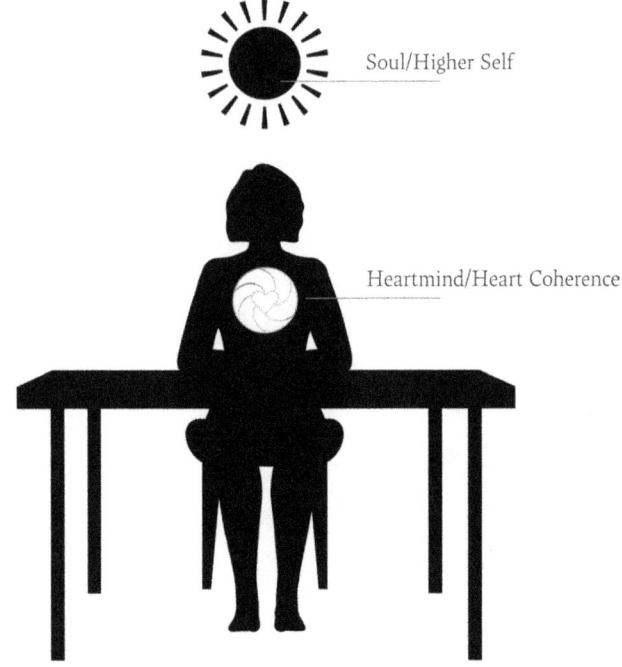

"Feet on the ground, connecting to the Earth."

The Purpose of Step II

The purpose of Step II is for you to build a relationship with your Higher Self to help us mitigate our ego and the 3D programming of your culture and upbringing.

One could say that a goal is to become one's Higher Self.

The Energy of Step II

1. When you ask for a healing from your Higher Self you will increasingly feel it, experience it, as energy moves through the lower vibration density to bring in resolution.
2. The more you embody your Higher Self the higher your vibration and you experience yourself carrying more light.

BENEFITS

Meeting your Higher Self helps you gain self agency, wisdom, and discernment.

Putting Step II into Practice

Set Intention
- I intend to obtain a sound healing percussion healing instrument that will help me drop into my heartmind/heart coherence. Something such as a Tibetan ting-sha, singing bowl, tuning fork, didgeridoo. . . . I can take a minute to play this when I am in "monkey mind."
- I intend to ask my Higher Self for wisdom when I am hamster wheeling with this prayer: *"I ask my Higher Self to bring healing to _____, and I pray for insight."*
- I intend to build my relationship with my Higher Self. "I ask my Higher Self to clear our connection, to be with me."

Daily Life Tip
Set aside time for a daily conversation with your Higher Self.

Step II's Healing Meditation

Short Version
I ask my loving infinite soul to bathe me in self-love. (Repeat a few times and wait a minute or so before continuing). I ask my Higher Self to bathe me in unconditional love. (Repeat a few times.)

Long Version
- I ask my Higher Self to clear our connection, to be with me.
- I drop into my heart chakra and tune into a feeling of gratitude for Source. I tune into something that puts a song in my heart.

    Heart Coherence
    - Focus on your Heart
    - Generate positive feelings (Gratitude, Joy, Love, Appreciation)
    - Imagine breathing through your Heart

- Feel my self in the center of my body
- I invite the Sacred Element Ether to bathe any illusions I have that I am separate from Source in Eternal Love.
- I ask my Higher Self to bathe me in unconditional love. Repeat frequently for 10 minutes.
- *Listen to the long or short version of Self-Love. You just receive, receive, receive.*

THE TRANSMISSION

Audio Meditation Step II

Sound Healing

Self-Love (short version, 9 minutes)

Self-Love (long version, 27 minutes)

Crystals
Self-Love

STEP 11 HIGHER SELF WORKBOOK

· · · · · · · · · · · · · · · ·

Stoneman insight

The excitement and joy never ends when you are embodied and connected. Guidance, teaching, wisdom, love, companionship—what more could you want?

Assess Yourself and Your Higher Self

What is your relationship to your Higher Self?

> *Annie's Example:* I've come a long way. I have more to go but I am trusting this essence of me, and have come to revere its messages and most importantly, its heart.

How do you know where you are at with your Higher Self?

> *Annie's Example:* By my centering, by my knowledge about myself, by my understanding of myself, and most of all by my feeling of coherence.

Daily Step for the Higher Self

> *Annie's Example:* I ask my Higher Self to be with me. I could definitely send much more gratitude.

Daily Action for the Higher Self

> *Annie's Example:* Thy will be done. (This is going to be an adventure for me.... It isn't easy to give up control.)

STEP III: CHARGE - REPLENISH YOUR BATTERY
(-) AND (+), YIN AND YANG, SHAKTI AND SHIVA, FEMALE AND MALE, MOTHER AND FATHER

"For the true path to wholeness can only be the one that passes into and through the world of opposites." —**Joseph Jastrab and Ron Schaumburg** "Sacred Manhood, Sacred Earth," p. 96

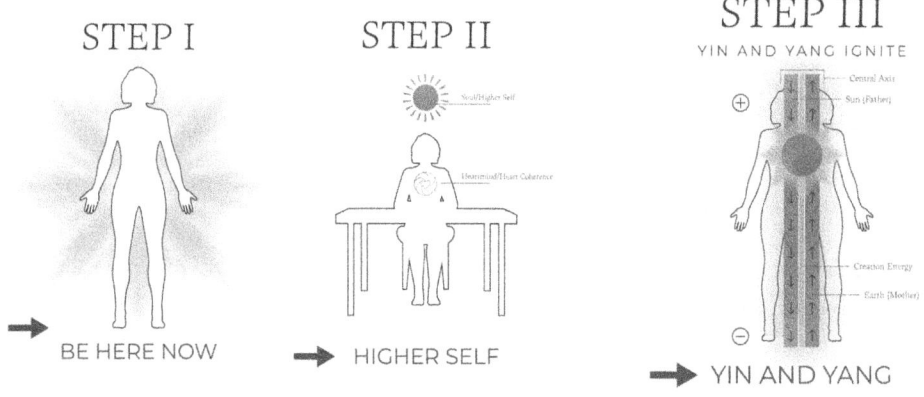

Step I - Embody (the Sacred Elements)
Step II - Connect [Higher Self/Soul]
>>>>>>>>>> You are here: **Step III Charge - Replenish Yin and Yang** <<<<<<<<<<
Step IV - Power Up (Ignite the Vortex)
Step V - Release (Remove lower vibration density)
Step VI - Meet (Source/Source)
Step VII - Increase Voltage (Pranic Tube Draws Prana)
Step VIII - Conduct Energy (All Systems Go, Toroidal Flow)
Step IX - Awaken (Come into Complete Flow with Source)

The Purpose of Step III

To establish your electrical charge, equal amounts of the (-) feminine, Yin current are brought into equal balance with the (+) masculine, Yang current.

Step IV is a step where you are actively moving and receiving energy and working with the bioelectric technology of the energy body.

BENEFITS

This step jumpstarts the entire energy body. In the car analogy, this is the battery!

The Energy of Step III

1. As you invite the Yin and Yang energies inside of your body, mind, and spirit to come into equal balance you will feel a wholeness, a balance.
2. You will also be creating the alchemy that ignites a powerful healing Vortex, which you will learn how to create in Step V.

Putting Step II into Practice

Set Intention

- I have willpower; I am willing to change, to work through balancing Yin and Yang energies in myself.
- I intend to connect to Mother Earth and Father Sun every day.
- I ask the currents of the divine feminine and divine masculine of Source to come into equal balance in The All That Is About Me.
- I intend to pay attention to how I might be out of balance with Yin and Yang in my personality when faced with cultural and family issues.

Daily Life Tip

Send love and gratitude to Mother Earth and Father Sun whenever you think of it.

Step III's Healing Meditation: The Charging Station

Short Version

A. Imagine You Are A Tree

TREE ANALOGY
Imagine Yourself A Tree

YIN COMES UP AND YANG GOES DOWN

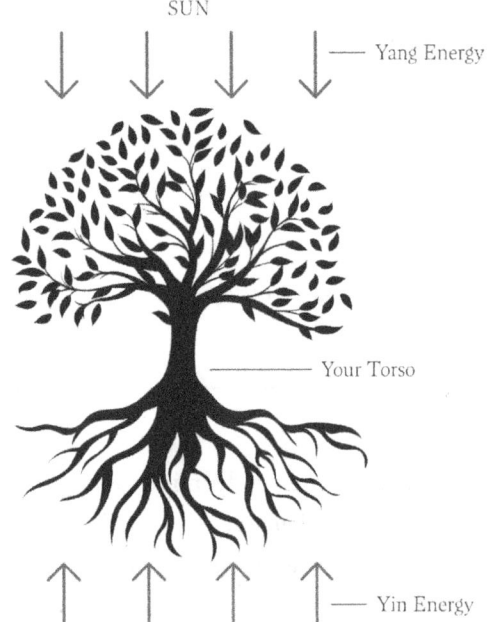
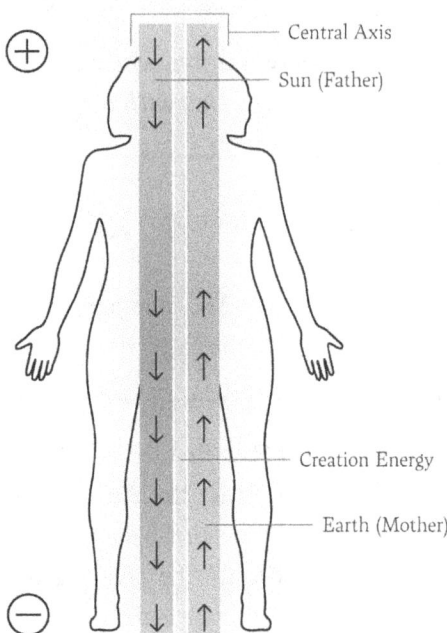

A. While Imagining you are a tree:
- Drink up Mother Earth energy through the roots.
- Drink up Father Sun energy down to the leaves.
- Mother Earth (Yin); Father Sun (Yang)
- Imagine yourself a tree to drink up the Yin energy.
- Imagine yourself a tree to drink down the Yang energy.
- The energies of Yin and Yang will meet in your heart.

Long Version
- "I send love and gratitude to the heart of the Earth. I send love and gratitude to the heart of the Sun."
- "I send love and gratitude to my soul mother and feminine aspect of my Higher Self. I send love and gratitude to my soul father and masculine aspect of my Higher Self."
- "I send love and gratitude to the Divine Mother. I send love and gratitude to the Divine Father."
- I ask Mother Earth to anchor me down, to help me be grounded. I ask Mother Earth to bring me healing.
- I ask Father Sun to fill me with light. I ask Father Sun to bathe me in light.
- I ask to activate my soul mother to bring me healing. Repeat.
- I ask to activate my soul father to bring me healing. Repeat.

THE ENTRY POINT FROM SOURCE

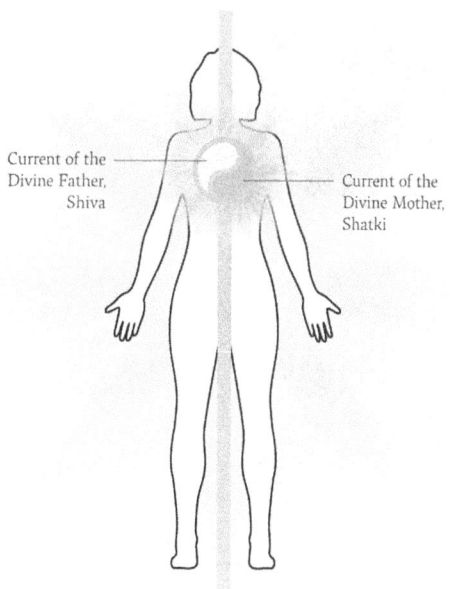

- I ask to activate my soul mother and father to bring me healing.
- I ask the current of the Divine Mother, sacred feminine aspect of Source, to come to me wherever it is needed and in the highest good.
- I ask the current of the Divine Father, the divine masculine aspect of Source, to come to me wherever it is needed and in the highest good.
- I ask the currents to fill up what is needed so that they come into equal balance.
- The current of the Divine Mother and current of the Divine Father
- I offer a prayer for healing to Source to remove any resistance to these currents.
- And I ask the currents of the Divine Mother and Divine Father to come to me where they are needed and are in the highest good, to fill and fill, to replenish where it's needed.

If you feel resistance to either filling, use this:
"I offer a prayer to the Creator to bring healing to any resistance I have to the Divine Mother or the Divine Father."

THE TRANSMISSION

Audio Meditation
Step III

Sound Healing
Yin and Yang
Time: 9 Minutes

Crystals
Yin and Yang

YIN/YANG WORKBOOK

Stoneman insight
The time for heralding in the sacred feminine is here now, and this is the time for rebellion against the old ways that don't serve. It is time for change. It is an imperative.

Assess Yourself and Your Higher Self
What is your relationship to your feminine and masculine?

> *Annie's Example:* The Divine Father is still a sticking point as there is resistance due to the experience of cultural dominance. My mother wound is healing hence I am more nurturing of myself.

How do you know where you are at with Yin and Yang?

> *Annie's Example:* The health of my body.

Daily Step for the Yin and Yang

> *Annie's Example:* Build the Vortex—drinking in Yin and Yang.

> *Daily Action for the Yin and Yang*
>
> *Annie's Example:* Work on cultural constructs I carry that limit me in yin and yang compartments; work on my resistance to the current of the divine masculine energy of Source.

STEP IV: POWER UP!
VORTEX ~ OUR MOTOR

"We work to create a Vortex because it carries a transmission of Source, the spark of Source." — **Stoneman**

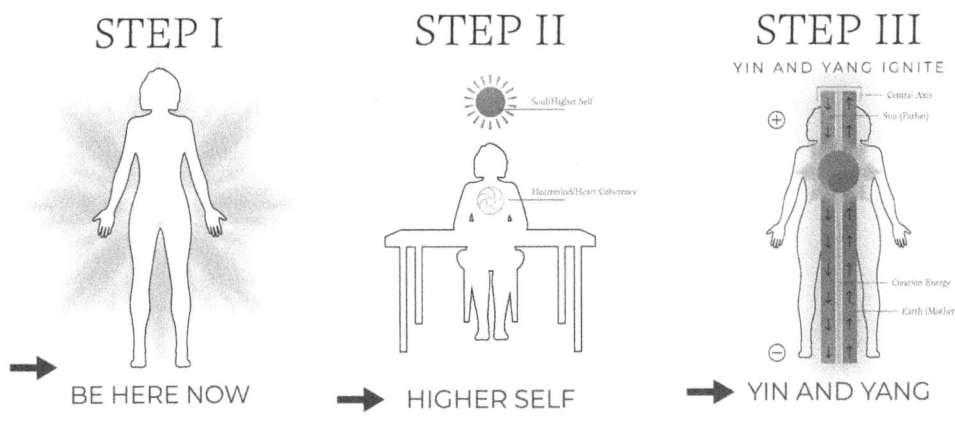

Step I - Embody (the Sacred Elements)
Step II - Connect (Higher Self/Soul)
Step III Charge - Replenish Yin and Yang
>>>>>>>>>> You are here: **Step IV - Power Up (Ignite the Vortex)** <<<<<<<<<<
Step V - Release (Remove lower vibration density)
Step VI - Meet (Source/Source)
Step VII - Increase Voltage (Pranic Tube Draws Prana)
Step VIII - Conduct Energy (All Systems Go, Toroidal Flow)
Step IX - Awaken (Come into Complete Flow with Source)

The Purpose of Step IV

To create a powerful Vortex of prana from Yin and Yang energy in equal balance coalescing to ignite as a Vortex, creating the spark of the Source.

The Energy of Step IV

Yin and Yang connect and ignite the Creator spark and the spark organizes a Vortex, the movement of Yin and Yang into a counter-rotating vortex.

The energy is both that of Source and destruction. The currents of Yin and Yang balance, coalesce, ignite, creating a powerful Vortex that becomes a master blaster of lower vibration density, allowing the Source lines to flow to us, bringing us into a matrix of light.

Putting Step IV into Step

Set Intention

- I intend to invite in the current of the Divine Mother and the current of the Divine Father at least one time a day to help strengthen my prana Vortex, wherever it is in the highest good.
- I intend to connect to my Central Axis every day by connecting to the above, asking that energy to flow down and by connecting to the below, asking that energy to come up.
- I intend to ask Yin and Yang to come into equal balance in my whole being.

Daily Life Tip

Ask to hear the sound of the vortex (inside your head) of the Central Axis and entrain to it.

Before listening to the following sound healing, a default intention is to always seek "Whatever is in the highest good."

Step V's Healing Meditation

Short Version

- I ask the current of the Divine Mother, the sacred feminine aspect of Source, to flow unimpeded into my heart chakra, or wherever is in the highest good.

- I ask the current of the Divine Father, the Divine Father aspect of Source, to flow unimpeded into my heart chakra, or wherever is in the highest good.
- I ask Yin and Yang to connect and ignite the Creator spark and that the spark organizes a vortex, the movement of yin and yang into a counter-rotating vortex.

Long Version

A. Refresh from Part III meditation—asking the currents of the Yin and Yang to come into balance wherever is in the highest good on your behalf.

B. Ask the Divine Mother and Divine Father to **connect and ignite** to create a prana Vortex.

CREATING THE BIOELECTRIC VORTEX

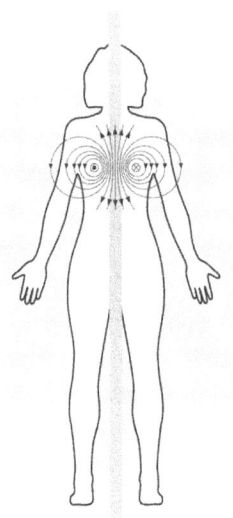
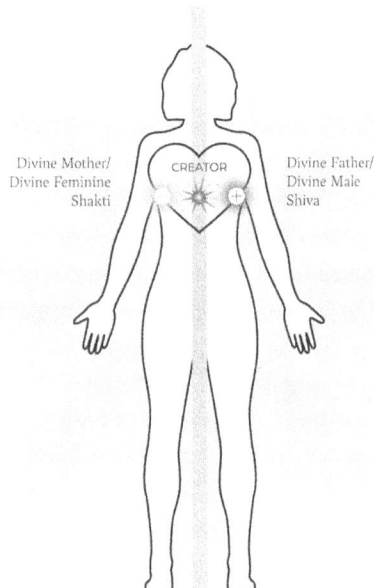

- I ask the currents of the female Yin and masculine Yang to come into equal balance wherever is in the highest good on my behalf.
- Ask the Divine Mother and Divine Father currents to connect and coalesce.
- I invite their energy and magnetism to each other. I ask that magnetism to pull more and more in of the Yin and the Yang, and for those energies to connect and coalesce.
- There they ignite—they create a SPARK—the SPARK of Source, life force energy. This spark of Source energy organizes to create a Vortex, the movement of Yin and Yang into a counter-rotating vortex, a Vortex flowing with life force, of prana, and I understand that the strength of this Vortex is the key to my well-being.
- I ask to connect to that spark of ignition, to feel that life force.
- I keep filling the Vortex, keep asking for more of the Yin and the Yang to continue to pour in, pour in. (Repeat frequently.)
- The Yin and Yang energies counter-rotate, making a powerful Vortex.
- I continually invite in more and more Yin and Yang currents to strengthen the Vortex.

- As the Vortex strengthens it becomes a "master blaster" blasting out lower vibration density, removing our trauma and heavy programming, illness, making way for the light.
- I ask it to grind away lower vibration density so that the light can get through unimpeded. Almost like a gear, grinding away.
- I ask it to grind away lower vibration density so as to open the receptor points to my physicality so that Light Force energy can flow through unimpeded.

THE TRANSMISSION

Audio Meditation
Step IV

Sound Healing
Vortex

Crystals
Align

VORTEX WORKBOOK

· · · · · · · · · · · · · · ·

Stoneman insight
This is the dance, this is the energy, this is the explosion of prana into your energy body system! This is radiance, this is where transformation begins.

Asses Yourself and the Vortex
What is your relationship to inner Vortexes?

Annie's Example: If I ask to hear the sound of the inner vortex it is like a gushing waterfall and I need to ask for this more frequently!

How do you know where you are at with inner Vortexes?

Annie's Example: Feeling of the freedom of my energy body, of being in flow.

Daily Step for inner Vortex healing

Annie's Example: Mother Earth and Father Sun connection on the rebounder.

Daily Action for inner Vortex healing

Annie's Example: Imagine a straw drinking the energy up and a straw drinking the energy down: pranic breathing.

STEP V: RELEASE

WE CAN RELEASE NEGATIVE THOUGHTFORMS, PHYSICAL DEPLETION AND TRAUMA!

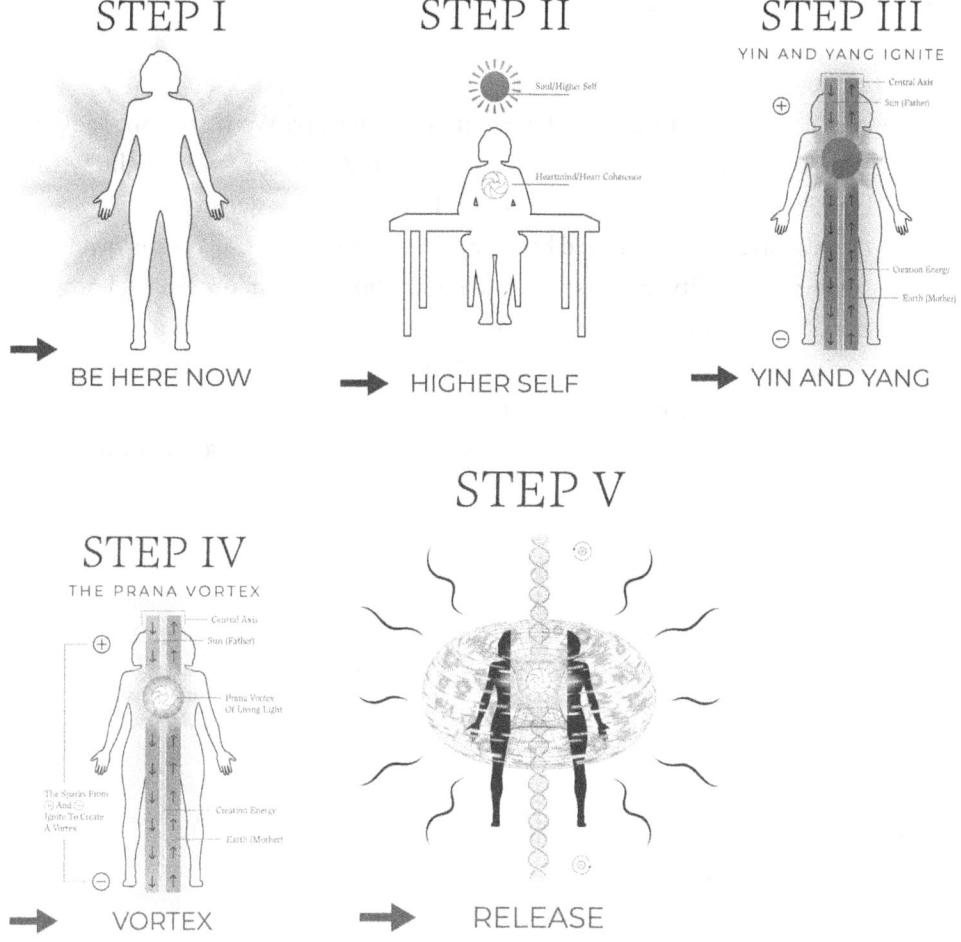

Step I - Embody (the Sacred Elements)
Step II - Connect (Higher Self/Soul)
Step III Charge - Replenish Yin and Yang
Step IV - Power Up (Ignite the Vortex)
>>>>>>>>>> You are here: **Step V - Release (Remove lower vibration density)** <<<<<<<<<<
Step VI - Meet (Source/Source)
Step VII - Increase Voltage (Pranic Tube Draws Prana)
Step VIII - Conduct Energy (All Systems Go, Toroidal Flow)
Step IX - Awaken (Come into Complete Flow with Source)

The Purpose of Step V

Without releasing we are bogged down with a lifetime of stress and strain. It is holding us back, it is curtailing our energy, it is crippling our ability to find new patterns. Without releasing, we become stagnant.

Refreshing your energy body for new adventures!

The Energy of Step V

The Vortex acts like a pump to remove lower vibration density. We then want to remove it. To release lower vibration energies. It also brings in the spark of Source light, which is LOVE, and LOVE is an alchemy that also dissolves lower vibration density.

Illness, trauma, stress, and required behaviors that run our lives, all create lower vibration density in our physicality (as a disease) and energy body (as a neurosis). Old programming such as trying to fit into a culture where one is not a perfect fit, or to please a parent.

It envelops us in a lower, darker, vibration. Some of it is so powerful it is solid, even hard. Entrenched and resistant to recalcitrant.

The Vortex, master blaster, removes lower vibration density so that light can enter.

Putting Step V into Step

Set Intention
- I work with the Elements every day by thanking them, asking to be of service, and then asking each to release what can be released:
  - Earth to magnetize it down
  - Water to wash it away
  - Fire to burn it away
  - Air to blow it away
  - Ether to remove it.
- I ask to release what I can release to the sun to be purified, whatever is in the highest good.
- I ask the Angels of Manifestation to help the flow of LIGHT FORCE to bring

healing to the lower vibration density blocking the LIVING LIGHT from flowing into my receptor Energy Centers.

Daily Life Tip
Realize that releasing energy is important to your well-being.

Short Version
The law of vibration states that higher vibrations will always win out over lower vibrations but the higher vibration needs to be around for a long enough time to deplete the lower, wear it out, so that it eventually dissipates and is removed.

One way to do this is to ask the high vibration of your Higher Self to remove lower vibration density/vibration for you. You do this by asking it to do this for you.

"I ask my Higher Self to please remove that which can be released."

Long Version
- I continue to fill the Vortex with the sacred feminine and sacred masculine currents to make it a strong master blaster of lower vibration density. Fill with the soul mother and soul father, with mother Earth and Father Sun.
- I ask the Supreme being to vacuum out all that I can release.
- I ask the Sacred Elements to help release the lower vibration density: earth to magnetize it down, water to wash it away, fire to burn it away, air to blow it away, and ether to remove it.
- I imagine a cloud in front of me and release all that I can release into the cloud, until it is filled and ask it to go to the sun to be purified. I ask in another cloud.
- Again, I ask the Supreme being to vacuum out all that I can release.

THE TRANSMISSION

Audio Meditation
Step V

Guided Releasing

Unguided Releasing

Crystals
Align

RELEASE WORKBOOK

• • • • • • • • • • • • •

Stoneman insight
Releasing is central to understanding yourself as an energy body. EXHAUST. You create exhaust when you process feelings and emotions, if they aren't released they clog the system!

Assess Yourself and Step V.
What is your relationship to Releasing?

> *Annie's Example:* I hold on to interactions with people way more than is to my benefit. Learning to release every day will make a major difference in the energetic log jams I can find myself immersed within.

How do you know where you are at with Releasing?

> *Annie's Example:* I know that I am not releasing well when I don't feel in flow with my life and the Universe.

Daily Practice for Releasing

> *Annie's Example:*
> **Take an elements walk every day:**
> I ask Earth to magnetize down;

I ask Water to wash away;
I ask Fire to burn away;
I ask Air to blow away;
I ask Ether to remove.

Daily Action for Releasing

Annie's Example: I will be conscious when I have a shower that I took a step to allow water's power to wash away all energy that doesn't serve.

STEP VI: MEET

"All this is the Atman*. From it the universe comes forth, in it the universe merges and in it the universe breathes. Therefore a man should meditate on the Atman with a calm mind." — **Chandogya Upanishad XIV:1**

* Atman: The Source of all that is beyond all mind, body, intellect and ego.

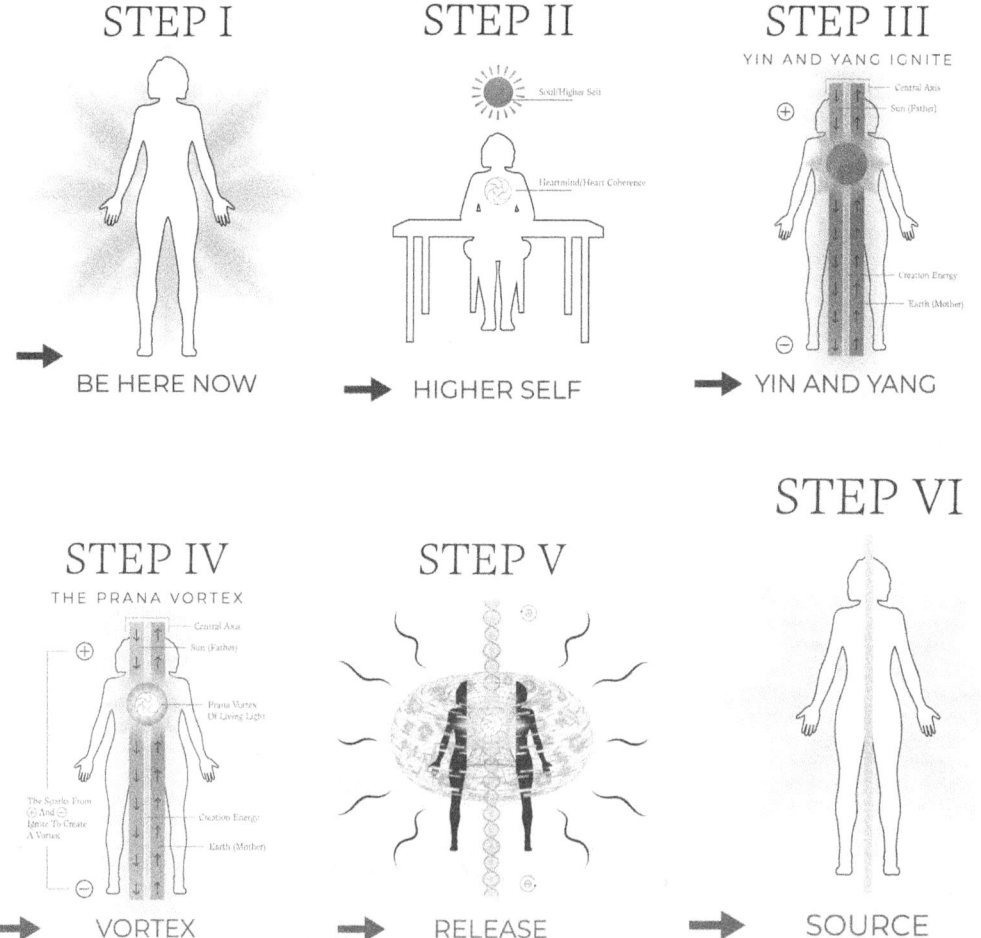

Step I - Embody (the Sacred Elements)
Step II - Connect (Higher Self/Soul)
Step III Charge - Replenish Yin and Yang
Step IV - Power Up (Ignite the Vortex)
Step V - Release (Remove lower vibration density)
>>>>>>>>>> You are here: **Step VI - Meet (Source/Source)** <<<<<<<<<<
Step VII - Increase Voltage (Pranic Tube Draws Prana)
Step VIII - Conduct Energy (All Systems Go, Toroidal Flow)
Step IX - Awaken (Come into Complete Flow with Source)

The Central Axis: The Current of Life Force Energy
The Central Axis is in front of the spine.

The Purpose of Step VI
The purpose of Step VI is to *feel and even hear* the essence of Source: it is visceral, not an intellectual exercise. You enter a place beyond thought or thinking. You enter a vibration, an *experience*. This current of life force flows down to your crown and down through you from there. This brings an experience of expansiveness over time.,

The sound of OM is the quintessence of the Central Axis. It represents the All That Is. It represents the fundamentals of Source. It is the sound of God/Source/Source, a place beyond words, a place of sublime grace. This is the field of energy that holds the messages of the sacred imprint, the holder of all the keys of the Universe.

BENEFITS

The Central Axis is your master healer. It carries your perfect blueprint.

The Energy of Step VI
You'll entrain to an energy of radiance and luminosity. You'll feel this through experience.

Putting Step VI into Practice

Set Intention
- I intend to connect to the light coming down from above that comes into my crown, out through my first chakra, and into the earth.
- I intend to hum OM with my awareness in my heart chakra.
- I intend to tune into the vibration of the cosmos.

Daily Life Tip
Feel that you are One with the All That Is.

> **BENEFITS**
>
>
>
> **Benefits of Humming**
> +Increase oxygen in cells
> +Lowered blood pressure and heart rate
> +Increased lymphatic circulation
> +Increased levels of melatonin
> +Reduced levels of stress-related hormones
> +Release of endorphins
> +Increased levels of nitric oxide
> +Release of oxytocin

Step VI Healing Meditations

Short Version

"I ask to entrain to my quantum self, whatever is in the highest good." If you have a specific issue you are concerned about, you can add that, such as "I ask to entrain to my quantum self to bring healing to the perfect blueprint of my ankle."

Long Version

Connecting to the Hum of the Central Axis

- Drop into heart chakra.
- Ask to hear the hum of your Central Axis. Hear the pitch. Stay with the hum for a few minutes.
- Ask to entrain to the hum of your Central Axis. Stay with this for a few minutes: it brings intense, profound healing.
- As the lower vibration density is removed I open to the experience of my Central Axis, that powerful beam of light coming down through me, up through me... the energy of my connection to the Universe, to the Source, the sound of OM, the luminosity of Source. I ask to entrain to the sound of OM.

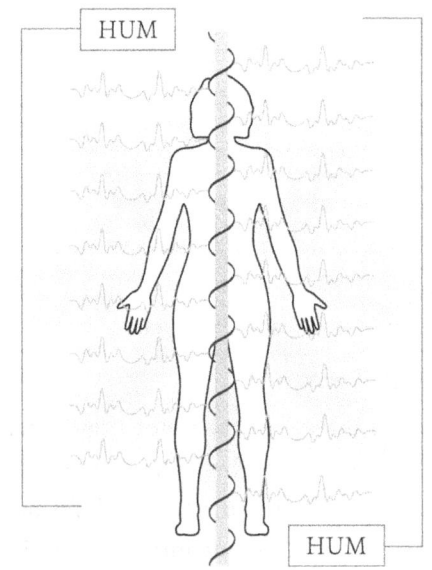

ASK TO HEAR THE HUM OF THE CENTRAL AXIS

- I ask to entrain to the sound of OM.
- As lower vibration density is removed and I can open to more light, I ask to entrain to the sound of OM.
- I open to receive the life force energy from my Central Axis carrying the light, color, and sound codes, the data carriers of my perfect blueprint, of the perfect blueprint. The life force prana that is center stage for my transformation.
- I ask to entrain to the sound of OM.

THE TRANSMISSION

Audio Meditation
Step VI

Sound Healing
7 Keys Long

7 Keys Short

Crystals
Align

SOURCE WORKBOOK

Stoneman insight

You know who this is—what this is—you have it inside of you. Remember that always. You feel it in your connection to the All That Is, in your knowings, in your heart. You know it because it is LOVE in all its splendor.

Assess Yourself and Source

What is your relationship to Source?

> *Annie's Example:* Nature is for me the centerpiece of how I connect, but I need to learn to trust more.

How do you perceive yourself within Source?

> *Annie's Example:* How "awake" I am. How well I am able to quiet my ego. I toggle back and forth between my "head" and heart coherence as a check-point.

Daily Step for Source

> *Annie's Example:* Trust. Trust. Trust

"The winds of grace are always blowing; however, you must raise your sail to catch them." — **Sri Paramahamsa Ramakrishna**

Daily Action for Source

> *Annie's Example:* Tune into a feeling of love in my heart. Hum OM four times out loud and say OM four times to yourself.

STEP VII: INCREASE VOLTAGE
THE PRANIC TUBE

The Pranic Tube is the pathway of light that connects the physical body to the spiritual body. It is the channel through which prana, or life force energy, flows.

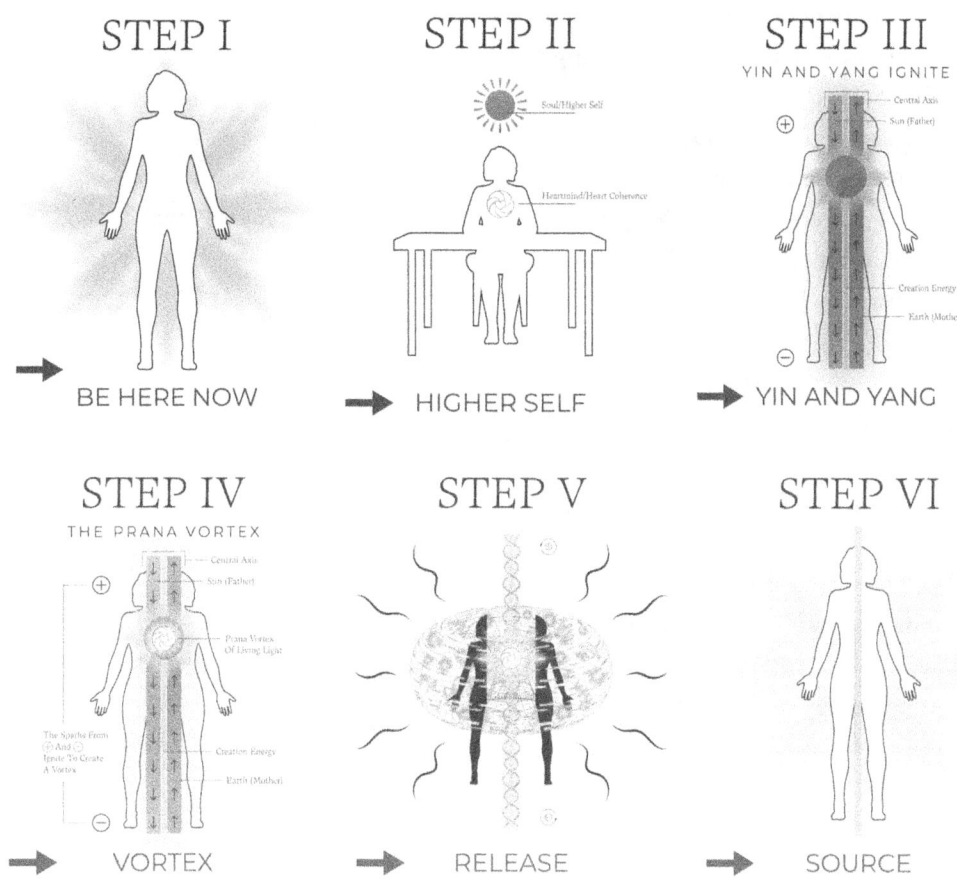

STEP VII
PRANIC TUBE

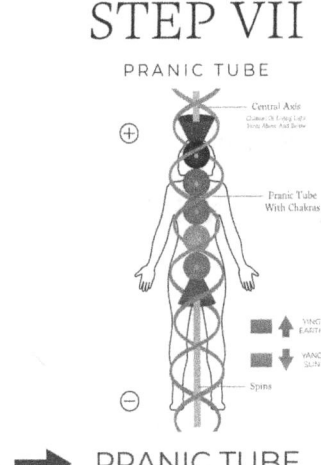

➡ PRANIC TUBE

Step I - Embody (the Sacred Elements)
Step II - Connect (Higher Self/Soul)
Step III Charge - Replenish Yin and Yang
Step IV - Power Up (Ignite the Vortex)
Step V - Release (Remove lower vibration density)
Step VI - Meet (Source/Source)
>>>>>>>>> You are here: **Step VII - Increase Voltage (Pranic Tube Draws Prana)** <<<<<<<<<
Step VIII - Conduct Energy (All Systems Go, Toroidal Flow)
Step IX - Awaken (Come into Complete Flow with Source)

The Purpose of Step VII
The Pranic Tube is the prana receiver, building the tours around us. It continually flows with polarity energies that support the Torus and is always strengthened by the blasting away of lower vibration density from the Vortex.

The Energy of Step VII
Voltage in the Pranic Tube happens by drawing the prana into it from above and below and from the Central Axis. The more energy the Pranic Tube draws in, the higher the voltage of the entire energy body. The Pranic Tube continually flows with (-) Yin and (+) Yang *polarity*, counter-rotating around each other, creating the Torus (see Step VIII). Energy from the Earth and Sun. The Pranic Tube is the inside sleeve of that Torus.

Putting Step VI into Practice

Set Intention
- I intend to connect to the energy of the Earth.
- I intend to connect to the energy of the Sun.

- I intend to feel the magnetism of Earth and Sun to each other inside of me.
- When doing visualizations, remember that energy follows awareness. Focus on the area of the body described, and the energy will go there.

Daily Life Tip

Find a time to draw prana up and down into you every day!

Step VII's Pranic Tube Healing Meditation

Short Version

To help facilitate pranic breathing, imagine a straw at the top of your head and at your base, drinking in the energy from above and below.

When doing visualizations, remember that energy follows awareness. Focus on the area of the body being described, and the energy will go there.

Long Version
- I pick up on the energy of the Vortex, the powerful counter-rotation that makes a Pranic Tube around the Central Axis, the inside sleeve of what becomes the Torus around us. That inside sleeve pulls in the Mother Earth energy from below and the Father Sun energy from above. **The two magnetize to each other**, creating a powerful counter-rotation of currents.
- I pull in more and more energy from below and above, and work to increase its voltage, to feel the energy coming up, imagining myself once again to be a tree with deep roots, and the roots are drinking up and up the Yin energy from below. And from above, the branches are drinking down and down the Yang energy from above. Filling and filling the Pranic Tube to create a Torus.
- A powerful counter-rotation that creates our Torus.
- Increasing voltage by drinking up Mother Earth and Father Sun currents.
- I ask the sun to bathe the All That Is About Me in all the colors of the rainbow to assist this reconnection and awakening. Red, orange, yellow, green, sky blue, indigo, and violet.
- I ask the Sacred Elements to come into their highest possible balance, relationship, and vibration in the All That Is About Me to come into coherence, and for them to invite in all the sounds they want to work with, and those sounds to breathe into whatever is in the highest good.
- Once again, I ask the flow of the Yin coming up and Yang coming down to strengthen and strengthen to increase voltage and build a powerful Torus around me.

THE TRANSMISSION

Audio Meditation
Step VII

Sound Healing
The Awakening

Crystals
Self-love

STEP VII PRANIC TUBE WORKBOOK

Stoneman insight

This is harder than you might think until you see that your system is already aligned to drink into your pranic tube from above and below. You can think of straws drinking in but also think of suction pulling the prana into yourself.

Assess yourself and your Pranic Tube
What is your relationship to your Pranic Tube?

> *Annie's Example:* I am still a bit resistant to pulling the energy down through me, but when I do it is amazing as I feel so much more grounded.

How do you know where you are at with your Pranic Tube?

> *Annie's Example:* I feel a bit mudded and stuck in negative thoughtforms.

Daily Practice for your Pranic Tube?

> *Annie's Example:* Drinking in the energies.

Daily Action for my Pranic Tube.

> *Annie's Example:* Leave negative thoughts immediately.

STEP VIII: CONDUCT ENERGY
TORUS- THE CONDUCTOR OF ENERGY.

"The Torus is a blueprint for the universe. It is the shape of energy flow, both within and without our bodies." —**David Wilcock**

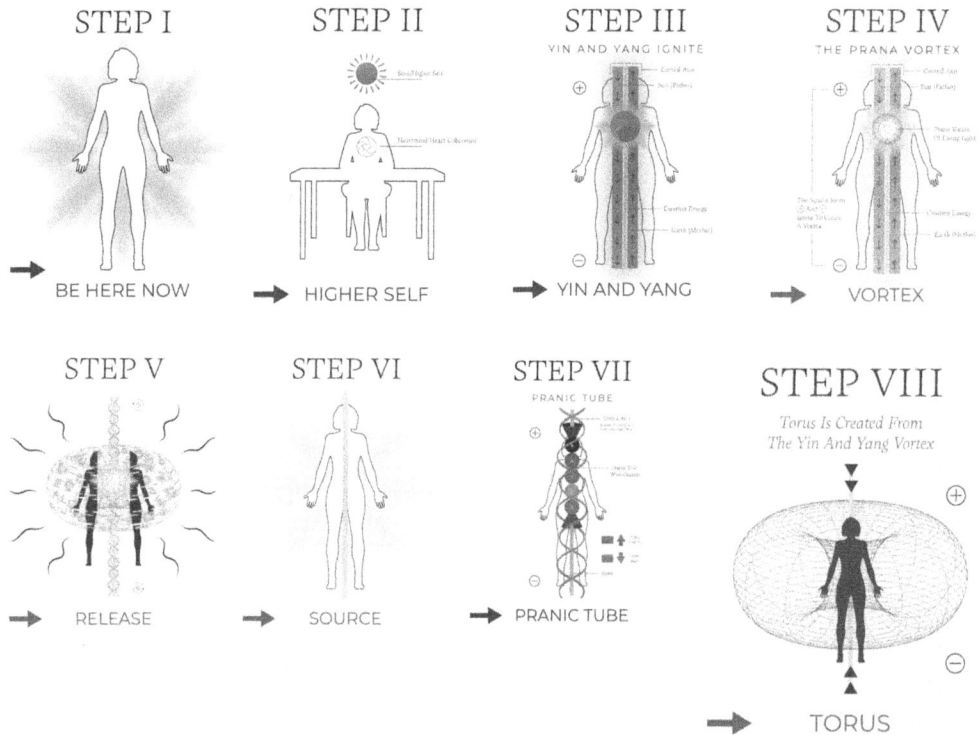

Step I - Embody (the Sacred Elements)
Step II - Connect (Higher Self/Soul)
Step III Charge - Replenish Yin and Yang
Step IV - Power Up (Ignite the Vortex)
Step V - Release (Remove lower vibration density)
Step VI - Meet (Source/Source)
Step VII - Increase Voltage (Pranic Tube Draws Prana)
>>>>>>>>>> You are here: **Step VIII - Conduct Energy (All Systems Go, Toroidal Flow)** <<<<<<<<<<
Step IX - Awaken (Come into Complete Flow with Source)

The Purpose of Step VIII

We Are Cradled In The Torus

The Torus cradles us in an energy system of unimaginable light and love, that of our soul, of our consciousness, of Source. The stronger our connection to our Torus becomes, the more cradled we become, the more of this light we receive, and the more in flow with our lives.

The Energy of Step VIII

The concept of the energy body as a toroidal system is a way of understanding the human energy field as a dynamic, interconnected whole. A Torus is a three-dimensional shape that has a continuous flow of energy. In the context of the energy body, the Torus represents the flow of energy through the physical, emotional, mental, and spiritual aspects of ourselves.

Putting Step VIII into Practice.

Set Intention
- I intend to practice self-love for myself.
- I intend to practice unconditional love for myself.
- I intend to ask my Higher Self to bring the masculine and feminine energies of the Earth, my Soul, and Source, into harmony and equal balance.

Daily Life Tip

Love is the key element of supporting your Torus. Self-love and unconditional love.

Short Version Meditation
- "I ask to activate my soul's Divine Father to bring healing to my Torus. (Pause.) I ask to activate my soul's Divine Mother to bring healing to my Torus." (Pause.)
- "I ask my loving infinite soul to bathe my Torus in self-love."
- "I ask my Higher Self to bathe my Torus in unconditional love."

Long Version

And now I begin to feel the flow of the Torus around me. A powerful energy field of prana that brings currents of life force energy to my physicality. Fed from the Pranic Tube, that powerful central channel that rotates around my Central Axis.

- I tune into a feeling of love in my heart chakra. I feel its resonance.
- I ask my loving infinite soul to bathe my Torus in self-love.
- I ask my Higher Self to bathe my Torus in unconditional love.
- I feel my Torus flow around me.
- I ask the Supreme being to vacuum out any low vibration density that has not yet been released, and take it to the sun to be purified.
- I ask the Sacred Element air to flow all along the currents of my Torus, helping the energy to flow.
- I feel the flow of the Torus move around to my back, into my spine, to all that All That Is About Me.
- "I ask the Source to remove any resistance I may have to this flow."
- I ask the Sacred Element Ether to bathe my Torus in eternal love.
- I tune into a feeling of love in my heart chakra. I feel that resonance.

THE TRANSMISSION

Audio Meditation
Step VIII

Sound Healing
Torus

Crystals
Self-love

STEP VIII TORUS WORKBOOK

Stoneman insight
Your Torus is like the hummingbird, it requires nectar to run. For humans, nectar consists of love and reverence, unconditional sweetness, compassion, and prayer.

Assess Yourself and your Torus
What is your relationship to your Torus?

> *Annie's Example:* My torus has been a bit depleted and once I became conscious of that I have worked hard to support its flow and integrity. I've found that self-love is a key piece to its health!

How do you know where you are at with your Torus?

> *Annie's Example:* How sensitive I am to my surroundings.

Daily Practice for your Torus?

> *Annie's Example:* I will bathe my self in unconditional love daily at least eight times, and my Torus will strengthen.

Daily Action for your Torus?

> *Annie's Example:* I do the 5-minute audio of the nine steps every day.

STEP IX: AWAKEN!
COME INTO COMPLETE FLOW WITH SOURCE

"The light body is the embodiment of your divinity. It is the vehicle that will carry you into the new world." —**Matthew Fox**

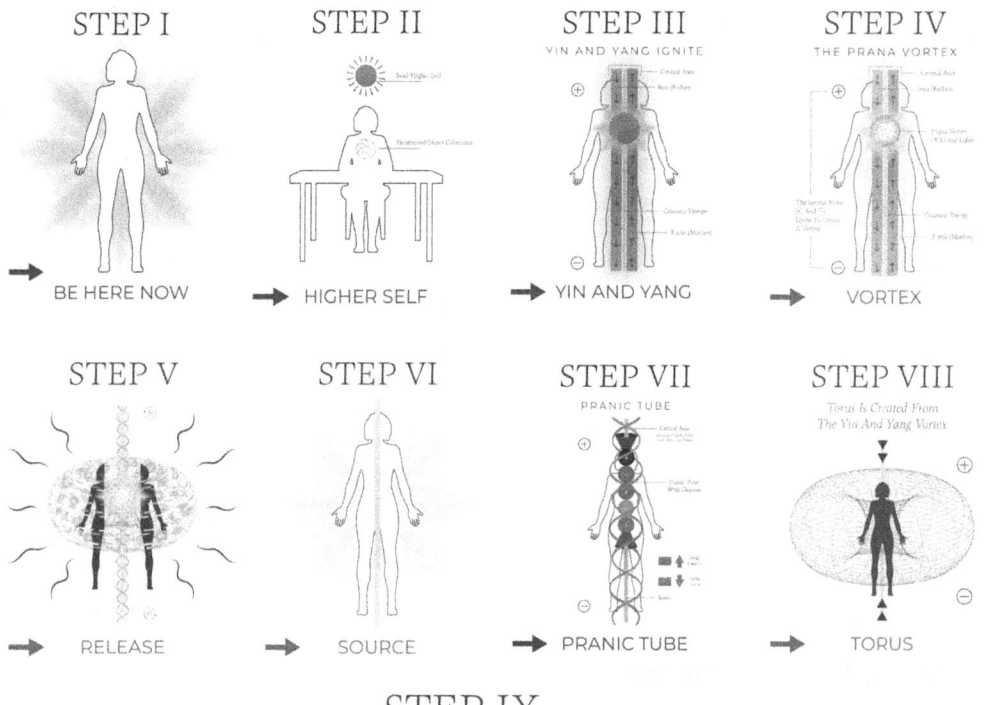

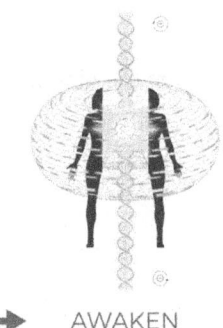

Step I - Embody (the Sacred Elements)
Step II - Connect (Higher Self/Soul)
Step III Charge - Replenish Yin and Yang
Step IV - Power Up (Ignite the Vortex)
Step V - Release (Remove lower vibration density)
Step VI - Meet (Source/Source)
Step VII - Increase Voltage (Pranic Tube Draws Prana)
Step VIII - Conduct Energy (All Systems Go, Toroidal Flow)
>>>>>>>>>> You are here: **Step IX - Awaken (Come into Complete Flow with Source)** <<<<<<<<<<

The Purpose of Step IX

Reconnecting to Source

Now we have reached the point of renewal, regeneration, radiance. The light of the Source can reach us and transmute that which no longer serves our well-being and higher purpose into a regeneration of our perfect blueprint.

The Energy of Step IX

Here and now, light can reach us from our Central Axis and remove that which no longer serves our higher purpose and health. When we are grounded and present, we can receive the light streams, the true vibration of our being, and regenerate into our perfect blueprint. We renew every cell from the dim aspects of ourselves that have awaited lumination. We have come home.

The 12 R's of regenerative healing are:
Remember | Return | Re-experience
Re-connect | Reactivate | Rejuvenate
Restore | Refresh | Repair
Radiate | Regenerate | Renew

Putting Step IX into Practice

Set Intention
- I intend to listen to the 5-minute meditation of the nine steps every day when I am able.
- I intend to take the time to experience the full meditation once a week.
- Every day I can send love to the Elements and get grounded, and send love and gratitude to the heart of the Earth and heart of the Sun.

Daily Life Tip Cheat Sheet
Weave the Steps into my day, as many as I can:
- Get grounded, connect to the Elements

- Ask my Higher Self to Clear our Connection
- Ask Source to bring Yin and Yang in equal balance in my being.
- Ask to hear the sound of the inner vortex igniting.
- Release all that I can release and ask it to go to the sun to be purified.
- Ask to connect to my quantum self and/or hear the sound of OM.
- Drink up Earth and drink down Sun energy.
- Ask my Soul to bathe me in self-love and my Higher Self to bathe me in unconditional love.
- Open to the matrix of light coming to my physicality.

Meditation

Short Version
"We ASK the Source to:
Align us with Source;
Make us whole;
Renew us to our perfect blueprint;
Return us to the abundance of who we really are;
Unify us with Source, our Soul, and our Atman self;
Entrain us with our Central Axis, quantum essence;
Reconnect our disembodied appendages, long disconnected from Source, be they in body, mind, or spirit, so they awaken with radiant Life Force from the Source of all Source;
Reconnect us all to become one at last. Let our regeneration free us into whole, healed, repaired, reconstructed, realignment with Source.

The Light Lines

"I ask my life force energy to flow along the light lines,
the ancient energy lines connecting me to the Source.
I ask this light to flow to me unimpeded and
for it to go where it is in the highest good and needed the most."
— A'ho Mitakuye Oyasin

Putting it All Together

Long Version

Self-Healing Protocol Checklist
The complete meditation Steps 1-9
- Become grounded, and connected to your Higher Self.
- Ask the current of the Divine Mother and the current of the Divine Father to come into your heart chakra. Fill and fill and replenish and balance.
- Ask those energies to meet and ignite and create a Vortex. Ask this master

blaster to blast away lower vibration density so that life force energy can get through to your physicality.
- Release the lower vibration density. This will reveal your connection to the sound of OM. The source of trauma is in the auric fields and then the lower vibration density that piles up from over-thinking manifests in life, including by clogging the chakras.
- Ask Mother Earth to come up and Father Sun to come down along your Pranic Tube to increase the voltage. Make it stronger and stronger to create a strong Torus.
- Ask the Source Life Force energy to come to you along the ancient energy lines to enter your physicality unimpeded to bring healing where needed.

Preparing for the Full Meditation
Consider creating an altar to the five sacred Elements. If you have this set up, you simply start the nine steps by lighting the candle, and sending love and gratitude to each.

Earth: A stone, crystal, flowers, whole food.
Water: In a bowl, in a glass, in the vase for flowers, sea shells.
Fire: A beeswax candle or other natural candle, such as one made from soy.
Air: A feather, image of bird; pure essential oils, incense, symbol of the sun.
Ether: Something to represent eternal love, reverence—a bell, mala beads, the symbol OM.

Full Meditation
Set an intention for a healing for a specific issue and/or for a healing that is in the highest good. If a specific issue, choose a physical issue the first round, next time you can expand to mind, and then Spirit.

(Embody the Elements - Step I)
- I send love and gratitude to the heart of the Earth. I ask Mother Earth to send her beautiful energy up to my earth star chakra, about eight inches below the ground, and from my Earth Star Chakra, up my Pranic Tube, along my Central Axis, and the energy goes where it needs to go.
- I ask the Sacred Elements Earth, Fire, and Water to help support my connection to Mother Earth.
- I send love and gratitude to the heart of the Sun. I ask Father Sun to send his beautiful energy down to my soul star chakra, about eight inches above my head, and from my soul star chakra, down my Pranic Tube, along my Central Axis, and the energy goes where it needs to go. I ask the Sacred Elements Air and Ether to help support my connection to Father Sun.
- I send love and gratitude to the Sacred Elements: Earth, Fire, Water, Air, and Ether.

(Connect to our Higher Self - Step II)
- I ask my Higher Self to clear our connection, to be with me.
- I drop into my heart chakra and tune into a feeling of gratitude, for Source. I tune into something that puts a song in my heart.
- I invite the Sacred Element Ether to bathe any illusions I have that I am separate from Source in Eternal Love" repeat
- I ask my Higher Self to bathe me in unconditional love. Repeat frequently for ten minutes.

(Replenish with Yin and Yang - Step III)
- "I send love and gratitude to the heart of the Earth. I send love and gratitude to the heart of the Sun."
- "I send love and gratitude to my soul mother and feminine aspect of my Higher Self. I send love and gratitude to my soul father and masculine aspect of my Higher Self."
- "I send love and gratitude to the Divine Mother. I send love and gratitude to the Divine Father."
- I ask Mother Earth to anchor me down, to help me be grounded. I ask Mother Earth to bring me healing.
- I ask Father Sun to fill me with light. I ask Father Sun to bathe me in light.
- I ask to activate my soul mother to bring me healing. Repeat.
- I ask to activate my soul father to bring me healing. Repeat.
- I ask to activate my soul mother and father to bring me healing.
- I ask the current of the Divine Mother, sacred feminine aspect of Source, to come to me wherever it is needed and in the highest good.
- I ask the current of the Divine Father, sacred masculine aspect of Source to come to me wherever it is needed and in the highest good.
- I ask the currents to fill up what is needed so that they come into equal balance.
- The current of the Divine Mother and current of the Divine Father
- I offer a prayer for healing to Source to remove any resistance to these currents.
- And I ask the currents of the Divine Mother and Divine Father to come to me where they are needed and is in the highest good, to fill and fill, to replenish where its needed.

(Power Up our Motor by Creating a Vortex - Step IV)
- I ask the currents of the female Yin and masculine Yang to come into equal balance wherever is in the highest good on my behalf.
- Ask the Divine Mother and Divine Father currents to connect and coalesce.
- I invite in their energy and magnetism to each other. I ask that magnetism to pull more and more in of the Yin and the Yang, and for those energies to connect and coalesce.

- There they ignite—they create a SPARK—the SPARK of Source, life force energy. This spark of Source energy organizes to create a Vortex, the movement of Yin and Yang into a counter-rotating vortex, a Vortex flowing with life force, of prana, and I understand that the strength of this Vortex is the key to my well-being.
- I ask to connect to that spark of ignition, to feel that life force.
- I keep filling the Vortex, keep asking for more of the Yin and the Yang to continue to pour in, pour in. (Repeat frequently.)
- The Yin and Yang energies counter-rotate, making a powerful Vortex.
- I continually invite in more and more Yin and Yang currents to strengthen the Vortex.
- As the Vortex strengthens it becomes a "master blaster" blasting out lower vibration density, removing our trauma and heavy programming, illness, making way for the light.
- I ask it to grind away lower vibration density so that the light can get through unimpeded. Almost like a gear, grinding away.
- I ask it to grind away lower vibration density so as to open the receptor points to my physicality so that Light Force energy can flow through unimpeded.

(Release - Step V)
- I continue to fill the Vortex with the sacred feminine and sacred masculine currents to make it a strong master blaster of lower vibration density. Fill with the soul mother and soul father, with mother Earth and Father Sun.
- I ask the Supreme Being to vacuum out all that I can release.
- I ask the Sacred Elements to help release the lower vibration density, earth to magnetize it down, water to wash it away, fire to burn it away, air to blow it away, and ether to remove it.
- I imagine a cloud in front of me and release all that I can release into the cloud, until it is filled and ask it to go to the sun to be purified. I ask in another cloud.
- Again, I ask the Supreme Being to vacuum out all that I can release.

(Meet Source - Step VI)
- As the lower vibration density is removed I open to the experience of my Central Axis, that powerful beam of light coming down through me, up through me... the energy of my connection to the Universe, to Source, to the Source. The sound of OM. The luminosity of Source. I ask to entrain to the sound of OM.
- I ask to entrain to the sound of OM.
- As lower vibration density is removed and I can open to more light, I ask to entrain to the sound of OM.
- I open to receive the life force energy from my Central Axis carrying the light, color, and sound codes, the data carriers of my perfect blueprint, of the perfect blueprint. The life force prana that is center stage for my transformation.

- I ask to entrain to the sound of OM.

(I Increase Voltage in the Pranic Tube - Step VII)
(Counter-rotate)
- I pick up on the energy of the Vortex, the powerful counter-rotation that makes a Pranic Tube around the Central Axis, the inside sleeve of what becomes the Torus around us. That inside sleeve pulls in the Mother Earth energy from below and the Father Sun energy from above; the two magnetize to each other, creating a powerful counter-rotation of currents.
- I pull in more and more energy from below and above, and work to increase its voltage, to feel the energy coming up, imagining myself once again to be a tree with deep roots, and the roots are drinking up and up the Yin energy from below. And from above, the branches are drinking down and down the Yang energy from above. Filling and filling the Pranic Tube to create a Torus.
- A powerful counter-rotation that creates our Torus.
- Increasing voltage by drinking up Mother Earth and Father Sun currents.
- I ask the sun to bathe the All That Is About Me in all the colors of the rainbow to assist this reconnection and awakening. Red, orange, yellow, green, sky blue, indigo, and violet.
- I ask the Sacred Elements to come into their highest possible balance, relationship, and vibration in the All That Is About Me to come into coherence, and for them to invite in all the sounds they want to work with, and those sounds to breathe into whatever is in the highest good.
- Once again, I ask the flow of the Yin coming up and Yang coming down to strengthen and strengthen to increase voltage and build a powerful Torus around me.

(Conduct Energy in the Torus - Step VIII)
And now I begin to feel the flow of the Torus around me. A powerful energy field of prana that brings currents of life force energy to my physicality. Fed from the Pranic Tube, that powerful central channel that rotates around my Central Axis.
- I tune into a feeling of love in my heart chakra. I feel its resonance.
- I ask my loving infinite soul to bathe my Torus in self-love.
- I ask my Higher Self to bathe my Torus in unconditional love.
- I feel my Torus flow around me.
- I ask the Supreme Being to vacuum out any low vibration density that has not yet been released, and take it to the sun to be purified.
- I ask the Sacred Element Air to flow all along the currents of my Torus, helping the energy to flow.
- I feel the flow of the Torus around my back, into my spine, to all that All That Is About Me.

- I ask the Source to remove any resistance I may have to this flow.
- I ask the Sacred Element Ether to bathe my Torus in eternal love.
- I tune into a feeling of love in my heart chakra. I feel that resonance.

(Awaken - Connect to the Matrix of Light)
From my Central Axis, I ask the Source Life Force energy, of prana, to come to me from my Central Axis, to flow to me, to enter my physicality unimpeded to bring healing where needed.
- I ask this life force energy to flow to me from my Central Axis, bringing to me the currents from Source to my perfect blueprint—the perfect blueprint.
- I ask this life force energy to flow to me unimpeded and for it to go where it is in the highest good and needed the most.
- I ask to connect to this matrix of light. That matrix of light that carries the light codes, the data transmissions for my transformation—my perfect blueprint.
- I ask this living light to come to the connector points of my physicality, so that Source energy can come into my physicality unimpeded
  - to align me with Source
  - closer to Source, the prana of Love
  - to make me whole
  - to renew me to my perfect blueprint
  - to be One with the All That Is.
- I send love and gratitude to Mother Earth, and I send love and gratitude to Father Sun.
- I ask this Awakening Prana! opening on my behalf to seed profound healing for me as per my intention, to assist in my finding my way on the path, and through me, bring healing to others and the planet. I authoritatively say my name to myself and ask for the healing issue to be gone and stay gone, and for all healing to be in the highest good.

Aho Mitakuye Oyasin . . . All my relations. I honor you in this circle of life with me today. I am grateful for this opportunity to acknowledge you in this prayer . . .

THE TRANSMISSION

Audio Versions

Short, 5-minute version:

Long, Full Version

Sound Healing

The Awakener

Crystals

Merkabah

STEP IX AWAKENING! WORKBOOK

Stoneman insight

Here at long last you come home to the natural regeneration that your body and soul always knew but your personality and ego were separated from. This is a collective separation—nothing you did wrong. The ego is a dominant feature in all of your lives on the planet. Now you can expand beyond your ego and here you will now find joy.

Assess Yourself and the Awakening Prana! Kriya

What is your relationship to yourself?

> *Annie's Example:* My ego, my marker of the ego-based operating system has become much more quiet and I am more in my love-based operating system.

How do you know where you are at with the Awakening Prana! Kriya

> *Annie's Example:* How driven I am by programmed training from my family and culture.

Daily Practice for the Awakening Prana! Kriya

> *Annie's Example:* Feel the matrix of light from the nine steps every day.

Daily Action for the Awakening Prana! Kriya

> *Annie's Example:* Set a time for this, a time you can honor.

CLOSING

"You are here today because you had a calling to wholeness. You are here today because you had to come find yourself in the midst of chaos. You are here today to begin the journey of soul memory, the remembrance of all who you must become because yes, it has already been agreed upon. You are here today to become who you are, a radiant being full of light and luminosity. This will take you far. This brings leadership from the stars. Your path is laid out with light. A ho." —**Stoneman**

Bardor Tulku Rinpoche, founder of the Tibetan Buddhist center near where I live, Kunzang Palchen Ling, once told me, when I asked about the state of the damaged environment of the planet, that it is a reflection of our consciousness.

Consciousness.

My conversation with Bardor Tulku Rinpoche changed my professional and personal life. Up until then I was the author of five books on green living, and my entire career had been spent as a writer and an editor in the environmental health arena. A shift happened in me, and I focused more on my spiritual growth.

Spiritual consciousness is a state of awareness in which we are connected to our Higher Self, to the sacred, or to the interconnectedness of all things. It is a state of being that is characterized by peace, love, joy, and a sense of purpose.

Connection.

Peace.

Love.

Purpose.

In general, spiritual healing and the increasing expansion of my consciousness has come to me from the mechanical. Attention to the energy body, such as in Awakening Prana! The search for healing of the physical has led me to these spiritual realms because, once you get into energy healing, there grows an intuitive understanding that it is in this energy system that we are cradled.

Once we feel our energy body flow we want it to empty of all our trauma and the programming of our personality. More flow, please! Just as when I wrote my green living books and readers would write to me to say that one thing led to the next, that they cleaned their bathtub in a nontoxic way and the next thing they knew, they were composting! So, too, with spiritual growth. We feel drawn to be empty. To build self-love. We want to activate our life channel. We want to heal and recharge.

For me, with the months and then years of clearing out old emotional wounds and trauma every day, attending to what is showing up, my life has moved into arenas I could never have dreamed. As the lower vibration density discussed throughout this book has been released, I feel more and more like a hollow flute, more like an empty vessel who can be in flow with the flow of the Universe.

Every day one wants to integrate the messages of the 9 Steps of the Awakening Prana! practice. With this we can increase attributes such as gratitude, forgiveness, self-love, feelings of love and being part of the Law of Reciprocity, and being of service. In other words, we come into a time of expanded spiritual consciousness. It is from this place, as Bardo Tulku Rinpoche taught, that we can be of better service to the planet, each other, and ourselves.

Prayer of St Francis

Lord, make me an instrument of your peace;
where there is hatred, let me sow love;
where there is injury, pardon;
where there is doubt, faith;
where there is despair, hope;
where there is darkness, light;
and where there is sadness, joy.

O Sacred Master,
grant that I may not so much seek to be consoled as to console;
to be understood, as to understand;
to be loved, as to love;
for it is in giving that we receive,
it is in pardoning that we are pardoned,
and it is in dying that we are born to Eternal Life.
Amen.

DEFINITION OF TERMS

Akasha: The Akashic Records, also known as the Akasha, is a term used in spiritual and metaphysical circles to describe a universal field of information—a non-physical library of information—that contains the record of every soul's journey throughout time.

Discernment: (Viveka in Sanskrit) occurs when we harness the ability of the intellect to distinguish between the permanent and the impermanent, the gross or dense, and the subtle. It is the ability to see through the illusion of the world and to understand the true nature of reality. Discernment is essential for spiritual progress because it allows us to see the world as it really is, without attachment or aversion.

Quantum Energy: Quantum mechanics is a branch of physics that studies the behavior of matter and energy in terms of probabilities and wave functions. One of the key features of quantum mechanics is superposition, which means that a particle can exist in multiple states simultaneously. Another important concept is entanglement, which describes the correlation between the states of two or more particles, even when they are separated by a large distance.

Yin/Shakti/Sacred Feminine: Yin is a concept in Chinese philosophy and medicine that represents a passive, receptive, feminine, and cool energy. It is often associated with the moon, darkness, water, and earth. Shakti: In Hinduism Shakti represents the primordial cosmic energy that is responsible for Source. As a feminine force, she is considered the embodiment of fertility, power, and creativity. She represents the sacred feminine aspects of Source, such as intuition, nurturing, and compassion. Sacred Feminine Energy: These are the strands of DNA that feed your receptivity to matter. Your love of nature, your body, your heart and lungs, the daily needs of nourishment and the sacredness of childbirth and fetus and leaves and trees. Yin is feeling, it is love, it is engagement. Yin is matter.

Yang/Shiva/Sacred Masculine: In Chinese philosophy, the "Yang" principle is associated with masculine, active, bright, and warm qualities. The Yang principle is associated with the sun, light, heat, and energy. It is considered to be the force of expansion and outward movement, associated with growth, creativity, and change. Shiva: Shiva is often regarded as the embodiment of male energy or the sacred masculine. Shiva represents the sacred masculine energy in Hinduism, embodying qualities of strength, transformation, wisdom, and spiritual growth. sacred Masculine Energy: These are the strands of DNA that Source your matter from the universe, that conceive of the idea, that sprout the thought, that absorb the time, that think through the cosmos, that bring you to matter. Yang is thought, it is consciousness, it is understanding.

Yin and Yang: According to Chinese cosmology, the universe is composed of two opposite and complementary principles, "Yin" and "Yang," which are in constant interaction and balance. Yin represents the feminine, passive, dark, and cool aspects of nature, while Yang represents the masculine, active, bright, and warm aspects of nature.

Yin is considered to be the complementary opposite of Yang, which represents active, masculine, and warm energy. Together, Yin and Yang are believed to be the two fundamental forces that create and balance the universe.

DNA: DNA (Deoxyribonucleic acid) is a long, double-stranded molecule that carries the genetic instructions used in the growth, development, functioning, and reproduction of all known living organisms and many viruses.

Prana: "Prana" is a Sanskrit term used in Hindu, Buddhist, and yogic philosophy to describe the vital life force or energy that permeates all living things. It is often translated as "breath," "vital energy," or "life force." Its free and unobstructed flow is essential for physical, mental, and spiritual well-being.

Higher Self: The Higher Self is believed to be the aspect of ourselves that is connected to the sacred, universal consciousness or Source. It is said to be a Source of wisdom, guidance, and spiritual insight that can help us navigate life's challenges and fulfill our soul's purpose.

Entrain: "Entrain" refers to the process by which two vibrating systems of different frequencies begin to synchronize or resonate with each other, causing their frequencies to become more similar over time. For the purposes of spiritual healing we entrain to a higher vibration, that of our soul, Higher Self, or Atman self.

ACKNOWLEDGMENTS

It is unlikely that this book would have been written without the pandemic. I was hunkered down, isolated, looking to work for a meaningful way to pass time. Many months were spent in front of the wood stove in my slippers, doing research into the energy body. I fully stepped into being a mystic. I started writing.

A wonderful team came together to help. First to come in was Shannon Marie Baldwin, who was able to take my sketches about the energy body and put them into beautiful form. She has openheartedly followed my lead despite entering a territory that was completely new to her (and me, too, to be truthful).

Next, I began to work with Nick Raineri, a Level III Awakening Prana's Path to Healing student of mine who is also an electronic music producer. I'd give him Stoneman's transmission of the Hz needed for transformation and Nick would masterfully produce the sound healing with the highest integrity, dedication, and skill of a healer.

The stars aligned to help me find Alexis Houston when I was looking for a developmental editor. She and I spent many months working closely on a Google Doc with the book, and she brought so much erudite expertise about many different spiritual faiths that the book was immediately upleveled because of her touch. It was a joy to co-create with her.During this whole time, I shared these new healing protocols with clients, family, and students and they helped me refine them by sharing their experiences. I was also heartened by the benefits they received.

I've loved working with Epigraph Books, too, and lucky they are local to me. It is great to converse in person and they have been so professional, supportive, and have provided invaluable expertise.

Suzanne Giesemann's generosity in agreeing to write the Foreword to the book took my breath away. How did I ever get so blessed? I couldn't be more honored. She and I met each other by happenstance and have valued each other's work and friendship ever since. Her devotion to her path of work is so extraordinary and open-hearted, she is always an inspiration.

ABOUT THE CREATORS

BY ANNIE B. BOND, FROM THE STONEMAN DIARIES

Annie B. Bond is a mystic who can see energy systems clairvoyantly. Through this connection, Annie finds insight and understanding for anyone on their personal and spiritual growth journeys. She has developed the Awakening Prana healing modality, works with clients from all over the world, and founded her first Healer School in 2016. Awakeningprana.com

Stoneman is the name Annie has given to a stone that is her portal to working with a masterful Being, a Hathor. He says about the Hathors that "We are highly ascended Beings who are rooting for the Earth as she comes into her ascension. We've been working with your planet since well before Egyptian times, back to the Lemurians. We have seeded the sound healings of many ancestral lineages, especially Native American, Tibetan Buddhist, and Taoist. Today we are working with a louder sound, bringing it to those of you who can hear it and translate it to seed the new path of the WAY."

Alexis Houston, LMT, Certified Family Herbalist, has practiced alternative medicine and taught yoga for over twenty years in Vermont and also India. She is a health and wellness writer and editor and dedicated Vedanta student.

Nick Raineri is a sound healer and energy healer who is a Masters Level III graduate from Annie's Awakening Prana Path to Awakening schools. Cubicalsunrise.com

Shannon Marie Baldwin is a graphic designer with a Bachelor of Science in Graphic Design and over a decade of experience working with fellow creatives, small businesses, and entrepreneurs. Her business Running with Foxes is based in Rhinebeck, NY. running-with-foxes.com

www.ingramcontent.com/pod-product-compliance
Lightning Source LLC
Chambersburg PA
CBHW081836170426
43199CB00017B/2751